THE
STONE MEN

Book Two

Kathy Lyons
Anna Argent

Cover by The Killion Group www.thekilliongroupinc.com
eBook design by eBook Prep www.ebookprep.com

August, 2017
ISBN: 978-1-61417-985-6
ePublishing Works!
www.epublishingworks.com

CONTENTS

ROCK CANDY

The Stone Men Series

Kathy Lyons

CHAPTER 1

"Serve me."

Thabo, runner and general clown of Zeva's army, leapt at the sound of his goddess' command. It was a favorite game of hers. She demanded service, but never specified what. Her slaves had to guess what she wanted, and special rewards were given to ingenuity. She claimed it encouraged her warriors to understand how she thought. Privately, he believed the bitch just wanted to punish someone and this was the easiest way to create a combat trial. That was her real lust: to see men, women, and children fight for dominance. Only one could ever win the combat, but all lost to her in the end. Thabo's only survival was to obey, to serve, and to never, ever think of what he'd lost.

Fortunately, he'd discovered a pattern in Zeva's thoughts. She loved seeing dangerous tasks performed with skill. Every soul here knew that, but he knew that she enjoyed it more if everyone nearby—including the performer—became bloody somehow. So he leapt into the press of slaves knowing that to delay action would be certain pain.

He began simply, killing the nearest slaves and stealing their weapons. Bodies collapsed at his feet, then disappeared to inhabit their Earthly statues. There was no true death in Idola. No one escaped Zeva so easily. Their lives were filled with pain, dismemberment, and the slow death of sanity. He felt no guilt in dispatching his fellow servants to their stone bodies. For a few of them, such a respite was almost pleasant. Not for him, though, which is why he worked especially hard to win at these trials; so his consciousness stayed forever in Idola and not his broken statue.

As soon as he had weapons at hand, he began to juggle because that was his greatest skill. A stone knife, a battle ax, and a pistol flew into the air. He preferred the pistol because with it he could perform what made him extra special.

His opponents knew this trick and scrambled to hide behind each other, but it was not enough. As opportunities arose, he would snatch a weapon with a hand, then throw or shoot it. The dance of his feet was simply to keep a rotating circle of weaponry above his head.

Others aimed at him. Flying weapons made him a huge target, but he'd had two centuries to practice avoiding or killing those who would bloody him first. And still he kept the weapons spinning in the air. He'd picked up more guns now, dispatching everyone else quickly. Then it was just him and Asha, the beautiful thief he had betrayed a century ago. Because of their history, she took special joy in besting him and this time she'd done it in spades. She stood with a goblet of wine in one hand and his own purse of shimmering opals in the other.

"Kuk," he cursed. When had she gotten close enough to take that? It proved that she could have killed him as easily as she had stolen his gemstones. Which made her the winner in this contest, unless he did something spectacular right now.

So he hit her with everything he had. Zeva loved it when he and his former lover attacked each other like enraged beasts. He shot the guns as quickly as his hands could grab them. He threw the blades, and even used the whip to snake around her torso. It could have been her neck, but his guilt kept him from killing her. Then, right as he jerked her toward him, he neatly grabbed the goblet of wine and offered it to Zeva.

Or such had been his plan.

Everything was executed perfectly up until the last second. To serve a goblet to the goddess required deft fingers and sure balance. The balance he had, the fingers he did not. Not in the tips. Not where it was needed most for this type of task.

So at the last second as he jumped over Asha's squirming body, the goblet slipped. The wine was cold, making the metal sides especially slick. And to his horror, the ruby liquid sloshed. His numb fingers over-compensated, making the entire thing worse. And rather than serve his goddess wine, he threw the entire contents onto her breasts.

Double Kuk!

All went silent in horrified glee. In a land of constant battle, such a thing never happened. A hundred years ago, Thabo would have begged forgiveness. Even fifty years ago, but he had learned that apologies had no place here. Neither did defiance. So he dropped to his knees before the bitch goddess and waited with bowed head for his punishment.

Zeva didn't respond at first. She did lift a droplet of wine off her cleavage and taste it, pronouncing it average at best. Then she waved her fingers and caused an assortment of knives to appear at his feet. Stone, metal, short, long. Some had spurs, others no true hilt. A glittering display, and Thabo wondered if he was to be used as target practice.

"Juggle those for me," Zeva said.

He glanced up, his heart thudding dully in his throat. Surely she did not mean so easy a task for him. Though challenging, he would be able to manage—

"Don't use your arms or even the palms of your hands. Just use your fingers. The very tips."

He swallowed. He could not do it. Not with his fingers numb and his hands going cold. In truth, that was why he had begun learning how to add his feet into the display.

Because since the moment his statue had lost its arms, he had slowly lost dexterity in his hands. He could mask it. Indeed, he had masked it for over a hundred years. But now the loss was unmistakable.

He thought about simply confessing. Sometimes Zeva prized truth, but she despised weakness all the time. So, he bent his head and began the task.

He started with a stone knife, a metal stiletto, and a simple eating knife. A rote task, even with numb fingers. He knew better than to grin, though he did allow himself a quiet grunt of relief.

"More," Zeva said.

Expected. And she would want something decidedly harder.

He grabbed a Roman short sword. Heavy for his fingers to manage, but one of the first weapons he'd learned to juggle. It flew into the air, the metal flashing dully in the sun.

"Another," Zeva ordered.

He picked up a shard of glass wrapped in leather for a hilt. The difference in weight between the sword and the shard were difficult, but manageable.

"Faster."

He complied because he had to. And though he managed it for a minute, he got his first cut. The index finger of his right hand sliced to the bone from the stone knife. Stupid. He'd been worried about the glass and had forgotten about the stone.

"Dance."

He was considered the fastest man in Zeva's army. That was how he'd gained her attention in the first place, back when he'd been a man. But to leap and slide while throwing knives would make everything too difficult.

He did it anyway.

And he bloodied two more fingers as he did it.

And then the wet made his throw off balance. The stiletto sliced off two of his fingers, but it was the short sword that took off his hand.

He stopped juggling. The weapons clattered to the ground. And as he stilled before Zeva, he felt nothing but a mild curiosity as to how she would try to hurt him now.

"You did not even flinch as you lost your fingers."

His blood was pooling on the ground. It wouldn't take long for him to pass out from blood loss. Once gone from Idola, he would wake in the stone body of his statue. He would remain there, his consciousness screaming from the boredom until Zeva called him back again. More souls had gone insane from neglect than from the goddess's capricious attention.

"You have trained me well," he said.

"I have seen you juggle more while the ground shook beneath you." She pushed up from her throne. Her wine-drenched armor shifted to a flowing robe of knives. "You have lost skill."

It wasn't a question. He bowed his head and watched the growing pool of blood at his feet. How long before he would wake in his statue, sunk to his nose while fish swam by? How long before he lost any hold on—

"It's because your curator has neglected you."

His curator was the man who had pledged his life—and his children's lives—to the protection of Thabo's statue on Earth. He was the man who cared the most for Thabo in this hell of an immortal life, and he had been the grandchild of Thabo's once best friend.

The man had drowned along with his wife and only child. The pulverized remains of their bones were mixed with the silt on the ocean floor. Thabo had ceased grieving for them decades ago.

"How much skill have you lost?" Zeva demanded in a sharp tone. He knew better than to evade her hard glare.

"I can still shoot and kill, as you have seen."

"But if your statue were intact? If you were recovered and healed? How many knives could you juggle at once? With just your fingertips?"

"A dozen," he said, wondering if it were true. It had been decades since he'd practiced seriously to stretch his skill.

But he couldn't take the statement back. He couldn't do much of anything now that blood loss was making every part of him sluggish. Spots already danced at the edge of his vision. He knew he should feel cold, but that sensation had been part of him so long, he would never know if it got worse.

Zeva grunted, a strangely erotic sound though the woman had little interest in sex. "It appears I shall have to create a storm wild enough to uncover a statue."

His head shot up, though it made him sway on his feet. Would he walk again in the world of men? He could barely conceive of it.

She shot him a glare. "And you shall have to do something spectacular to make it worth my effort. I will give you three days. Do you understand?"

"Yes, Goddess," he answered. At least he tried to. He managed a nod as his knees went out from him. His last conscious thought was that he had better think of something truly spectacular or Zeva was likely to shatter his statue—and his mind—into a million pieces before she gave him this opportunity again.

CHAPTER 2

Molly Parker swam closer to the incredible statue of an African man. She had to maneuver carefully amid the bones of the shipwreck, but nothing was keeping her from the statue she'd named *Mine*. He was gloriously naked, his expression fierce, and he was buried beneath silt up to his...well, his well-endowed, not-broken-off manly part. She couldn't say as much for either of his arms which had to be around here somewhere. But her first order of business was to retrieve him. Fortunately, she'd brought help for that.

Salvage was not her specialty. Neither was finding undiscovered shipwrecks, but what the hell. Luck and a faulty compass had brought her to this place a month ago. She'd come upon the wreck and since it had been her birthday, she declared the statue her present from the Universe. Sadly, it had taken her a month, most of her savings, and her entire credit card limit to come back for him. But the salvage crew knew their stuff and were already opening a large hole in the wreckage above Mine to haul him out. Her job, after the obligatory stroking of his chiseled torso, was to find his arms. Though looking away from the stone eye candy was unexpectedly difficult. But he would look even more delicious with his arms.

They had to be around here somewhere.

Good news, the left one was close. She saw his hand first, clutched into a fist as if he were trying to pummel the nearest fish. If she weren't in a breathing apparatus, she would have cheered. As it was, she did a victory wiggle before hauling up a forearm and bulging biceps. Three cheers for realistic anatomy in naked men statues.

She passed off the arm to one of the salvage crew, though God knew it was surprisingly difficult to let go. She had to remind herself that he was her find and she got to keep him. Even the dismembered parts. Then it was the laborious search for the other hand. This one had broken off just short of the elbow, so it was smaller than the left and it was absolutely nowhere to be found.

She stayed well after the crew got Mine out of the remains of the boat, but after a while, she had to admit defeat. Maybe she'd rename him "Lefty." Then just as she was flagging down her partner to go, she spotted a bright fish of a species she'd never seen before. It looked like a flameback angelfish wearing a tiara. No shit. The crown was luminescent and clearly spotlighted something round caught next to the bones of the ship.

She swam over, paying as much attention to the weird fish as the round…oh wow. That could be it. The fish was forgotten as she began to dig with her bare hands. Oy, this was sunk deep. Two minutes. Seven. She was well past her safety limit on her oxygen, but she hated the name Lefty, so she kept at it.

At the ten-minute mark she realized why she couldn't just haul the thing out. The statue's right hand was clutching something bigger than it. Something that looked a lot like a ship's wheel. *WTF?* Why would anyone make a statue holding a wheel? Whatever. She had no understanding of art. She just needed Mine's arm.

Fortunately, once she understood the problem, she saw the solution. Instead of gripping the forearm, she and her partner dug down far enough to grab the wheel. Way too much exertion later, they got it free. And voila, her present had all its pieces. Now she just had to figure out how to re-attach them, and she could fondle all of Mine to her heart's content.

She swam as fast as she was allowed, giddy with excitement. She had all of Mine's parts!

It was well after midnight when she finally made it back to shore. The boat was her neighbor's and Molly knew that he was particular about how it was treated. So, even while she wanted to supervise Mine's unloading, she was too busy messing with other details. She kept looking over to make sure everything was going well. The crew was careful as they gently transferred him to her pickup truck in the parking lot. Then they wanted to get paid, blah, blah, blah, and it wasn't until two a.m. that she could finally, blessedly, head for home with her treasure.

It was a short walk up the dock and out to the parking lot. Her gaze immediately went to where Mine stood tall and proud in the moonlight where they'd tied him to the truck. *WTF*? She'd told them specifically to lay him down. It would be hard as hell to drive him home standing up. Except now, as she rounded the corner she saw something even more disturbing. It looked like both his arms were in place, one still clutching the wheel.

No way.

She crossed the lot at a sprint, her mouth hanging open as she did, indeed, see both arms firmly attached. What—?

"Finally!" A woman's acidic voice came to her from the hidden side of the statue. "I've been waiting forever. I have better things to do than sit here in the middle of nowhere while you take your time."

Molly jogged to the back only to gape at a woman in bright blue coveralls and a headband that, sure as shit, looked like a glowing tiara on spiky obsidian hair.

"What the hell are you doing back there?" Molly demanded. "That's Mine!"

"I'm here fixing it, you simpleton. I can't let him stand around without arms. Not after I went to such lengths to have you find them."

So many responses clogged her throat as she glared at the woman. What lengths? What had she done? How had she heard? A zillion questions and the only thing that got out was, "How?"

The woman waved her hand dismissively. "Magic paste. It'll take a bit to set properly, so be careful with him." Then she squatted down until she was eye to eye with Molly. There was a weird color to her face, strongly reminiscent of the angelfish she had seen earlier in the ocean. It had the same flame color along the top and shimmery blue at the bottom. But that had to be a trick of the moonlight. And when Molly blinked, the crazy person looked almost normal, except for the tiara.

Then the woman spoke and Molly had to suppress a shiver. There was something different in her words. As if the sounds and shape of her question burrowed inside and burned deep into her bones.

"Is this statue yours?" she asked.

Molly nodded, her answer coming out with a stammer. "Y-yes. He's Mine."

"Great. There are rules. Do you agree to them?"

"What?"

"Under his right foot. Do you agree? You can't have him unless you agree."

Molly felt her anger surge. It wasn't that the woman's voice had lost its power. It's just that Molly had adjusted and was starting to think clearly. "Get the fuck off my truck, you looney." Then she leaped up onto the bed to look at what the bitch had done to Mine. At least that was the plan. She'd barely cleared the pavement when she was thrown back onto it hard enough to slam her head against the shrubbery. It was probably a good thing, because if she'd flown the other way, she might have been knocked unconscious on the pavement. As it was, she had a couple burning, probably bleeding, holes in her scalp and shoulders. But that didn't keep her down.

She surged forward—albeit a bit unsteadily—spitting profanities like a sailor. But once she ran through her expletives, she added, "I'm calling the cops." Except she never got a chance to pull out her cell phone. Instead, the woman appeared before her, nose to nose in a blink of her eye.

Jesus, she must have hit her head hard because she hadn't even seen the woman jump down. And that bizarre skin coloring was back, flame over blue, cleanly bisecting her face across the bridge of her nose.

"Fighting soul," the woman said, then she sneered as she added the rest. "Completely unskilled."

Molly didn't bother with a retort. She was grabbing her phone while simultaneously looking around for help. No go. At this time of night, the lot was completely deserted. And then she was talking, clearly not listening to the part of her brain that said, *don't antagonize the crazy woman*.

"I'll show you unskilled, you freak—"

"Do you accept ownership or not?" the woman interrupted.

"I told you, he's Mine. Now get out—"

"Rules and all?"

"Yes! Whatever! Now get the fuck away from..." Her voice trailed away. She must have blacked out for a moment. Her vision had gone all underwater-wonky. Like a murky cloud of silt and seaweed had washed across her face. And when it finally cleared, she was alone in the parking lot. She spun around, her heart in her throat as she scanned absolutely everything.

Alone.

Well, except for Mine. Who was still strangely intact, arms and all.

WTF?

It took her a moment to quiet down. And even longer to double-check her statue and all the ties securing him to the truck. He looked really good in a perfect eye-candy kind of way. There was marine life crusted on, but surprisingly little. The only explanation was that he'd been buried deep underground and only recently exposed. Probably after their last hurricane.

Whatever the woman had done to Mine had smoothed over cracks and set the arms right in place. Now that he was intact, Molly could see that he was holding onto the wheel and gesturing to the side, though at what and why she had no idea. Besides, it was his face that caught her attention. Even through the crustaceans, she could see that there was a look of resignation there. As if he knew what was coming and accepted it with dull fatality. Kind of heartbreaking to see; that total acceptance of inevitable death.

And how she knew that from a partially obscured face, she had no idea. But that was art. It spoke its own language.

She thought about trying to lay him down in the truck bed but everything was secured tight. And since it was the middle of the night, the streets would likely be deserted. She'd just be extra careful as she drove home.

She went at a whopping ten miles an hour on surface streets. Palmetto Bay was blessedly quiet because it was early January. They weren't into spring break season. But when she arrived home, she realized she had a problem. No way could she get Mine into the garage without decapitating him. He was too tall while standing on the truck bed.

Too tired to deal with it, she pulled in halfway and parked. Then she double-checked everything again. With the light on in her garage, she could see much more clearly the lines where his arms had been re-attached. She already knew about the pock marks along his body and the crap that had attached to his exposed face and torso, but all in all, not so bad. And she found it ridiculously funny that his impressive privates remained unscathed.

She stifled a yawn, torn between the need for sleep and the bizarre attachment she had to Mine. He was just a statue, but part of her wanted to sleep right here in her truck just to be beside him. Ridiculous, especially since she had a nice soft bed inside. She was just about to go inside when something caught her eye. A piece of paper underneath Mine's right foot.

It couldn't be.

She crept closer, her eyes narrowed as she peeled up a corner. The writing was large and dark, which made it easy to read, though she could only make out one word.

Rules

CHAPTER 3

There was no sound, and the silence was making Thabo insane. It was better than before when he sat fathoms deep in the silent ocean. Then all he was was the occasional fish, and that was only after Zeva had created a hurricane to uncover him. He was above ground now, but all was muffled and dim. He studied what lay before his marble eyes. He faced away from his new curator's house to stand sentry over a smooth street and houses so much more elaborate than the huts of his childhood. Trees so beautiful they made his heart ache. But none of them were *her,* the woman who would be his curator.

What a fierce little warrior she was! Hair like liquid flame, flowing over her head to coil around her shoulders. Even her white skin had freckles where her hair had flamed so hot, she'd burned.

His thoughts were fanciful, the imagery growing more elaborate the longer he stood in darkness; neither in her home nor out of it. But with nothing to do but think, he grabbed on to her as a way to stay sane. He thought about her breasts, large and tempting. He thought about the way he could see muscles in every part of her body, but not like the other women in Zeva's army. Her strength was softened by curves that made her beautiful. And he thought about hearing her voice clearly. Though he had listened to her negotiation with Zeva, he had not been able to capture the true notes of her voice and he longed to do so.

His view changed just as he was thinking about her pert chin. About how she'd lifted it in challenge to a goddess who could have easily killed her. But then, his awareness snapped back to his view as a car appeared before him. Only now could he pick up a muted rumble from its engine. He knew cars from his years training for War. This was a black SUV filled with large men, given the way it ran low to the ground. But he couldn't see if the windows were bullet proof or what weapons the men carried. He thought at first they would just drive by. He'd seen two other vehicles zip past, but this one stopped and pulled into the driveway.

Light burst across his senses. Floodlights triggered the moment the vehicle crossed the boundary of the property. Four men winced as they got out of their car. Thabo couldn't even twitch, so his vision was temporarily blinded. Didn't matter. There was nothing he could do standing here encased in stone and covered in barnacles.

"Well, well," a man's voice drawled. "That is impressive."

Thabo focused on a muscled man with a thick neck. He wasn't the largest by any means, but he wore authority the way some men carried a very large weapon. It was there for all to see and sometimes he used it just because he could. The man stepped to the back of the truck, peering up at Thabo's penis, as if measuring it.

Two other thick men flanked him, but the third—smaller and more wiry—bounced nervously around the truck bed, shaking his head as he tugged at the restraints that locked Thabo in place. "Dumb to leave him standing. One bad bounce and we could break him."

Thabo felt a rush of panic at the idea of losing his arms again. He had no idea how solidly they were re-attached, but he knew he wouldn't get full use until he animated at least once. The warriors who regularly went between Idola and Earth were always the most fit. Meanwhile, the leader reached out and rapped Thabo's calf with his knuckles.

"He's pretty solid. We'll drive him a couple blocks then lay him down once we're clear of here."

No! They were planning on stealing him. On driving him away from *her* and there was absolutely nothing he could do about it. And while that was disastrous for him, it would be death for her. Curators who lost their statues could be *disappeared*. Unmade, as if they had never been. Unless, of course, they made a different bargain with the goddess. And no one came out the better for that.

But what could he do? He was a statue and—

"Uncle Sully, what are you doing here?"

Her. She was somewhere behind him, out of sight, but her voice was getting stronger as she came closer.

"Molly. What are you doing out of bed?" the uncle asked.

Her name was Molly.

"Strangers are messing around on my property. Of course I'm up. And I thought we were going to meet tomorrow afternoon." Her voice was cold and angry, but Thabo could hear faint tremors underneath. She was frightened of this man she called family.

"Yah, but I heard about this little find of yours." He gestured to Thabo. "Had to come see it for myself." The uncle's voice was light, but there was iron underneath.

A shiver rippled down Thabo's spine as he anticipated the danger. One of Zeva's rules allowed him to animate without an expressed order. If his curator were in mortal danger, then he could help her. He could come to life and defend her against these hard-eyed men.

But as much as he willed his muscles to soften, his form remained locked solid. She wasn't in mortal danger yet.

"Well sure, Uncle Sully," she said, her voice taking on an edge of its own. "There's a pedestal inside. Just help me carry him there."

No one moved to do as she asked. They wouldn't. Not until the uncle agreed, and one look at the man's greedy eyes told him that Uncle Sully would release nothing to her.

Come closer, Thabo silently urged. He wanted to see her. He wanted to know how to best defend her when the danger escalated.

"Why's he holding a boat wheel?" the uncle asked as he gestured to Thabo's clenched fist.

Because he'd been the only one strong enough to manage the rudder during the storm, so many years ago. And when it became clear that they would sink anyway, he had turned to stone while still gripping it.

"Haven't a clue," she answered. "It's a miracle he's still intact, even buried so deep."

"How old is it?"

"No idea."

"What was the boat's name?"

"No idea." Her voice was getting more clipped, her tone annoyed. If only she would step around in front of him. If only he could see...

There! She'd moved to confront her uncle, nose to much smaller nose. At least now Thabo could see her.

She'd clearly just risen from bed. She wore loose clothing up top, and next to nothing below. Her breasts bobbed and her hair waved messily about her head. But she was still small enough—and fierce enough—to step between the truck and her uncle. And when she spoke, he heard the low, raw notes of fury.

"He's Mine, Uncle Sully. I found him. I salvaged him. And I'm not giving him up."

A heat burned at the base of his spine. A searing brand muffled through stone, but it was sharp and he wanted to howl at the pain. *Owned.* Never free. How far gone was he that he welcomed this woman as his mistress? She was a damned sight better than Zeva, but she was not freedom and part of him resented her for that.

Meanwhile, the uncle's hand settled thick and dangerous on her shoulder. A shift of his fingers would have him choking her. She didn't flinch at the contact, and Thabo couldn't see if her eyes blazed with fury the way his would if he were alive. And then the uncle spoke, his voice coaxing.

"I've been good to you these years, haven't I? No way would those boys have made college without me."

"I've paid you back for that, Uncle Sully. Every damned cent."

"Not the extra, Molly. Not what Bobby owes."

She shrugged his hand off her shoulder and Thabo could see she wanted to shove him across the garage. She hadn't the size or the strength. So she stood there, practically vibrating with her anger. "That's between you and Bobby. I got nothing—"

"He's in deep, Molly. And not just to me."

He could see the news hit her. Her shoulders bowed a bit before they straightened. "I can't save him, Uncle Sully. And that has nothing to do with this." Her head jerked to indicate the statue. Meanwhile outside of her field of vision, but ooh so clear to Thabo, the wiry one got into the truck.

"I'm taking him, Molly. As payment for Bobby's debt."

"Like hell you are!" she cried as she shoved her uncle away. He didn't budge an inch. His bulk was too big compared to hers. But with her attack, the uncle gestured to one of the waiting thugs.

Henchman One reacted with eager violence. He grabbed Molly by the elbow with one meaty fist to haul her backward, while his other arm wrapped around her chest. At her smaller size, she was held fast. But just to emphasize her vulnerable position, Henchman Two drew his pistol and waved it slowly in front of her eyes. It was a threat, and Molly took it seriously. She quieted, though her eyes blazed with fury.

That was the only benefit to that by-play. She'd turned now so he could see her face. For a split second, Thabo was able to memorize every detail of her expression, from the hard jut to her chin to the defeated cast to her shoulders. She already knew this was a fight she had no chance of winning and he ached to see that defeat in her. But then his line of sight was interrupted by the uncle. The man jumped onto the truck bed to inspect Thabo in humiliating detail.

"A lot of crusty shit on him," the bastard said. "How are you going to get it off?"

She wouldn't have to. It would rip away—quite painfully—the moment Thabo animated.

"I have no idea," Molly spat. "He's *Mine,* Uncle Sully. You can't steal him from me."

"Not stealing," the man returned as he walked around behind Thabo's extended arm. "Payment for Bobby."

"Bastard." Molly spit the word, but Thabo had been thinking it just as loudly. Didn't matter. The thugs reacted to her. She'd barely finished the curse when the guy holding her started to choke her. Easy to do with his arm across her neck, and Molly reacted like a cornered animal.

She fought with everything she had. She clawed at the arm across her neck and stomped down hard on his boot, but it was useless. Except in one regard.

Finally, her life was in danger.

Thabo concentrated with all his will, focusing on the image of Molly choked to death beside the truck. Was it enough? Could he...

Yes!

His stone body began to soften. The whole process took no more than a couple seconds, but to his consciousness it was a steadily increasing roar of deafening sensation. His extremities came first, fingers and toes burning with pain. Hundreds of years under the water had pocked his skin, and the pain of bringing life back to it was excruciating. Softness followed the pain in the way that a fire stoked hot enough it could melt stone. It roared up his legs and arms and left behind mobility. The shift of tendon and bone, and he began to shuck his restraints. His forearms slowly dropped, the weight of the wheel pulling them down as fingers riddled with holes grew slick from blood.

His shoulders screamed in agony. Barnacles had crusted over him in places, mostly his face, shoulders, and back.

The shift into human didn't dislodge them. They remained, biting into his flesh until movement shucked them off. His hips came next while pain burst into his belly. The last to soften would be his heart and his lungs. The things that gave him life, still frozen though straining to beat, to breathe, to move.

His face woke and he tilted his head back. Debris clattered to the metal bed of the truck, just as sound burst loud and painful through ears that could hear clearly again. He registered the roar of the engine—when had the truck started?—and Molly's scream. Not in pain. *Terror.* And she wasn't the only one.

Close to his ears, a man's voice erupted in horror. The uncle, just now seeing the statue turn to bloody flesh. He looked to the evil man, but then his vision shattered. The barnacles tore at his eyes and he screamed, but no sound came from lungs still hard as stone. His arms could move though. He'd already shrugged off the restraints. He was sure, even if no specific sensations lifted above the fire that was his entire body.

He threw the boat's wheel.

He had only his memory of where the uncle stood. His eyes burned too hard to open, but he knew the approximate direction. He heard a grunt of impact even as more sounds crowded into his consciousness. Curses in English and Spanish. And two words bellowed from the uncle.

"Shoot it!"

Then his heart lurched and his lungs drew breath.

Agony.

It twisted his senses, tangling them around each other into a confusing mass. He tasted the push of blood, heard the tang of air fouled with exhaust, and smelled the beat of his own heart.

She was still screaming.

He focused on that sound, turning toward Molly. But as he did, the world beneath his feet heaved. He fell backwards against the cab of the truck. Fresh agony burst through his body, but it was a small thing as he scrambled for balance. Everything was slick with blood. Now that his heart was beating, it pushed his life out of thousands of tiny cracks in his skin.

He dropped to his knees, a roar bellowing from his lungs. He had to stop the truck. He had to keep it from taking him away from Molly. His only choice was to smash through the back of the cab, but he never got the chance. The restraints on his body fouled his movements. They had been meant to hold a statue, but even slack, they twisted around his feet and hampered his action.

And while he removed the restraints, gunfire erupted. It banged in his eardrums and thudded against the metal vehicle. It also shattered the window and allowed him to reach through.

He grabbed the driver who squealed in terror. He guessed he'd grabbed the man's shoulder and the truck jerked sideways as the driver twisted away, spinning the wheel in the process. Thabo kept his balance this time, gritting his teeth against the pain, but then a bullet slammed into his shoulder and he toppled sideways into the bed of the truck. He kept one arm through the back of the cab, though, still holding onto the driver.

The thing about blinding agony is that it ate up concentration and left him with one overriding directive. For most men, it would be to find a way to make the pain stop. Thabo had long since learned to choose his focus. He picked Molly. He had to find her. He could protect her if he could get to her.

The wiry driver was being smart. Though he screamed, he kept driving, jerking the wheel left and right as he backed out of the driveway. It screwed up the others' aim which likely kept Thabo alive. Bullets pinged left and right, but none hit him. Still, it was a losing game as the truck backed further away from Molly. He could not abandon her so he had to jump. But without vision to know where he was going, he could leap onto anything.

No choice. He gathered his strength, scrambled for the side of the jerking truck, and jumped.

His bloody feet slid on grass and he went down, but that was what he wanted. Bullets pinged all around him, but he wasn't listening for that. He waited for Molly. She'd stopped screaming and he couldn't find her. Smart of the woman to hide herself in battle, but he needed to know where she was. So he took a breath that cut like knives through his insides.

"Molly!" he shouted.

She didn't answer, but he heard her squeak of alarm and centered on it. But if he went to her, he would draw the gunfire in her direction. The bastards were still shooting. So he set his back to Molly and roared in the direction of the men.

"Stop shooting!" he bellowed. Sometimes men got used to taking commands. They obeyed every order, no matter who it came from. It would only work for a second, and not at all with seasoned warriors. Fortunately, these men were not warriors and the gunfire ceased.

In the sudden silence, Thabo heard police sirens. He knew the sound only from description, but it could be nothing else. And in that pause, he heard Molly scream her own taunt.

"Run away, you shitheads! Run like the cowards you are!"

Thabo heard slamming car doors and the skid of wheels. It was the SUV rushing away. He couldn't see if all the men had left. Most important, he couldn't see if Uncle Sully remained. But as the roar of the SUV faded, Thabo felt the compulsion hit him.

Return to the pedestal.

Return to stone.

That meant the danger was past. Molly was no longer in peril.

He began to walk where the compulsion led him. He heard Molly squeak in alarm as she scrambled out of his way. He caught the scent of lemons and vanilla, and he turned toward it.

"Wh-who are you?" Molly stammered.

"Thabo," he answered even as the compulsion made him walk past her. "Of Zeva's army."

"You can't go inside!" she cried as she followed after him. She touched his arm and he hissed in pain. But it wasn't as bad as before, he realized. His skin was healing. Something about the halfway point between flesh and stone eased the pain. It wasn't just that his nerves were deadened. It was that as the magic took hold of his body, it also accelerated healing. It sealed crevices chipped away by time. It closed broken blood vessels and solidified cracked bones. Every moment he could hold off turning to statue was a moment when he grew stronger. But he didn't linger because of that.

He slowed his steps as much as possible so that he could remain with her. Molly with hair like coiling fire who smelled of lemons. His curator. But only if she grew a lot wiser, a lot faster.

"He will come back," he warned.

"Who?"

"Your uncle. Take precautions." There were stairs in front of him. He knew because he'd just banged his toes on them. Three steps as he went from garage to kitchen. It barely slowed him, though the dull flash of pain told him he had little time to get to his pedestal. He was nearly solid now.

Five steps. Six.

Through the kitchen, into the living room.

He knew his destination by the drag on his limbs. As if he were a metal man pulled to a lodestone. He lifted his knee to climb up, but there was no time. He solidified within inches of the base. Then he toppled forward, landing on his hip and belly. The magic thickened and he froze in this undignified position, ass up and face planted. Worse, his eyes were shut against the pain, so he could see nothing but blackness.

Well, he thought, at least no one would comment on his exposed privates.

CHAPTER 4

"That is one fine ass," purred the female Palmetto Bay cop, her eyes caressing the collapsed man statue.

She should see his front, Molly thought, but rather than speak that aloud, she buried her face in her mug of coffee. She didn't need the caffeine to wake up. She was wide awake and still terrified. But it was a soothing part of her morning ritual, so she sipped the dark brew and tried not to babble incoherently about what had just happened.

Meanwhile, the male of the police pair shot his partner an annoyed look then redirected his attention to Molly. "Let's go over this one more time."

"It's not going to make any more sense than the last time," she huffed. "My uncle came for my statue." She was pleased that she didn't stammer over the word "statue." Just because it came to life, fought to save her life, and then collapsed on a pedestal that hadn't been there yesterday, didn't mean it wasn't a statue. It was. Clearly it was. She'd gone over and felt its marble body, fine ass and all. "I salvaged it this afternoon...er, yesterday." It was now 5:00 a.m., with sunlight beginning to shine into the bullet holes that riddled her garage. "My uncle wanted it, and I said no."

"Then you had a gunfight."

She shuddered so bad she had to set down her coffee or spill it. But eventually, her words came out clearly. "He had guns. I screamed and ran."

The woman cop came over to her side and set a gentle hand on her shoulder. "The smartest thing you could do. But it was quite the rain of bullets out there."

Another shudder racked her frame.

"You're lucky you're alive."

She didn't feel lucky. She felt freaked and terrified and—

"Yes," drawled the man. "Just how did that work? They came for the statue, took aim point blank at you, and missed."

"They weren't aiming at me. They were aiming at the truck."

"Your truck?"

She swallowed and nodded.

"This one?" He flashed her a picture on his smart phone.

Molly took a look. Yup, there was her only vehicle now with a smashed back window, a crumpled side where it had slammed against her garage, and all those bullet holes.

"Yes," she choked out. She still couldn't believe her uncle had fucking shot at her!

"Why would they shoot up the truck?"

Her eyes drifted to the statue. She wasn't sure she wanted to call it Mine anymore, so she easily substituted "Thabo" in her thoughts. "The driver had gone nuts," she said. "He started backing out wild and…God I don't know." That last part was true enough. "It's all insane." Her uncle had shot at her! And she knew in her mind that it had been at Thabo but it all came out to the same emotional place. Her dead mother's only surviving relative had come to steal her statue, and when he hadn't gotten his way, he and his men had pulled out guns.

Sure, her uncle was a dangerous man. Mob ties possibly, big thug definitely. After Molly's mother died, he'd been all too willing to help…at a price, and not always in money. Shady packages picked up and delivered into his greedy hands. A credit card in her name that he always paid off.

Little things that spoke of petty crime that she'd escaped as soon as her three jobs covered what she needed. But he was always in the background, always ready to pounce on any weakness.

And apparently her brother Bobby had been weak.

She started to hyperventilate at what that might mean to her and her brother's lives. God, the terror of being under Uncle Sully's thumb had haunted her for the last ten years, and her mother for many years before that.

Then she felt the female cop press her into a chair. It was a welcome pull back to the present moment. Unfortunately, the cop pressed her into an overstuffed easy chair that aimed her vision straight at her statue. Thabo's finely sculpted ass was front and center, and she couldn't stop herself from staring. From replaying in her mind everything she'd seen.

The way he'd darkened in color, going from marble to black flesh in seconds. She remembered the way the crust of marine life had dropped from his body and the bright red blood that quickly replaced the black skin. Hell, he'd even left bloody footprints where he'd walked to the pedestal. She'd cleaned it up before the cops came in. Thank God she'd had the presence of mind to do that. But she'd missed the spot right below the statue's knee. It darkened the carpet, but what could she do about it? Nothing but pray no one else noticed, because how the hell would she explain that?

"Can we call someone for you?" the female cop asked. "You got a friend or family—"

"I…," she swallowed. "I've got a sister and two brothers," she finally said. "But it's too early to call them." And the last one she wanted to talk to was Bobby. Just what the hell had he been thinking to get in debt to Uncle Sully? And who knew how many others?

"I'm sure they'd want to know—"

"No!" She felt life and strength come into her body, and she invested it into her words. "They've got good lives now. Graduated from college and with good jobs." Did these cops have any idea how hard she'd worked to be able to say that?

To see her siblings not only surviving, but thriving? "Uncle Sully is my problem." And Bobby's.

"They're going to find out—" the woman began again, but Molly cut her off.

"I'll tell them in my way. I've spent my life making sure those kids make good. I'll be damned if my uncle knocks them off their feet now."

That shut the woman up. Her partner, too. In the end, they passed her their cards, told her to call them…blah, blah, blah. Molly barely heard it, couldn't wait to get them out of her house, and yet part of her didn't want them to leave. What if her statue came to life again? What if it didn't? What if she'd hit her head and none of this was real? Of course, the forensic guys in her garage were real. As were the bullet holes and the crumpled side of her garage. Hell, how was she going to pay for that?

She had no answers and she had to go to work soon. IHOP customers didn't serve themselves.

It was dark by the time she came home after one hell of a dinner shift. Her garage was wide open. Not a prayer that she'd ever get the door down again. So she thanked Frank, one of the IHOP cooks, for the ride and tried not to look at the dust and crap left behind by the forensics team. Then she walked steadily, determinedly straight into her house.

Don't look. Don't look.

It was an irrational thought. She'd spent the day obsessing about her statue coming to life. Of course she was going to look at it the moment she walked in. In truth, the only reason she'd managed to stay the afternoon at work was because she couldn't get anyone to cover her shift. If she had, she would have been back home and touching the cold marble just to reassure herself that it was real. That *he* was real.

She pushed inside and headed straight for her living room. But two steps into the door, she heard her sister's high trill of laughter. What the hell was Dani doing here?

She turned a corner and saw her sister at the kitchen table. Her freckled face was alive with humor as she gazed at Thabo—who was also alive and completely human-looking—where he lounged in the chair right next to her. Both had coffee mugs in front of them and both looked up when she appeared. Dani reacted first, her expression immediately softening to concern.

"Molly, oh my God, I can't believe you went to work—"

"What the hell are you doing here?" Molly demanded, not sure if she was talking to Dani or Thabo.

Dani pushed to her feet and adopted that same attitude the girl had perfected in adolescence. "I came to see if you were okay. I should have known that a *gunfight in the garage* couldn't keep you from work. Jesus, Molly, what the—"

Molly held up her hands in surrender. She couldn't take any more. Her shift had been one disaster after another and she just fucking couldn't—

"Molly," Thabo said. One word as he pushed to his feet and all that glorious body appeared. He was wearing Bobby's sweatpants and a torn wife-beater tee, both obviously too small. His muscles rippled as he moved, dancing in glorious display, and should have been terrifying. But the way he said her name—all tender and soft—made her head swim. He was a statue. A freaking statue she'd salvaged from the bottom of the ocean. And yet one glance at the pedestal showed that it was empty. Though that bloodstain from his knee remained, a dull brown on her faded blue carpet.

She swayed on her feet, the world much too unstable for her to handle. He was beside her in a moment, guiding her to that same easy chair that aimed right at the pedestal.

She closed her eyes.

"What happened?" her sister asked, being typically non-specific. Did she mean right then when she'd just about fainted? Last night, when Uncle Sully had come at her with a gun? Or how about when she was at work and her damned statue had come to life again to sit drinking coffee at her kitchen table?

"What have you heard?" she asked.

"Shots. Police. Thabo told me he was visiting and kept it from being worse, thank God."

"How long have you two been talking?"

Dani shrugged. "Long enough for me to give him our life story. But there aren't any answers about why Uncle Sully would suddenly start shooting at you."

Molly sighed and focused on the one thing she could tell Dani. "Bobby got himself in trouble with Uncle Sully. He came here to collect."

Dani's curse was impressive for being a half dozen profanities strung so tightly together they sounded like one word. Then she took a breath. "Look, I've got some money saved…"

"Don't you fucking dare," Molly hissed. Dani was saving every penny for an MBA. "This is Bobby's problem, and he's got to solve it."

"And if it kills you in the process?" Dani pressed. Molly was about to answer, but Thabo did it for her. He stood above them, his arms crossed and fury in his face.

"I will not allow that to happen," he said, and God help her, she believed him. She didn't even know who he was— *what* he was—but the moment his clearly enunciated words hit the air her entire body relaxed. He had a foreign accent of some sort. African, maybe? There was an odd rhythm to his words and it brought to mind exotic places and old movies, like *Casablanca.* Stupid to trust an accent, but damn it, she did.

She looked at him. "Why are you here?"

"I can be no other place," he stated.

"Of course he can't," Dani said as she nudged Molly's arm. "And why didn't you tell me you were dating?"

How to answer that? No way to explain how a hot guy was staying here and wearing Bobby's old clothes. "It's, um, really new." Like hadn't-happened-yet new. "And tell me again why you're here?"

"Because you got shot at!"

Molly huffed out a breath. "Yeah, but how did you know?"

Dani rolled her eyes. "Because half the freaking neighborhood called me. They've been bringing around casseroles all day looking for gossip." She gestured behind her to the kitchen counter. Molly had been too freaked to notice that every available space was filled with dishes of Tuna Helper or egg salad. There were probably six Jell-O molds in the refrigerator. "Why'd you leave your phone here?" she asked. "It's been ringing non-stop."

That's why. And because she'd forgotten to grab it when she realized she was late for work.

"Zach's been calling too. He's going to drive down from Chicago—"

"No." Her nearest-in-age sibling was not going to leave his architecture job for this. Out of all of them, he was on the most solid footing, but only if he kept working sixty-hour weeks.

"We're not leaving you alone in this."

Thabo shifted uncomfortably. "She is not alone."

Dani flashed him a warm smile. "Thanks. And I appreciate your support. But we're her family. Everyone needs to know that if one of us is in trouble, we're all in trouble."

Thabo's expression darkened. "Is Uncle Sully not part of your family? And Bobby?"

Molly grimaced. "Yes and yes." Then before Dani could say more, she squeezed her sister's arm. "I'm sorry I worried you and I should have called—"

"Ya think?"

"But this is happening really fast. I've put out a restraining order on Uncle Sully." That's how she'd spent her morning. That, plus all the insurance paperwork for her truck and her garage. "And I'm going to talk to Bobby—"

"If you can find him."

Right. "But for the moment, honey, please, please, please, will you give me a chance to get my wind back?" She glanced not at Thabo, but at the empty pedestal right behind him. "Thabo and I need to have a talk. In private."

Dani's eyes narrowed as she looked between her sister and the new man in the house. "I can hang out in the bedroom. Don't have to hear a thing."

"Right. Like any part of this house or neighborhood is sound proof." When her sister started to object, Molly pulled the girl's chin back to her. Just like she'd done countless times when they were little. "I need you to thank all the neighborhood for their gifts."

"Already done."

Right. Her sister was the most organized, disciplined woman on the planet. Once she got her MBA, the world was going to open up for her.

"Then you need to call off Zach. Tell him to stay in Chicago."

"He'll want to hear it direct from you."

Of course he would. "But you can delay him for me."

Dani nodded.

"And then I know you're going to try to put the fear of God into Bobby." Dani and Bobby were the nearest in age. When their parents had died, Bobby had gone off the rails. Dani had used all her wiles to keep it hidden from the rest of the world. She'd been trying to give her brother time to get his act together without having Zach or Molly get up in his business. And it had worked until Dani went to college. That was five years ago and Bobby had become increasingly rebellious ever since. The awful truth was that the only one he was rebelling against was himself.

Meanwhile, Dani's expression turned rueful. "I don't know that I can reach him."

"You're the only one who can."

Dani grimaced and nodded. "So you're not going to tell me what happened last night? About why there's a huge pedestal in the middle of the living room."

Molly sighed. "Uncle Sully wants that statue I told you about. The one I salvaged yesterday."

Fear came into Dani's expression, swiftly covered. That was her sister, brave to the core, but they'd all been raised on warnings to stay away from Uncle Sully. Dani knew that where Uncle Sully saw an opening, he would do whatever was necessary to turn it to his advantage.

"So he wants the chiseled eye candy, huh? Where is it?"

Good question. Fortunately, Thabo had a clever answer. "I have hidden it for now. Your uncle cannot capture it."

Capture. What an interesting word as opposed to "find" or "take."

"But is it valuable? I mean, there *are* bullet holes in the garage. The neighbors made it sound like the shoot-out at the O.K. Corral."

It had felt like that too, but Molly just shook her head. "I can't talk about that right now. I just can't." She probably couldn't, ever.

"You have heard most of the story from the neighbors," Thabo inserted quietly. "You should let your sister rest now. I will watch to be sure she is safe. Then maybe she will feel better tomorrow."

Maybe. Or maybe she would wake up in the looney bin. Meanwhile, her sister studied both of their faces very closely. Then she pinned Molly with a hard look.

"Is he a good thing or a I'm-not-sure thing?" The *he* in question was Thabo. "Because I can stay, and he could go."

Tempting, except that Molly was pretty sure that Thabo wasn't going anywhere. Not as long as his pedestal was in her living room. "Go home, sis," she said strongly. "Let me get some rest."

Dani didn't take the direction gracefully, but she did end up leaving. After all sorts of fussing and making sure Molly ate some lasagna. Then after one long, hard look at Thabo, she finally left. Which meant Molly could get some answers.

Except now that the moment was at hand, Molly wasn't sure what to ask. In the end, it was a pretty easy conversation to start. She just leaned back in her chair and said two words.

"Explain. Now."

CHAPTER 5

Thabo slowly lowered himself onto his pedestal, squatting there as he eyed his curator. She watched him warily, reminding him strongly of a sharp, bright cockatrice. The legendary creature had a rooster's face, eagle's wings, and the tail of a serpent. Her bright red hair and regal bearing were enough to make the similarity. But it was her eyes that froze him, just like a cockatrice. They seemed to pierce right through him, calm, clear, and so beautiful that he was dumbstruck.

She saw him. And she waited for him to speak. After two centuries of serving a fickle goddess with little patience, Molly's quiet attention was unnervingly powerful. And he could barely think for the wonder of it. What he wouldn't give to touch her as well. To feel the heat from skin that looked as soft as down. To remember what it was to caress a woman.

"It is a long story," he finally said.

"I'm not working again for twelve hours."

"I was an arrogant youth. I ran like the wind and boasted that no soul could beat me."

She arched a brow. "Kids brag all the time."

"I was no child. Only a youth in mind. Twenty-two when a woman appeared and offered to race me. I laughed at her. No female had ever come close to matching my speed."

Molly dropped her head back against the heavily cushioned chair, her expression weary. "I'm guessing she beat you."

He nodded. "She offered me riches if I won, but if I lost I had to serve her until she won a wager against her sisters."

"Which was what?"

"She must gather the largest and most unusual army of stonemen at the world's end."

"World's End? Where is that?"

He shook his head. "It is a time. When the Earth dies."

She didn't respond at first, but her expression said clearly what she was thinking. She did not believe a word of it. And if she doubted this part, how would she understand the magic that bound him?

"Go on," she prompted when he fell silent. "You're in her army until the planet dies. Hope you live a long life."

"I am immortal as long as I serve the goddess."

Her lips twisted in a wry smile. "Of course you are."

"I lost the race, so now I serve the goddess as her stoneman. I come to life on Earth when she has a task for me. Otherwise, I stay in stone or serve her on Idola."

"Idola?"

"That is Zeva's realm. And that is the last time I will say her name aloud."

"Zena? The Warrior Princess?"

"No. With a 'v,' and do not say her name. Swear this to me, Molly. For if you call her name, she may appear."

"Sounds like a good thing. Maybe this bitch needs a reminder that slavery is illegal in the United States." She was joking. He could hear it in her tone. She mocked his story, even as she pretended to believe him, and his temper flared.

"How can you laugh at me when you have seen me come from stone? When you have met her and made your own poor bargain?" He was on his feet now, glaring down at her as he tried to get her to see. His fists were raised, his body tense. If he spoke like this in Idola, he would already be in a fight. The battles between soldiers were as common as boredom, and he was prepared for any attack she would make.

Except she didn't attack. She tilted her head as she held her gaze.

"So you still have that arrogant temper, then."

At first he didn't understand what she was saying. He simply stared at her, adjusting too slowly to the idea that she wasn't about to fight him. Then he looked down at his fists and slowly opened them.

"I have been too long away from Earth."

She arched a brow. "How long?"

"The ship sank in 1835 and my curator drowned. Since then I have stayed in Idola, only returning to my statue as punishment." He looked down at her faded blue carpet. "Until the goddess brought you to me, I was buried deep beneath the ocean floor. Endless years of dark silence is not easy on a man's sanity."

She opened her mouth as if to comment, but then shut it again. She was watching him, weighing his words, and giving nothing away as to her thoughts. He had faced off with thousands of opponents, each canny in their own way. They had to be in order to survive in Zeva's army. But Molly was different. She didn't wait in the way of a predator, watching for an opening to attack. She simply waited. As if she had to remain patient while he discovered something. And without knowing what it was he needed to find, Thabo became uncomfortable under her stare.

"You must listen to me, Molly. You agreed to be my curator and that makes you beholden to the goddess just as much as I."

"I never agreed to—"

"You said I was yours. You claimed ownership and she gave you the Rules."

Molly paled, the shift in blood clear on her very white skin. "The woman in the truck? The one who…" she waved vaguely at him. "Put your arms back on?"

He nodded. "That was…the goddess. Her name loosely translates to War, and you can refer to her as such."

"And I told War you were Mine."

"Yes."

"Because you're the statue now on earth, come to life. After she had me find you." Her tone wasn't as mocking as before, but it was still heavy with disbelief.

"How did you find my ship?" he challenged. "There, at the bottom of the ocean?"

"I was sailing with a friend and we…" She shrugged. "My compass got screwed up and the GPS was wonky. But I went diving anyway, and I found you."

"After a storm. One that seemed to shake the very foundations of the Earth." He had felt the deep rumble and watched as tons of ocean floor was moved from around him. And he had watched as Zeva stood hip deep in the silt, her hair wild and her body encased in scales of gold, as she whipped the ocean into a frenzy. Even knowing she was powerful, the sight had awed him.

"Florida gets lots of storms."

"War uncovered me, and she brought you to me. She is nearing completion of her wager, and she wants all her army intact." He gestured to his arms. "For me, that meant I needed repair and a curator." He met her gaze. "You."

"Because you're a statue who serves a goddess. And I promised a crazy woman that you were mine."

"Yes."

A long pause, then…

"How long have you been off your meds?"

Her phrasing was confusing, but her meaning was clear. So he responded with his own challenge. "You have seen me turn from stone. Why do you doubt the evidence of your own eyes?"

She had no answer to that. Just a haunted expression that told him she doubted her own sanity. So he moved close enough to touch her face. A slow caress of her cheek such as he had wanted to do since first seeing her. And a shiver went up his spine at the exquisite softness of her skin.

"What would it take to convince you?" he asked. "Should I turn to stone again while you watch?" The shift to and from was painful, but for her, he would do it as many times as she required.

"Maybe," she finally said.

He stood and crossed back to his pedestal. But on the way, he accidentally kicked something small that he had not seen there on her carpet. It pinged against the wall where'd kicked it.

"What's that?" she asked as she pushed forward out of her chair.

He looked at the floor, finally locating the object where it had landed near the corner of the room. Ah. He quickly picked it up. "It's the bullet. I was shot in the shoulder last night. Do you remember?"

Her hand started shaking as he pressed it into her palm. "I, um…"

She had never been in a battle before, and certainly not a gun battle. That much he could tell from her face, and his heart ached to meet such innocence. He'd seen violence almost from his earliest days, long before becoming trapped by Zeva. "Fear not," he said gently. "A single shot is nothing to me. I have received much worse."

She swallowed and folded her fingers over the misshapen bullet as if blocking it from her sight. "How did you get it out?"

"It had to fall out as I shifted from stone to flesh to stone again throughout the day. It was necessary to repair the other cracks in my body as well." It was an incomplete answer. Normally such a thing wouldn't work, but Zeva had covered the worst of his damage in her magic paste while she was setting his arms. And then when he'd reappeared in Idola after the night's battle, she had commanded him to heal as fast as possible. That meant he could shift between life and stone through the day, steadily repairing the remaining cracks in the most painful way possible.

Molly blinked as she stared at him. "None of that makes sense."

"And yet it is true. The longer to you take to accept this, the more danger you are in."

Her eyes widened at that and again he indulged himself by touching her. He stroked across her jaw and fluttered his fingers down her neck. No warrior would ever allow him to touch so vulnerable a place. She did not push him away. In fact, the fine tremors that racked her body were something else entirely. Fear? Confusion? Or could it be lust?

His groin surged at the thought. Sex was not something he had considered for two hundred years. Zeva was not one to indulge in that, though rumor whispered her sisters enjoyed it immensely. To have a soft woman beneath his fingers now had desire surging so powerfully that his hips jerked in hunger. He held himself back, stunned by the need. Part of him considered the many thousands of ways he could take Molly, right here, right now, whether she willed it or not. But he had lost so much of himself while serving Zeva. His honor and sanity were shreds of what had once been. Even so, to take an unwilling woman was a line he hadn't crossed. He would not do it now no matter how much the blood pounded in his ears and his organ throbbed with need.

He took a hasty step back, though his movements were unsteady.

Her eyes widened at his awkward movement, but he did not allow her the chance to comment.

"I will turn to stone now. When you are ready, ask me to return, and I will." Then he hesitated. "But do not take too long. I only have three days and much to accomplish in that time."

She pushed to her feet, clearly unsteady. "And if I never ask you to return? Will you stay a statue?"

"Is that what you want?" he rasped. Pain lanced through him at the thought that she would want him to stay away. That she would never let him touch her again, even in the briefest way.

She shrugged. "I've gone looney tunes. Who the hell knows what I want?"

"You do," he challenged. The woman who had so boldly faced down the goddess in her truck would not be one to hide in insanity. She was too fierce for that. "You know that this is real, and you know exactly what you want."

She glared at him, but he had the impression that her annoyance was for herself, not him. "Fine," she eventually bit out. "You're real. Bitch Goddesses are real. And my garage is really shot to hell." She gestured to the pedestal. "Go on. Show me how insane the world really is. I promise I won't take long staring at your marble self."

"And when I return," he said, "we will talk about how you will survive being my curator."

She jolted. "What?"

"Did you read the Rules?"

"I couldn't. They were in the truck under your foot."

He suspected as much. "Call me back quickly, Molly. We have much to discuss."

"Oh goody," she drawled. Then she folded her arms across her chest and nodded her readiness. "Rock on."

CHAPTER 6

Molly wasn't exactly sure what she expected when Thabo stepped onto the pedestal. Last time it had been so fast and she'd been completely freaked out. One second he was crawling, the next she had a statue of a collapsed man lying on her living room floor. This time he stood tall and faced her square on. He stripped off the wife beater tee, holding it out and to the side. And then he flashed her a rueful smile.

"I will try to go slowly so you can see," he said.

And then it happened. Ebony flesh seemed to fade to gray before her eyes. All that huge expanse of glorious chest turned zombie-gray starting from dead center. The expansion of that sickening stone was slow enough to see, but still happened in the space of a single held breath. His chest, his arms and legs, and his face. Oh God, his face just hardened in that rueful expression, half smile and half grimace. Damn. That had to hurt. It just had to.

And then he was solid marble. Every part of him was a whitish-gray color frozen in place, staring right at her. And still wearing pants. Even more bizarre, his hand still gripped the shirt. She walked over to that, gingerly touching the fabric, still warm from his body. Then she tried to pull it free. Nope. It was gripped in his fist and wasn't going anywhere.

Damn.

Something about that just terrified her. The warm fabric gripped by a stone hand. She stared at it a long time, her breath coming in short jerks. She would not freak out, she ordered herself. If she'd kept it together during a shoot-out in her garage, then she'd keep it together now. It was just a statue. A magical cursed statue.

Magic was real.

Her mind stuttered to a halt, echoing those last words until it seemed to throb in her entire body.

Magic was real.

Her knees started to give out and she dropped onto her scarred coffee table. It creaked under her weight, but it had withstood two teenage boys, so it damn well better not collapse now. And why the hell was she thinking about a coffee table when Thabo was a stoneman?

She swallowed, her gaze drawn back to his face. God, what would it be like? Trapped in a stone body while the world passed by? Unable to interact. Unable to do anything but just watch. And shit, he'd been in a sunken ship for years. Hundreds of years. Oh God. The thought had her shaking in horror.

She touched his chest, startled to realize she was standing. More than standing, she was inspecting every part of his body. The man was cut, that was for damn sure. Ripped abs, lean build, and every muscle clearly defined. Also, the scars and moles. Pock marks and subtle imperfections everywhere. No chisel had made those marks. They were the raised bumps of puncture wounds or the ridge of a cut long since scarred over. And then there was his chest hair. Tightly coiled ripples in the stone. She looked up to the top of his head. His hair was cut close, but even there she could see the delineation of every single strand. She was tempted to tug down his pants to check there, but called herself a perv for even thinking it. And for wanting to see up close and personal exactly what was there. Well, wanting to see it *again*, because she'd spent a bunch of time looking at it when he was underwater.

So. Magic *was* real.

The thought wasn't banging as loudly in her head anymore. Instead, it sparked a low giggle of humor, all the funnier because of its hysterical edge. Were fairies and goblins real too? Did a four-leaf clover really bring luck, and could she find a pot of gold at the end of a rainbow?

She was Irish by heritage, and the idea that all those lovely stories were true gave her a deep thrill of delight. She'd always wanted a fairy to clean her home while she was at work. And why did Pete get a dragon when she didn't? There sure as hell had been a few monsters who'd needed slaying when she was growing up. God, why hadn't the magic shown up then? No, it had waited until now when she was finally free of sisterly duties, just to give her another freaking dependent. Not three traumatized siblings this time, but a magical statue man.

And now she was moving from hysterical to pissed off. None of this was rational. Not the magic and certainly not her reaction. But she figured she'd left reason behind the minute she'd poured all her savings into salvaging a statue instead of buying a mutual bond.

"Okay, Thabo. You can come back now."

She hadn't even made the conscious decision to call him back, but now that the words were spoken, she didn't regret them. Since her list of Rules had disappeared with her truck, she'd have to get them directly from Thabo.

He unfroze as quickly as before and in much the same way. Only this time zombie gray grew darker, richer. She thought it might look like a black hole taking over, but it was different than that. His skin was vibrant even when looking like lickable dark chocolate. His flesh was supple and beautiful, pulsing with life. She watched in amazement as his body softened. His eyes sparked bright and his expression tightened in struggle. Then he took a slow, tortured breath that rasped in his throat until the exhale.

That came out in a sigh as the hand holding the tee dropped to his side.

"You see?" he asked.

"Yes."

"You believe?"

"Hard not to."

"Then you will care for me?"

Her eyes jumped to his. She'd been watching the steady lift and lower of his chest. Seeing the way his scars now moved and his belly shifted as he bent forward. She stepped back to give him room to step down off the pedestal. She banged painfully into her coffee table, and he caught her elbow with a reaction time faster than human.

"I have questions," she said.

"Whatever you need."

His words were more than a simple statement. It had the echo of a vow, and she searched his expression for...something. She read honesty in his face and desperation. But she also felt a pull. That same attraction she'd felt when she'd first seen his statue, and right there was her answer.

"This is part of the magic, isn't it?" she asked.

He frowned. "What?"

"This..." She reached out to touch his chest, flattening her hand there as she felt his breath and his heartbeat steady beneath her fingertips. "This draw I have to you. The connection." It was like a live wire stretched between them. "It's the magic, isn't it? So I'll be your curator."

He frowned. "There is no magic for that. Not even the goddesses can force you to feel anything. They can only bind you after you have agreed."

She shook her head. "That can't be true. Everything I've done around you has been weird. Damn it, I spent most of my savings to salvage you."

He swallowed. "And I am grateful beyond words."

"I don't want your gratitude!" she snapped. "I want my life back. And my garage!"

He stroked his hand down her arm, the gesture meant to be soothing. But she felt so many things when he did that. His calluses were rough but his touch was gentle. Heat followed his fingertips and desire sparked low in her belly. She'd felt lust before in her life. Lots of times, but this was stronger than ever before. Her reaction came so swiftly as her nipples tightened and her body softened toward him. Everything in her wanted to touch him, and that had been true when he'd been a statue sunk up to his groin in the ocean. But now that he was alive? God, it was insane.

She took a forceful step back. "This is not normal."

He didn't argue with her. He just stood there looking. And while they watched each other, she noted how his sweatpants shifted as his erection thickened. He moved his hand to cover himself and turned away, clearly ashamed.

"See?" she pressed. "That's not normal!"

He looked back, his expression startled. "That I would react to a beautiful woman? That I would want what any man would desire?"

She swallowed and tried to get a hold of her rioting emotions. She shouldn't have bothered. There was no managing this particular ride. She just had to hold on and hope she came out the other side intact. "So how long has it been for you? Since you, you know, were with a woman?" And why the hell was she asking that? Of all the questions that were fighting to get out, why would that be the one to surface first?

"Since before boarding the *Duncan*. I do not know what year it is now."

"Was that the ship that sank?"

He nodded. "We were heading here to grow tobacco. My owner purchased a farm."

She noted that he said "owner" as opposed to "curator." Had he been a slave? Meanwhile, she gestured to her wall calendar. "Today's the third." And when he turned and stared at it, she wondered if he knew how to read it. Well, a part of her did. The rest of her was thinking that ship went down two hundred years ago, and he'd been celibate that long. She knew men who couldn't go a week.

As least he thought she was beautiful. Though, to someone who'd been away as long as he had, a deformed senior citizen would probably look like a supermodel.

And this was a silly, fruitless conversation! What the hell was going on in her head? She'd never had this much trouble focusing, even when lip locked with her high school crush. But damn if she wasn't aching to touch Thabo even now. Worse, she wanted to lick him from head to toe like a lollipop. Jesus, she was depraved!

"Okay, let's try and keep it together here." She was speaking to herself more than him, but she watched him square his shoulders and face her directly.

"What do you need from me?" he asked.

And right there all those carnal bells started ringing. He wanted to help her and damn if she didn't want everything he had to offer. She shoved all of that down as far as she could and tried to focus on what was important. "Tell me the basics."

Thabo nodded smartly. Clearly he'd been in some kind of military. Then he started rattling off information in a rapid-fire staccato of facts. He gave her nicknames of goddesses with their approximate military strengths. He talked about stonemen throughout the world and to what ends they were deployed. Apparently, there was a skirmish right now between Chaos and Justice which Zeva was watching with great interest. He explained that the goddesses occasionally interfered in events, but they feared their father's wrath if they mucked about too openly. He was about to detail the organization of Zeva's army when Molly held up her hand.

He stopped speaking mid-word.

"I meant the Rules, Thabo. Let's start with those." He blinked, and she rolled her eyes. "Why do men always make it so complicated?" she asked. It was meant to be a rhetorical question, but he answered it anyway.

"Because women don't ask for simple things."

She arched a brow and her first flash of humor hit. Finally, a chuckle that wasn't born of hysteria. "You got me there. But can we start with my rules?"

"You have agreed to take care of me. That means you cannot sell or discard me. And any damage that happens to me can be inflicted upon you." He paused for a moment, his expression grave. "War enjoys giving pain."

It took a moment for that to sink in, and when it did, she had a host of other questions. Not to mention a full minute of panic. Eventually she pulled herself together and reached for the first question. "So you can be hurt?"

"Yes. In all the usual ways. I am stronger and faster than typical for a man, and I usually heal faster. But in all other ways, I am exactly like a normal man."

If other men were cut warriors with extra special training. "So if a building falls down on you and you get crushed—"

"The goddess will crush you as well."

Oh goody. "Well, let's avoid collapsing buildings then. What about your last curator?"

"He died when the ship sank."

"And you were at the helm—"

"Because I was the only one strong enough to manage it." He shook his head. "And even I failed."

Clearly that weighed on him. "And now I've got you," she said softly. "So how do you I take care of you?"

"I…" He frowned, his words abruptly cut off. "I believe there is a board that has all this information on it. One of the newest warriors said as much. He claimed that curators from all the goddesses were speaking with one another. He believed that War could learn things to her benefit from these people."

Her head jerked up. "A board? What kind of board? Where?"

He shook his head. "I do not know it. A single place where people throughout the world can speak to one another without the need to travel. It seems inconceivable."

That's because he'd been sunk in the ocean for the last two hundred years. She grinned as she reached for her tablet and thumbed it on. "Welcome to the modern age, Thabo. Let me introduce you to something called the internet."

She was just pulling up her browser when Thabo gripped her arm. "What weapons do you have, Molly?"

"What? None!"

"Then you must hide. Someone is hunting you through the back yard."

CHAPTER 7

Thabo expected Molly to run into a back room. She was an untrained warrior, and she was woefully unprepared to face another fight. He should have known better. Certainly she had been terrified in her garage, but today was different. She'd had time to realize just how much her life had changed. Not enough to get smart, just enough time to be angry.

So while he pulled a knife from a block on her kitchen counter, she stomped to a glass door and hauled it open.

"Just who the hell do you think you are skulking in my back yard? Show yourself, you coward!"

Thabo was already leaping to her side, shoving her protectively behind him. Thanks to modern electricity, the back was abruptly flooded with light and he saw his target immediately.

It was a boy in his young twenties. At the prime of his youth and with no maturity to keep him alive. His face was slack with surprise but quickly shifted to the sulky anger of a child. And his eyes darted from Molly to Thabo and back. Given that the boy's soft chin and hazel eyes mirrored Molly's, he guessed the intruder's identity. But even if he didn't, Molly cried out when she saw him.

"Bobby! Why can't you come through the front door like a normal person? You scared the hell out of me!"

"Who's this?" the boy returned, his stance aggressive as he thrust his chin at Thabo. "Put that knife away. Looking all bad ass with a pointy stick. That's not going to do shit against someone with a gun."

The child had no idea what he could do with a knife and Thabo didn't move. Not even when Molly tried to push him aside to get through the door. He would not let her expose herself to this boy who was a great deal more dangerous than Molly seemed to understand. All children were when thrust into a man's body without the understanding of how to use it.

"This is Thabo," Molly said as she touched his right arm. Then she tugged at it, trying to get him to lower his knife. "That's my brother Bobby. Don't gut him."

Thabo addressed the boy. "Your sister asked why you did not come to the front door. Please answer the question."

"Or what? You'll gut me?" the boy mocked.

"I could in a dozen different ways."

"Thabo!"

"But I will not unless you try to enter this house without permission."

"It's my fucking house!" the boy cried.

"Really?" Molly drawled. "So you've come back to live here?"

The boy opened his mouth, but then shut it with a furious scowl. "It's mine, same as you."

"No, Bobby, it's not. I paid the mortgage here. Every last cent."

His expression shifted to upset, though Thabo could see the calculation, not in the boy's expression, but in the way he adjusted the conversation. If his goal was to get inside, then attacking his sister's emotions was the way to do it. "It always comes down to money with you, Molly. I'm your brother and I just came to see if you were okay. I heard about the shooting." His eyes scanned her anxiously. "You're not hurt, are you?"

Molly huffed out a breath and once again tried to push Thabo aside. And again, he remained rooted. "I'm completely freaked. Damn it, Bobby, he shot at me!" Her voice shook as she spoke, and Thabo wanted to reassure her but he didn't know how.

"But you're safe, right?" the boy pressed. "You're not hurt, right?" His voice wavered enough that Molly relented. She squeezed past Thabo to hug her brother. He could have stopped her, but that would not have helped his ability to defend her. It would merely put her more firmly on her brother's side.

"I'm fine," she said into her brother's shoulder. "I'll be fine."

The boy hugged her back, and Thabo watched with a distant twinge of longing. He'd had family once. Two older sisters and an aunt had pecked at him as women often do. But they had loved him with all their hearts.

"He shouldn't have done that," the boy was saying into Molly's hair. "He shouldn't have come here like that."

She sighed, pressed a kiss to Bobby's temple, though he was six inches taller. Then she pulled back. "You told him, didn't you? About the statue. I only told Dani, but you saw all the paperwork and pictures when you came last week. And you told him."

Bobby jolted backward, his shoulder hunched in defense. Only now did Thabo see the way the boy protected his right leg and that there were bruises on his arms almost hidden by his clothing. Bobby had taken a beating lately. Probably more than one. Thabo guessed the boy had been resisting his uncle's pressure. That spoke of a good heart, but the child had clearly lost the fight. He was now cowed and definitely working with his uncle.

"I didn't see nothing!" Bobby snapped. "I wasn't here."

"You were. It was Sunday while I was at work. You ate the bananas and my ice cream."

"Damn it, it wasn't me! Maybe it was your new boyfriend!"

Molly sighed and she stepped back. Thabo could see that she was tired. Not just from everything that had happened, but bone weary of fighting with her brother. "Bobby—" she began, but Thabo cut her off.

"Do not give in. He has worn you down, but you must be like stone."

She shot him a look filled with resentment. It was a defensive response to hate the messenger. But did she also know that he spoke the truth? He couldn't tell, and he couldn't allow her to jeopardize herself.

"Uncle Sully is your enemy," he continued, his words delivered with precise language. "This boy is his informant. You must not allow him access to you."

"I'm not some fucking spy!" the boy spat. Then he rounded on his sister. "And when did you start slutting yourself out to some black guy?"

Molly reared back with shock which gave Thabo the space to act. He didn't use his knife, though it was desperately tempting to do so. Instead, he grabbed the boy by the arm and slammed him onto the ground. Bobby's head bounced on the grass, but not hard enough to break. And by the time the boy recovered, Thabo had put his bare foot on the child's throat.

"You fuc—" Profanities flew from the child's mouth, rapidly cut off when Thabo pushed harder. Meanwhile, Molly was hauling on his arm, trying to pull him back.

"Don't you dare hurt him!" she screamed.

Thabo didn't move for either of them. He held his ground, keeping the boy silent while he turned to Molly.

"Thabo! I order you to let him go!"

Coldness washed through him. It froze his explanations such that they caught thick and hard in his throat. Other words formed to drop like ice from his lips. "You do not command me, Molly. You are as much a slave as I, and we obey War."

"I don't—"

He pointed at her. Not with the knife. That remained aimed at the child's nose. He used his finger on Molly and spoke clearly. "Hear me, Molly. You do *not* command me."

She swallowed, clearly absorbing the fury in his words. "You're right. I'm sorry. I shouldn't have ordered you." Then she looked down at her brother. "But you can't go hurting—"

"I have known thousands of boys like him."

The child stiffened. "I'm not a boy, you fuck—"

Thabo increased pressure on the child's throat and the curses stopped. And while he stared at Molly, he felt the boy's body shift as he tried to grab Thabo's pants. It was an obvious move and Thabo stopped it with a flick of the knife. The child gasped, his arm flinching back. Thabo didn't even have to look to know that he'd cut the boy. Deep enough to scar, but not maim.

Meanwhile, he continued to speak.

"War delights in these children. Bodies of men, but minds like arrogant children. They are easy prey. They respond to taunts and seduction. And once they are in her clutches, she breaks them to her will. It takes less than two days until they are lost to everything but her."

The boy objected to what he said. Bitter anger boiled through his body, but it was Molly who interested Thabo. Her eyes teared up, and she looked away.

"He'll grow out of it," she said.

"No, he won't," he said. And when she rose to argue with him, he held up his hand. "I was one such man child. If War hadn't taken me, I would have died in some other way." He glanced down at the boy. "It is too late for this one. You must harden your heart and send him away."

Molly straightened as if slapped. She was reacting in the way of all mothers, living in hope for a child even when all was lost. "I do not give up on those I love! Never. He's my brother and you need to get your foot off him." And when he didn't move, she grimaced then blew out an angry breath. "That wasn't an order. *Please,* get your foot off his throat."

"I will not allow him to hurt you. You are too important."

She dropped her hands on her hips. "Me? Why? Because I'm your..." She glanced at the boy. "Because I have your pedestal?"

"No! Because..." His words faltered. She was his curator, and that made her important. He had been so long without one. And yet, he knew that if she died, another would claim him. Another who perhaps was better at defending himself. Her uncle certainly qualified. That man might help Thabo do something spectacular as Zeva had ordered. Molly was nearly useless in matters of war. She had no great wealth or skill. And yet, every part of him wished to protect her.

And while he stood there struggling with his words, Molly's expression flattened out to bitterness. "Like I said. It's because I've got your pedestal."

He shook his head. "You do not understand." But without a better explanation, he gave in to her request. He stepped off the boy, though he kept his knife hand ready.

Meanwhile, Molly geared up to argue more. He saw her gather her breath, but before it translated into words, the weight of the last twenty-four hours defeated her. Her eyes still sparked with anger, but her shoulders slumped and her gaze dropped to her brother. A moment later, she addressed the child. "How deep are you in to Uncle Sully?"

"I ain't—"

"I'm too fucking tired, Bobby. Sully told me, okay? He said you owed him big. And others too."

The boy's body broke then. Not in the way of a bone, but in the way of a kicked puppy. His eyes teared up, his muscles quivered, and every part of him appeared wounded and tragic. If Thabo still had a heart, he might have been moved.

"He tricked me, Molly. He offered me a job, and I needed the money. It was a craps game, and I just had to stand watch."

Molly wasn't moved. She was disgusted. "You played. Damn it, Bobby. You know his games are rigged."

"It wasn't." He pushed up on his elbows while keeping a wary eye on Thabo. "I made sure of that. I watched everything and..."

"And yet you still lost. And you kept playing—one way or another—trying to recover. Not just with Sully but with others."

"I had it worked out, Molly! I did. It wasn't gambling, it was—"

"A sure thing? Jesus, Bobby, you're a fucking idiot. How many times are we going to play this game?"

Predictably, the boy rose at the insult. "You never had any faith in me! You always helped the others, but I was just the whipping boy..."

The words continued while Molly seemed to shrink with every accusation.

"Let him go," Thabo said, his voice pitched deep so that she could hear him beneath her brother's higher toned rant. "Surely you can see he has been broken by your uncle. Not all slavers are goddesses."

He saw acceptance in her expression, but still her heart could not let the child go. She raised her hand to silence the boy and in a space between a curse and another accusation, she voiced her question.

"What do you want, Bobby?"

"A little fucking respect from my sister who used to love me."

"Stop it, Bobby! What do you want?"

"I came to see if you were okay!" He spoke so angrily, he spit the words.

"I'm not!" She shot back, equally angry. And then her eyes narrowed as she finally understood. "Uncle Sully sent you over here, didn't he? He wants to know about...about the statue." To her credit, she didn't even look at Thabo. They both knew that if her uncle realized that he was a magic statue, the man would stop at nothing to possess him.

Meanwhile, Bobby's gaze did narrow on Thabo. "Is this the guy? The one who attacked Uncle Sully with a boat wheel?"

"No—" Molly said, but Thabo saw no reason to deny it.

"Yes, I am the one. Your uncle sought to take that which is not his. He brought men and guns. I had merely the wheel of a boat to save her life."

"Nobody was going to hurt her!" Bobby blustered.

"If that were true, I would not have been able to help." The boy wouldn't be able to understand what he said, but Molly could. "I can only help if you are about to die."

He saw the meaning hit her. That she could have died in that confrontation even though the panicked gunshots had been aimed at him. Worse, he saw the realization crush her. She stumbled as her knees went out. He cupped her elbow and eased her back inside. She went like a doll, and the boy followed. But this he could not allow. As soon as Molly was seated safely, he rounded on Bobby.

"Go back to your uncle. Tell him that your sister has no part in your debt. And tell him as well that I am more dangerous than any man he has ever met. It would be best if he left us alone."

He thought it would be over then. Even the boy could see that no good would come of staying. But the child was in more distress than he thought. His skin paled and he swallowed convulsively. Then he spoke with a wretchedness that was not faked.

"I can't, Molly. He bought out all my other debt, so I'm in really deep." He stepped around Thabo. "Please, Molly, can't you help me out this once? He just wants the statue." He glanced over at the pedestal. "Where is it?"

"No." Her voice was hard and cold.

"But Molly—"

"No. He can't have it. He can't steal it. He can't send you to beg for it." Her voice broke as she spoke. "I could give you anything else, Bobby—"

"He doesn't want anything else!"

She turned to give him a hard, defeated stare. "It's not possible, Bobby. I couldn't even if I wanted to. You have to think of something else."

That wasn't exactly true. There were certainly ways to change curator and not all of them included death. But they were all dangerous.

Meanwhile, Bobby saw the truth in his sister's eyes, but typical of a child, he could only complain about it. "There has to be a way. Maybe you could loan it to him. Maybe we could borrow money from the bank. Maybe…"

A thousand maybes rolled of the boy's tongue and neither Thabo nor Molly listened. In the end, the child sputtered back into accusation. "You're not even listening! You have to help me!"

"I can't," Molly said.

"You can!" the boy screeched. Then he abruptly stood and pulled out a gun, aiming it with shaking hands at his sister. It was a small caliber pistol. Pitiful, really, when compared to what his uncle carried. Or what any of Thabo's typical opponents used. "Tell me where the statue is! Tell me!"

Molly's eyes widened, but she didn't even try to move. She just stared at her brother with tears spilling quietly down her cheeks. "I can't."

But even a small caliber weapon could kill, especially when this close. Molly had barely finished speaking when Thabo struck. He moved with precision and speed, chopping down with his hand hard enough to break the boy's arm. The gun dropped free, straight into Thabo's other hand. And while the child was still screaming in reaction, Thabo picked him up and threw him outside.

The child landed on soft grass, rolling with the throw, and then he was up and running into the darkness. Thabo watched him disappear and listened carefully for even longer. He heard the boy sobbing as he scrambled into a waiting car.

"Where's he going to go?" Molly asked from his elbow.

"He has been picked up by someone. There was a car."

"Oh." Such acceptance in that one word. Acceptance of pain and difficulty. "This was supposed to be my glorious rest. No more tuition to pay. Everyone out on their own. I've been working at least two jobs since my parents died. I fed and clothed them. I made sure they got their homework done and worked summer jobs. And now, finally, I get to rest." She snorted, the sound half laugh, half sob. "I was on my first vacation trip in years when I found you." Her voice trailed away as she shut the back door.

He let her, but when she turned back toward the main room, he pulled her into his arms. It wasn't a conscious movement. It had been too long since he'd given comfort to any person, much less a woman. But he tucked her tight to his chest and buried his face in her hair. He smelled her lemon scent and felt the way she melted against him. And in that moment, his heart was lost.

She was an innocent caught up in things she could not handle. Her brother and her uncle were bad enough, but that was nothing compared to the war the goddesses waged. He did not want to complicate her life any further. And yet, how long had it been since he'd touched such sweetness? How many centuries had it been since he knew tenderness from anyone? It ached, this feeling in his heart. And it made his breath stutter inside him.

She felt the tremors in him. She pushed away enough to look up at him, a question in her hazel eyes.

He tried to speak. He tried to find a way to give voice to the riot of feelings let loose inside him. How had she broken him in one day? Even Zeva had taken nearly a week for him to devote himself, heart and soul, to her bidding. But this woman who bravely faced down uncle and brother, who had cared for her siblings as fiercely as any mother, she'd taken his heart in one day.

"How has this happened?" he asked her, knowing she had no understanding of his thoughts. "I…You…" He swallowed, searching her face for an answer that he knew wasn't there.

"What?" she whispered.

"I…admire you," he finally said. It was not close to what he felt, and the least adequate word for the depth of his emotion.

She smiled. "Well, I suppose that's fair. I've spent a good deal of time admiring you."

She meant his body. He had felt her caress so many times. Always, he had been stone, first sunk in the ocean depths, and then earlier today when she explored his scars. But even as stone, her touch had reached to his core. And now she was locked against him and he could not bring himself to release her.

"Will you let me, Molly?" he asked. His voice was a harsh rasp, but he had no control over it. He wanted so badly that it was all he could do to stand still and not take what he wanted.

"What?"

His hand shook as he touched her face. He stroked his finger over her cheek and outlined the curve of her lips. He wished he remembered how to be gentle. "I want to kiss you, Molly, but I'm not sure I remember how."

She snorted. "It's not complicated. You just do it."

Lust slammed through him, hard enough that he clutched her to him rather than take her while so out of control. He held on to her and waited for the madness to recede enough that he could manage it. And while the maelstrom surged through him, she held him equally tight until she became his touchstone.

"I've got you. It's okay. Take a breath. I've got you." She was crooning to him, her voice a steady murmur of reassurance. She was an innocent, unaware of the nightmare that he could be. He was War's slave, a weapon in so many ways. And yet just then, he was only a man in a woman's arms. How had he forgotten how beautiful it was to be held?

"I won't hurt you," he vowed. "I swear it."

"I know," she said.

She didn't know. She couldn't. And he couldn't explain. So they stood there wrapped in each other's arms while he lost more and more of himself to her.

"I will keep you safe."

"Thabo, calm down. It's just a kiss. One we haven't even had yet."

She peeled herself back from him then, far enough to touch his face. Far enough that he could see the individual striations of her beautiful eyes. So many colors. A man could get lost in those colors.

"It's easy," she said. Then she pushed up on her toes and pressed her lips to his.

It was light. It was tender. And he had to work to allow himself to soften into it. Rarely did a warrior go slow. Not when he finally chose to act. But he held himself in check. He would take only what she wanted to give. And in this way, he would honor her gift.

He kissed her back. Gently, measuring his pressure by the push of her lips. And when she nipped her teeth against his lower lip, he bit her back. Playfully. Though every cell in his body strained toward her.

Then he dropped her back onto her heels. He forced himself to unlock his arms from around her. It was an act of will to let her fall, even so tiny a space as an inch.

"See?" she said, her eyes wide and darkening to cobalt. "Simple."

"I do not want—"

"To hurt me," she finished for him. "I get it. But you know what? I've been a good girl most of my life. I've been responsible for my siblings, I paid the bills, and I even managed to date a couple very respectable, boring men."

"Do not tell me of these other men," he warned darkly. His emotions were so keyed up that jealously burned hot beneath his skin.

She chuckled. "I said *boring*. But you know what?" she asked, as she squeezed his buttocks. Both palms, squeezing hard. He was so startled he gasped out his question.

"What?"

"I'm on vacation, remember?"

He didn't. That's not what she had said. But before he could contradict her, she stretched up on her toes and nipped at his lip again.

"So come on. Let's share a little *vacation* together, okay?"

"Molly," he said, her name coming from deep within. "Even I know that this is not usual for women. And most especially not for you."

She laughed, then intertwined her fingers with his. Then she tugged him toward her bedroom. "Vacation, remember? God, quit making it so complicated." Then she paused and turned to look back at him. "For one night I don't want to think about anything except making a few dozen of my fantasies come true. Do you understand that Thabo? I just want fantasy." Then she touched his chest, stroking her fingers slowly down his torso while his body throbbed. "I want magic. Delicious magic."

"I am made of magic," he said.

She flashed him a brilliant smile. "So come razzle-dazzle me."

CHAPTER 8

Molly tugged him down the hallway. She could tell by the bulge beneath his sweatpants that he wanted her, but the fine tremors in his body told her he was fighting it.

"It's okay, Thabo. I want this." And she really did, though rationally, what she was doing was insane. She didn't understand why she felt so deeply for a man she didn't know. But he'd risked his life for her when the bullets had been flying. That was enough to make her like him. Then he'd allowed her to make the decisions about Bobby even though he disagreed with them. Respecting her decisions? That was the truest way to melt her heart. Then add in his constant awareness of when she was overwhelmed and that he tried to protect her emotionally as well as physically. Well, that was enough to make her a wet puddle of lust.

So she tugged him to her bed. It would be small for him, which meant they'd have to tuck tightly together. And that was quite all right with her. But when she attempted to pull him onto the mattress, he resisted. He just stood there, looking at her with an intensity that set her blood on fire. God, what woman didn't dream of being looked at just like that? With such hunger it set her toes to curling in excitement.

Absolutely magical.

His tee was long gone, so now she stroked her hand down his abdominals. They rippled beneath her fingers and she smiled at the play of muscles. But when she went to pull off his sweatpants, he gripped her wrist. She looked at his face and saw the clench of his jaw and flush of his cheeks. It took him two tries to speak, and when he did, his voice was like rocks being ground together.

"It has been too long for me."

Ah. Yes, she could understand that. But they had all night, and she could be patient. "So let's take the edge off, okay?"

She could see he didn't understand. She didn't know if it was modern day slang or that he was holding himself so rigidly that he had no extra focus for words. Either way, she gently uncoiled his fingers from her wrist. Then, with a couple quick tugs, she was able to lift the sweats away from his massive erection and drop them to the floor.

Wow, he was big. Dark, full and uncircumcised. She'd left the light off because she usually didn't want to be distracted by how a guy looked. But with Thabo, that all changed. He was eye-candy to the Nth degree, so she flicked on her bedside lamp and let it bathe him in a soft, warm glow.

"You're like an ebony god," she whispered.

"I am no god, Molly." He sounded insulted by the suggestion, and given that he was slave to a goddess, she supposed that made sense.

"I meant it as a compliment." She glanced up at his face. "I'm afraid I won't compare well."

He cupped her cheek, his hand so gentle she almost wasn't sure he was touching her. "You are astonishing, Molly."

Astonishing sounded good. And so while he held her gaze she quickly undid her uniform. It was a button down dress, quickly opened and discarded, leaving her in a utilitarian cream bra and basic hipster panties. His gaze left her eyes, then moved slowly down her face. Rather than let him see her boring underwear, she quickly popped the clasp and let the bra fall away. Her breasts were average, just like the rest of her. Average size, average height, average—

His breath caught on a gasp and his hand dropped from her face to hover just above her left breast. She took hold of his fingers and gently pressed them down. His hand was large and the heat of it encompassed her breast. The sight was even more erotic: dark fingers on her flushed pink skin. Then he squeezed. She wasn't even sure it was on purpose, but she felt it all the way down to her toes. Then his thumb rolled across the tight bud of her nipple.

Electricity shot straight to her core. She gasped and lifted her breast deeper into his hand. His other hand came up and she guided that one as well, loving the feel of both his hands on her body.

"That feels amazing," she said. A massive understatement. And while he continued to caress her nipples, she reached down to take him.

The moment she wrapped a hand around his penis, he hissed out a breath. She felt his thighs contract as he thrust forward. Then he did it again and again. It was quick and his eyes held an apology. He couldn't stop himself. She could see it in his eyes. He wanted to go slow, he wanted to make it good for her. She knew it, but he couldn't stop. And all she could do was hold on as she gave him what pleasure she could.

"We're taking the edge off," she said.

His breath rasped and his hands slid to her hips, gripping her in place as he thrust harder and harder into her hand.

"Molly!" His entire body jerked with his orgasm, and he half collapsed forward.

She caught him, steadying him though it was a losing battle. He was breathing hard, and his forehead was pressed into her neck. He still held her hips, his grip alternating between a hard grip and a soft caress. And then she realized, he wasn't breathing hard, he was murmuring her name over and over.

"Mollymollymollymollymolly."

"Shhh," she said as she shifted to stroke his sides and back. "It's okay."

He took a deep, shuddering breath, but beyond that, he didn't move away from her. Then he spoke, his words coming from deep in his throat. "It is shameful. To treat you as such."

It took a moment for her to understand his words. "Treat me how?"

She felt him swallow and a bit of his weight left her as his legs found some strength. "A woman's pleasure should come first."

Really? "Where did you learn that?" Then she rushed her next words. "I'm not arguing, mind, just wondering where—"

He pulled back. "The leaders of my village always said so. It was part of every young man's education. What they are taught in the water hut after first growing their adult hair."

So many words there that she wanted to understand. But she was getting tired standing, and so when he straightened off her, she allowed herself to drop onto her bed. Then she reached for a tissue to clean herself, only to be stopped by him.

"This is my shame. Allow me to clean it, please?"

"It's not shameful, Thabo. It's been a long time for you and—"

"Please."

She nodded, and he left her side to go into the bathroom. He returned with a wash cloth and basin. It was a decorative bowl she kept there for knick-knacks, but he'd emptied it and filled it with warm water. Then he guided her to lay back on the bed as he gently stroked her belly to clean her.

Oh God, what he was doing set her on fire. The utmost tenderness in his strokes as he wiped her belly. He wasn't even touching anything sensitive, and yet she had to clutch the sheets to keep herself from jolting in pleasure.

"Tell me about your village," she said as a way to calm herself. If he thought his release was shameful, how would he react to her coming just from a washing?

"It is gone now," he said, his voice flat.

She blinked. "Gone?"

"It happened many years after my service to War began. Perhaps if I had been there, I could have saved my home."

Wow, the guilt this man held would crush a normal man. It was a wonder he was sane. "Did they come with guns? And your people had...what? Spears? Bows and arrows?"

He nodded, a single hard slash to his chin. "My best friend survived. He was my curator in a city where War recruited many youths. Eventually, he and all his family died, the last perishing when the boat sank."

What would it be like to watch the last survivors of your family drown beside you? While you remained stone, watching the end and knowing there was nothing you could do?

"I'm so sorry, Thabo."

"There is nothing left of the Conteh people now." There was a mournful note in his voice and she realized it was the closest he ever came to self-pity.

"They survive through you. You're here. You remember."

He didn't answer, and so she took hold of his empty hand and drew it to her mouth, pressing a kiss to his knuckles and then she twisted it over to press her lips into his palm.

"We can't change the past, Thabo. Let it go."

"My past is all I have. The goddess has taken everything else."

Molly pushed up on her elbows. "Not true. You have me, right now. You have a future—"

"No."

Oh wow. That was one flat, cold word. With absolutely no possibility of change. Or even hope. How awful to live like that for centuries. But she supposed it made sense. When enslaved to a goddess, that was probably the only way to survive.

"Okay. Then let's concentrate on right here, right now."

He looked at her, his gaze dark in the soft light. Chocolate brown, rich enough that she could sink into just his gaze. And while she was looking at his eyes, she felt the washcloth slide across her breast. A rough brush that abraded her nipple enough that she gasped. And then he did it again on the other side. It was enough that she collapsed back into the pillow.

"Did you learn that in the water hut?" she asked.

"This is the first lesson. How to bathe a woman."

"Really?"

"I will show you."

She meant to object. She'd never been bathed by a man before in her life and found the idea rather bizarre. But before she could say anything, he stroked the wet washcloth across her breasts again. Not a horizontal stroke like she might do in a bath, but a slow circular caress that lifted her breast, cupping it gently before finishing at the peak with a soft tweak of her nipple. Never had she felt anything so lovely. Her mouth opened on a gasp and her thighs went liquid as he began with her other breast.

It was a slow process; erotic, not just for the touch, but the way he seemed to worship her skin. He lavished attention everywhere. Her hands and arms, belly and legs. He watched her face intently as he worked, and when he began to stroke her thighs open, she was so wet he didn't need the cloth. But he used it anyway as he bathed the crease between thigh and groin, then stroked her most private folds open with fingers and cloth. Then he used his lips.

She was so dazed by the sensual fog, the shift in texture was nothing more than one more amazing sensation. But eventually she knew the difference. She learned that his tongue was way more clever than his fingers. And while her belly tightened and her thighs quivered, she looked down to see his dark head between her thighs. He was still watching her, his eyes alight with mischief. Mischief! As if he delighted in her every cry or moan.

She wanted to laugh, but she hadn't the breath. Especially since he apparently decided that he'd kept her hovering on the edge of orgasm long enough. His gaze never wavered from hers, but oh, what he did to her clit! Gentle sucks that grew stronger. Her back arched, and her eyes fluttered as she fought to keep looking at him. But then he nipped her, and she lost the battle. Her hips thrust upward. He held her pinned with his arms and his broad shoulders kept her legs wide. Twice more he licked her. Twice more she tightened unbearably far. And then he sucked her.

Detonation!

Every part of her rolled into an orgasm that made her scream. Never before had she seemed to compress so tiny before waves of pleasure shot her outward. There was no controlling this expansion, so she let it carry her where it willed. As *he* willed, because just when the pulses started to fade, he pushed her back into the ocean with a flick of his tongue. He kept her soaring for eons. And when he finally let her settle, boneless and sated, he grinned up at her.

"Bathing," he said. "Lesson one."

She tried to say something, but hadn't the breath. He waited a while as he gently petted her thighs. Eventually she had enough control to speak.

"Just how many lessons are there?"

"Twenty-two, but I only mastered fourteen. When you are rested, I would love to practice numbers fifteen and above."

Laughter spilled out of her, joyous and so filled with delight, it made her feel buoyant. Especially when his rich, mellow chuckle joined her.

CHAPTER 9

Thabo woke slowly, his body lethargic in an alarming way. He felt as if each arm weighed a thousand pounds and his thoughts scrambled to form something other than panic. What had happened? Where was the goddess? Why was he smiling?

That last question burned brightest in his mind. It was so odd to feel the pull of his cheek muscles and the ache that came from using his face in such an unaccustomed way. It was so bizarre that he kept his eyes closed in pretend sleep while he figured out what was going on. He recruited his other senses and felt the soft mattress and cotton sheets beneath him, then he smelled Molly.

Molly.

She was the reason for all of this. His joy in their lovemaking last night. His first, real sleep in two centuries. And this exquisite sense of being a man again, not a goddess's plaything.

Except, even as he reveled in his unaccustomed wholeness, he knew that his deadline was fast approaching. Zeva had given him three days to learn something spectacular. Today was his second day and he had done nothing to further that goal. When tonight came, he would be forced back to his pedestal to face Zeva, and who knew when she would next allow him to return to Earth. To Molly.

He spent a single panicked moment trying to figure out something that would impress a goddess. He'd had two centuries to study the bitch and knew how impossible that task that was. She was familiar with all the new war toys and strategies. He could add nothing there. And she had little interest in anything that wasn't violence. Although she did have a strange curiosity about Ghandi and his idea of peaceful resistance. This drugging quiet of the soul would impress her, but he could think of no way to give it to her.

So he had a choice. He could spend his time in a fruitless search to impress Zeva, or he could devote himself to Molly. Phrased that way, there was no choice at all. So he opened his eyes and reached for the woman who was not in her bed. Fortunately, he could hear someone typing in the main room so he didn't panic. Instead, he rolled easily out of bed, his earlier lethargy gone, and went to find Molly.

She looked up as he entered the main room. She was stretched out on the couch, a tablet and keyboard on her lap. And when she saw him, her cheeks flushed pink.

"You are the most gorgeous man I've ever seen."

He grinned, pleased even as he turned the compliment around. "I am pale compared to you."

She snorted as she reached out to touch his arm. Warmth spread from her touch, glowing bright all the way to his heart. "Pale you are not." Then her eyes turned hungry as she studied his body. "I love the shades of your skin. The softer browns, the darker blacks. I never realized how much subtle variation there is on a man like you."

"A man like me?"

"An African." She shrugged. "I've never dated a black man before, and it's just one more part of you that I find fascinating."

He stared at the admiration in her eyes. He saw desire and excitement as well, and his cock thickened in response. What would it be like to see that every morning when he woke? To spend his life making sure that she was as happy as he felt? He could do that, he thought. He could enthusiastically devote himself to giving her everything she wanted. If only he were free. If only he could find a way to escape Zeva.

"Would you like to practice some more, Molly?" he asked, his voice a low rasp. "I would like to bathe you again."

If her cheeks were flushed before, now they burned scarlet. He stalked around the couch, ready to scoop her up, but she held up a hand.

"No! No, wait!" He froze and she took a deep breath. "I would love that, Thabo. You have no idea how much, but first…" She twisted her tablet around so he could see. "Look at what I found. It's an entire website on the stonemen."

He understood a little about computers and the Internet. Zeva had spent a great deal of time playing with the devices, but he had never been allowed to look himself. So it was with a great sense of privilege that he sat down beside Molly and touched the device.

"I do not know that Stone Woman," he said as he looked at a statue.

"Hmmm? Oh that's Jacqueline, the woman who owns the site. I've already emailed her. She's devoted to finding a way to free all the stonemen, especially those in Zeva's army."

"Don't say her name aloud!" Thabo snapped, his entire body tense as he waited to see if the goddess would appear.

Meanwhile, Molly flushed and tapped the screen. "Right. Sorry. We're calling her War. Here's the description of her. It says here that she thinks she's close to winning their game."

Thabo nodded. "Yes. She believes she will have enough stonemen to end the world and thereby win the game."

"You mean win the game at the end of the world, right?"

He frowned. "Yes, the game ends when the world ends. So once War believes she has a large enough army to win, she will set all her warriors to destroy Earth."

He watched as Molly absorbed that information. "You're serious, aren't you? She's going to blow up the world. How soon? And how—"

"I don't know. I only have guesses."

Molly took a deep breath. "Okay, well first things first. Let's get you free. This website says that every stoneman has an out clause. Something that will free them. Do you know what yours is?"

"Yes."

She looked at him, waiting for him to say more. He didn't. The shame was too great.

"Thabo, we have to get you free."

"I will not do it, Molly."

She cupped his cheek and gently guided him to look at her. He hadn't even realized he was looking away, but with her caress, his gaze inevitably locked back into hers.

"Just tell me what it is. Exactly. We'll figure it out from there."

He swallowed and spoke, unable to deny her anything. "I must get two others to serve in my stead."

"Serve? How?"

"Many years ago—before I sank in that boat—I was commanded to steal a weapon in Kambia. There, I met a beautiful thief and I..." He looked away. "You must understand. I was desperate for a way out of War's clutches."

"Oh hell," she said, her voice filled with sympathy. "What did you do?"

"I seduced her. I gave her love and convinced her that War could give her immortality. She need only serve in my stead as War's thief."

"She agreed?"

"She wanted immortality with me. So she stole the weapon and pledged herself to War." He felt Molly's hands grip his and he clung to them as he confessed his shame. "I tricked her. I told her every lie she wanted to hear, and I stood by as she enslaved herself so that I could get free." The acid pain of what he'd done churned in his gut. "I was heartless and cruel. And worse, she sits beside me in court as we wait upon the goddess. It amuses War to keep her near me. Every day I apologize for what I have done. She is a slave because of me, and I cannot make up for that." He dropped his head back against the couch and wished for the millionth time that he had been a better man. "Of all the things I have done, this is why I despise myself. Even the arrogance that doomed me in the first place was nothing compared to this. If I could save her, then I would give everything to make up for that."

He thought Molly would push him away. He deserved to be thrust from her side. Instead, she wrapped her arms around him and pressed a kiss to his temple. "You made a mistake out of desperation. We'll find a way to break her free."

His eyes teared as his heart broke into a thousand pieces. "I do not deserve forgiveness. And I cannot ask you to help me atone."

"Of course you do." Then she turned his face to hers so she could kiss him. Soft. Sweet. So tender that every part of him shattered. "And we're going to fix this together," she added. "We're going to break you and her free. Right now."

"It cannot be done."

"Of course it can. Someone has to serve in your stead, right?"

"I will not—"

"I know. What about her? What's her out clause?"

"Asha must give away her heart's desire."

Molly frowned. "Probably pretty hard for a thief."

He touched her face. He stroked her soft cheek and pressed his thumb against her red lips. He saw his darkness stark against her white skin and he marveled at her open heart. "You risk too much," he whispered. "We must find a way to keep your uncle from hurting you."

"I've been dealing with Uncle Sully for years. He can wait a bit." She said the words, but he could feel the stiffness in her body that came from fear.

"I want to defend you from him. I want him gone so that you never worry—"

"How much time do you have?" She spoke quickly, her question laid right over his words. And from the way she spoke, he knew that this question had been burrowing at the back of her mind for a time now.

"You do not need to worry—"

"How much time?"

"War will summon me back tomorrow night."

He felt her flinch. They were pressed so close that her recoil tore at every part of him.

"We're going to fix this, Thabo. I swear—"

He pressed his fingers to her lips. "We cannot do—in two days—what I have worked for centuries to accomplish. Do not poison yourself, or our time together, with fruitless hope. I am not worth it."

He watched his meaning sink in to her and tensed for her reaction. A warrior had one of two responses to his statement. She would either tense and fight his words or slump in grim acceptance. Molly did neither. Her expression softened as she stroked his thigh where it pressed against her.

"You need to feel love, Thabo. Before all things, you need to feel that you are worth saving."

He was not. But she was so good that she believed in him with all the passion in her spirit. It broke his heart to see it because he knew the inevitable disappointment to come.

"Molly," he began, but she cut him off.

"This was my vacation. I told you that, right?"

He paused. "Yes."

"No more tuition to pay. No more sisters or brothers at home. No more work except for myself." She nuzzled her cheek against his as she whispered into his ear. "I was free to do whatever I wanted so long as I could meet the mortgage payment."

"And can you?"

She pulled back to look into his eyes. "I can. But you know what? Without my siblings to hound, without Bobby around to worry about, without the constant threat of bills…" She shook her head. "Thabo my life was empty. I was so bored I went scuba diving."

"When you found me."

She smiled. "When I found you. You've brought magic into my life and given me a purpose again."

He gestured to his pedestal. "Another burden."

"A gift, Thabo. A purpose." She pressed her lips to his. "Thank you."

He kissed her with all his strength. And with it, he gave her all the worship he had in him. The gratitude, the blessing, and most of all, his heart. He gave all those to her because she had the audacity to love a slave. To give hope to a man who was made of stone.

"What can I give you?" he whispered into her mouth. "How can I serve you?"

She pulled back. "Don't serve me. Be with me. Share with me."

"What?"

Her gaze turned mischievous. "Shall we try Lesson two?"

"No," he said as he slid his hands beneath her cami. "No, I would like to show you something better. Lesson seven."

She giggled as his hands spanned her ribcage, the tremor in her belly revealing excitement and delight. "Sounds good to me, but on one condition." She touched his chest, holding him back from her as she slowly slid her hand down to engulf his penis.

He tensed at her touch, spirals of delight radiating outward. "Molly," he groaned, the word a plea.

"We do lesson seven only if it ends with you inside me."

He looked at her. "It could. It can. But…"

"We're in this together, Thabo. You and me. Together in all ways." And so saying, she began to squeeze, stroking him from tip to base while his mind splintered from the joy of it. "Say it, Thabo. Promise me—"

"Together." Then he scooped her up and carried her to bed.

CHAPTER 10

God, Molly loved Thabo's strength. Sure the physical ability to just pick her up was thrilling, but there was more to him than just his body's power. The fact that the man had survived two centuries enslaved to a bitch astounded her. And that he'd only had one moment of weakness in all that time? And that he regretted it to the depths of his soul? Well, that spoke of a man of honor, and that was more erotic to her than the wonderful things he was doing to her breasts. He was sucking on them slowly, deliberately. A steady pulse that pulled at her womb and made her belly go liquid and hot.

She already knew it would kill her to see him go back to a statue, and she swore with every kiss from his lips that she would free him. But first she had to save his soul. She had to make him believe that he was worth saving and that meant giving all the love in her heart to him right here, right now.

"S-so what's lesson seven?" she gasped out.

"It is the slow thrust." He raised over her on the bed. He was a large man and in the muted morning light, he could have looked menacing above her. Instead, she felt sheltered and surrounded by all that was Thabo. And she loved it.

"That sounds promising," she said.

His expression faltered. "I do not know if I can do it, Molly. You push me to the edges of my control."

Her smile widened into a grin. "That sounds *very* promising."

His eyes danced and she felt another warm glow expand through her heart. How she loved making him smile. "I should wear a sheath. I do not know if I can get you pregnant, but—"

She touched a finger to his lips. "You're the only one who could tempt me to have a baby," she said, "but I'm not going there until things are more settled."

He nodded. "That is wise."

"Doesn't mean I'm not thinking about it. For someday."

His mouth opened in shock. "Someday," he echoed softly. And the longing in that one word touched her deep.

"Someday," she echoed. Then she stretched to the drawer in her nightstand. "And in the meantime, there's a condom in there."

He pulled out the foil packet and stared at it, his expression faltering. "Molly, the goddess did not train us in all modern things. Language, weapons, even some things about computers were part of our training. But this was not one of them."

What? Oh! "No problem. I'd love to show you how to do this." Then she sat up and took the foil packet from his hand, ripping it open with a flick of her wrist. "You're sure you're ready, big guy?"

She was teasing him. She could see he was more than ready. In fact, she was a little worried she had the wrong size condom. He touched her face, drawing it up for a deep kiss. And when they were done, he whispered, "I will always be ready for you, Molly. If you want me."

"I want you," she said and no truer words had ever been spoken. So she leaned down and took him in her fist. She spent a moment enjoying the feel of him. She stroked him and rubbed the liquid around his mushroom cap. He wasn't circumcised, and so she got to explore him as if she'd never seen a man's cock before. It was really quite fun until he gripped her wrist.

"Is this part of putting on the sheath?" he asked, his breath short and tight.

She grinned. "Nope. It's just fun."

He chuckled. "Then you must choose which fun you want because this is not lesson seven."

"Hmmm, hard choice." And it was. "What do you want?"

He guided the condom to the tip of his penis. "This."

Okey-dokey. Deep thrusting coming up. She could hardly wait. She rolled the condom on him with shaking hands. And then she took a moment to strip out of her sweatpants. No need for him since he'd not dressed when coming out to the living room. And then his hands were on her waist, gently pulling her to lie back down on the bed. A moment later he was on his knees between her thighs.

"Are you ready?"

A rhetorical question because he could feel the answer. He was stroking his knuckles between her folds, spreading the moisture everywhere including in circles over her clit that made her gasp.

"Molly?" he asked, humor in his tone.

"Yes!" she cried. "Quit teasing me."

"I am having fun," he said, using her own words to taunt her.

She stuck out her tongue at him as he took hold of her thighs. His hands were large as they pulled up her knees, slowly lifting them high as he spread her open. She felt vulnerable in this position, especially as he looped his elbows under her knees and then rolled forward. Her bottom curled up slightly as he positioned himself at her entrance. She felt the cool latex quickly turn slick and hot, but that was nothing compared to the way his eyes burned as they looked at her. He looked hungry.

"I wish I could speak poetry," he said. "Your beauty astounds me."

"God, Thabo, you slay me," she answered. Because absolutely everything he said cut straight to her heart.

And then he rocked forward into her. The tiniest fraction, slow and not nearly enough.

She arched to let him go deeper, but he withdrew. Rocking back as gently as he had gone in.

"You don't have to go slow. I can take more."

"This is the slow, deep thrust, Molly. Trust me, you will take more."

And so he rocked forward again, slightly further, but not by much. The tiniest increase before rocking back once again.

"Oh my God," she gasped, finally understanding what he meant to do. "You're going to drive me insane with anticipation."

He grinned. "Then I will have done Lesson Seven correctly."

Again with the slow press in and slow withdrawal. Over and over, barely deeper with each thrust. And each time he pushed inside, she ached for more. Each time he pulled back, she arched to keep him inside.

Steady increase.

Steady thrust.

He took an eon until he gave her his whole cock in deep, patient thrusts. Never had she thought the slow tempo could be so good. Never had she felt a man push so far inside her she thought he stroked her heart. And all the while, her body tried to make him go faster. She squirmed as much as she could move—which wasn't much. She squeezed him when she thought it would help. She even grabbed his flanks and tried to drag him deeper. Harder.

But he was relentless in his penetration. Everything was at his speed, and she writhed on the spit of his pleasure. Her pleasure. Lord, by the time he became fully embedded inside her, they had merged into one creature compressing and expanding in tidal waves of sensation.

Her belly tightened and released with his motions.

His strength kneaded her in a steady pump of desire.

On and on until she lost herself in his power.

When her orgasm came it was simply more of what they had become.

And when she milked him to release, it was so perfect the way he juddered inside her. Hard and quick. A man who'd lost control. Because of her.

She loved seeing it. She loved causing it.

She loved.

Him.

Oh my. Oh wow. She'd fallen in love with a magic stoneman. Not just in the I'm going to show him love, way. But deeper and more profound. As in she could absolutely contemplate giving herself to War to stand in his place.

And that thought terrified her. How could she fall so deep, so fast?

"Thabo," she whispered as he collapsed beside her.

"Molly," he answered, as he tucked her close, holding her as if he couldn't bear for any separation between them.

She wanted to say more. She wanted to tell him what she'd realized. But the emotions were too raw, the feelings too frightening. And besides, she'd said it all when she'd whispered his name. Everything she longed for and feared was right there.

So she wrapped her arms around him, tucked her face tight to his neck, and pressed a kiss to his pulse point. A sweet kiss while her heart sang with love.

"When we're rested," she said as her eyes drifted closed. "When we catch our breath—"

"I will never have breath around you, Molly. You take it from me."

Her lips curled into a smile. "We're going to figure this out, Thabo. We're going to free you."

"I will try," he said as he pressed a kiss to her temple. "For you, I will hope again."

CHAPTER 11

For the rest of the day, they struggled to come up with a plan. But how could they win against an immortal goddess? Every idea led to a quick failure. By nightfall, they had exhausted all possibilities and Thabo knew his hope was in vain. And when he looked at Molly, all he saw was a frazzled desperation in her eyes.

They didn't speak. She allowed him to call her uncle. If he couldn't free himself, at least he could bargain with her family into leaving her alone. And when that was done, he kissed her one last time.

He refused to allow their last coupling to become desperate. But even as they both cried out their pleasure, he tasted salt from her tears.

"I love you," he whispered.

"I'm not enough," she said, her words choking on a sob. "I'm not smart enough to—"

"You are everything," he said. "My heart and my soul, I give everything I am to you."

CHAPTER 12

M olly barely cared when she saw her uncle's dark SUV drive into the IHOP parking lot. The sense of desolation that infused her made her want to curl up in a ball and howl, but she knew that would hurt Thabo even more. What had ever made her think she could outwit a goddess? She was just a waitress.

But she couldn't collapse yet, so she put on her brave face—and her uniform—and took Thabo to work because she hadn't been able to get out of her shift, and because she couldn't imagine losing one second of their remaining time together.

Besides, he'd struck a deal with her uncle, and the least she could do was honor his choice. Though when her trigger-happy uncle walked into the restaurant, she felt like punching him right in the face. Instead, she gestured him and his henchman to a booth where Thabo sat drinking a milkshake like it was ambrosia.

Uncle Sully's eyes narrowed and he swaggered forward, all broad shoulders and bluster. Molly just rolled her eyes, even as she wondered why she wasn't frightened of the man anymore. Sure he had guns and money, but she was about to go up against an immortal goddess. What could Uncle Sully do against that?

But then a second car pulled into the lot and out stepped another of Uncle Sully's men and Bobby, his arm in a cast. Hell, the boy looked haggard and terrified.

"What is he doing here?" Molly demanded. "This was between—"

"He's family," Uncle Sully interrupted, his eyes triumphant. "He needs to see that you need me as much as he does."

Translation: he wanted to show Bobby that she couldn't fight him either. Except that wasn't the case. She had an immortal warrior on her side. Or she did for another twenty minutes.

Bobby entered the IHOP, his stance defensive and his gaze slipping away from hers. Lord, when did he get that new shiner? Just what the hell had Sully's men been doing to him?

"Bobby—" she began as he slunk up to the hostess stand.

"Just give him what he wants, Molly. Please." His voice was a low undertone and Molly's heart ached to see him so broken. If Thabo could manage it, Bobby would be free from Uncle Sully. But that only worked if Bobby chose the straight and narrow path afterwards. But rather than say anything, she gestured to the back of the restaurant.

"This way."

She wanted him far away from the action against Zeva. And if Molly lost—or died—at least Bobby would see that good people fought for what was right. They risked everything for those they loved, even if it all ended in disaster.

Once Bobby and the second henchman were seated, Molly headed back to her uncle and Thabo. She made it in time to hear Sully's gruff question.

"What are you?"

"Magic," Thabo answered as he smiled warmly at her.

"Bull shit. If you think—"

Molly interrupted, echoing Thabo's words to her, way back when. "You saw him come to life from stone. How can you scoff at that now?"

Sully's eyes narrowed and he pushed up from his seat. "Don't know how I let you convince me to come here," he groused. "In the middle of the night."

"It's when you do your best work," she retorted. It was also the time least likely to have collateral damage if the goddess got pissy. Which, according to Thabo, was pretty damned likely.

"Not in an IHOP, I don't."

That was probably true. "This is where the magic is going to happen," she said. "Along with pancakes. So give me your order, and I'll make sure you get a prime seat."

"It'd better be worth it or Bobby pays the price."

Molly was ready to give an acidic retort back, but Thabo was faster. He didn't do anything more than grab Sully's arm. To Molly, it looked like he just touched the man, but Sully jerked backwards away from Thabo…and didn't go anywhere. Thabo apparently had him in an iron…er…stone grip. Because as she watched, Thabo's hand steadily turned to marble.

"Release Bobby as you promised," Thabo said in a low undertone.

"Get off me!" Sully's voice was high pitched in panic. His henchman scrambled to his feet, fumbling with his gun.

Molly slammed the man sideways. Not far. He was too big for her to do much damage, but it was enough to make him fumble the gun. It dropped to the floor and she kicked it away. Meanwhile, Thabo spoke, his voice gravelly and hard.

"If you shoot anyone here, I will become stone locked around your arm. You cannot hurt me."

Actually, they could cut off his arms and that would bring everyone right back to the beginning; except that Molly, as Thabo's curator, would have her own arm cut off. Fortunately, Sully didn't know that.

"What do you want?" her uncle rasped.

Thabo pushed a piece of paper forward. It had latitude and longitude numbers written on it.

"What is that?"

"Directions," she responded. "Coordinates to another statue, this one in South America. It's abandoned and available for the taking. In return, you release Bobby from all his debts and never talk to him again. You or any of your thugs."

"How do I know this is real?" he scoffed. That was enough to make all of Molly's anger spill over. All her frustration and pain boiled out in words that burned but felt so good to say.

"Don't you dare suggest I'm lying, Uncle Sully. I've never lied once to you and all you've done is manipulate and threaten. You're a damned weasel, and I've got a magical statue ready to break your wrist. So take the deal and get out."

He glared at her, but she wasn't fazed. And in the end, he grunted his agreement.

"Say it," Thabo rasped. "And know that you will be bound by your word. By magic. Whatever happens with that statue, Bobby is free."

Sully didn't want to do it. He was still looking for an angle as his gaze hopped from her to where Thabo's stone hand still gripped him tight. But in the end, he nodded.

"I agree."

And just like that, Thabo released him. His hand was no longer stone and he used his very human fingers to grab his milkshake and take a long sip.

"One condition, Uncle Sully."

"I didn't—"

"Just freaking listen." She glanced at Thabo, then back to her uncle. "A statue isn't as easy as it looks. Stay and find out what you're in for."

His brows drew together. "There's more?"

She nodded grimly.

He leaned back. "All right. Then get me the banana pancakes while we wait. And Jimmy here likes blueberry pancakes."

She exhaled slowly. Trust her uncle to remember to feed his stomach while her world fell apart. But that had been the plan. If Uncle Sully was indeed going to get his own stoneman, then he needed to know the lay of the land, so to speak. She turned to put his order in while his thug retrieved his weapon from the floor.

So much for keeping them unarmed. Then again, maybe they'd get trigger happy and dump a zillion bullets into Zeva. Maybe she wasn't as immortal as Thabo thought. It was Molly's only hope as she went to talk to her brother.

Except he wasn't talking. Not really. All he did was mutter his order as if she didn't know his favorite dishes. At least he looked as miserable as she did. Maybe that would help this particular lesson sink in. And if it didn't, she grabbed his chin and drew it straight up to her eyes.

"I'm pulling out all the stops here, Bobby. Because you're worth it. Do you hear me? I love you that much. But there isn't anything more after this. And you have no idea what I'm risking right now. You got that?"

He nodded once. It might be the kid was finally growing up because he didn't say one mouthy word back. And then she had to put the order in, which brought her near Thabo again. She blew him a kiss, tried to quiet her racing heart, and waited while he pushed up from his seat.

It was time.

"Wait!" she cried as she rushed to his side.

He caught her quickly, his eyes so rich and chocolate she could almost miss the agony swirling in their depths.

"Five minutes—" she began but he shook his head.

"My time is up. I feel it. If I fight it, things will go worse."

They couldn't be much worse. She had a vague plan that wouldn't work, but it was all she could think of. "No matter what it takes, I'll figure out a solution. I swe—"

He cut off her words with a swift, deep kiss. "I love you," he said. And then he set her gently aside.

"I am here, Zeva," he said in a loud voice. "I call you to me. Zeva, Goddess of War. Zeva the Bloody. I call you, for I am healed. I have something spectacular to show you."

How about Zeva the slaver bitch? But she supposed that wasn't a helpful thought. Instead, she stepped against the wall, pressing her back there as she waited for the goddess to appear. So did everyone else in the restaurant. Thabo's voice had boomed through the restaurant. But as time ticked by, Molly began to hope. Nothing was happening. Maybe the bitch had forgotten—

A low growl sounded behind her. That was startling enough, but there was only wall behind her. Except what had been solid dry wall was suddenly hot and vibrating. She leapt away, her heart in her throat, and saw something that wasn't possible.

A dog as a big as a Volvo. It was black. It had dark red eyes and paws that shot up flames as it walked. It came out of the wall and left a singed outline behind. She leapt backwards with a squeak of terror, banging herself painfully into a table. She would have fallen over it, but Thabo caught her, steadying her easily as he stepped between her and the dog.

Not a dog, she belatedly realized. A wolf. A big, freaking bad wolf, and it scared the shit out of her. And not just her because everyone else in the room shot to his feet. The two thugs pointed guns at it with shaking hands.

"I wouldn't do that," a sing-song voice said. Molly searched to find the source of the voice and found a lithe African woman with light brown eyes and a chest that rivaled Dolly Parton's jumping down from the ceiling. A ceiling that up until now had been nothing but sound-proofing tiles. "It's never a good idea to hurt the puppy."

"That's not a puppy," squeaked Bobby as the wolf-thing stalked forward, sniffing around him with big bellows of breath.

"Actually, it is," Thabo said sotto voce. "About half grown."

"Jesus, Mary, and Joseph," Uncle Sully muttered and that wasn't half of what the others were saying as it sniffed them each in turn.

"And don't do that either," Thabo said, his voice harsh. "Don't mention other deities."

Good to know, since Molly was mentally revisiting every single Sunday school class she'd ever attended. But if Zeva was real, couldn't she call on Jesus to save her? Possibly, but she hadn't been to church since childhood, so she doubted that would help. Which meant it was up to her and Thabo to pull this off.

Straightening, she turned to the African woman who was currently bouncing her ample cleavage in front of Uncle Sully, who was struggling to not stare.

Molly cleared her throat. "Well, um, Goddess Zeva, can I show you to a—"

Thunk!

Molly blinked, a scream tight in her throat. The goddess had whirled around and thrown a dagger straight at Molly. She hadn't seen more than a flash of silver when Thabo had leapt in front of her. The knife landed squarely into Thabo's shoulder, except it hadn't sunk into flesh. Somehow, the man had changed the left half of his chest to stone fast enough to block the weapon. That was good, but the goddess wasn't finished. She leaped onto a table, then half danced, half jumped over Thabo to head straight for Molly, another dagger in her fist.

"Asha, stop!" Thabo ordered, his voice sounding like two boulders crashing together. "Zeva needs her alive!"

He was spinning around as he spoke, but he wouldn't have been fast enough if his words hadn't halted the goddess…er, woman. Molly's brain was just catching up to the realization that this woman wasn't Zeva.

"She has insulted the goddess," the woman said. "It is my obligation to kill her." Then she frowned. "It is yours as well."

Thabo's expression tightened. "She didn't insult the goddess. She was just confused."

"To suggest that I am anything like Her Magnificence—"

"You appeared out of thin air with the puppy right after I called Her name. Your beauty mesmerizes all around. It was a logical mistake to make, not an insult."

"Stupidity is never a good excuse." The woman was taking a haughty tone, but her expression had visibly softened at Thabo's compliment. Clearly Asha liked thinking of herself as beautiful.

Wait, this was Asha? The woman Thabo had seduced into servitude? Well, hell. Sure, Molly had heard a great deal about this woman as they discussed ways to free her, but never had he mentioned her looks. Damn, the woman was gorgeous. But that wasn't important, she scolded herself as she shoved jealously aside. The main thing was that just like they'd hoped, Asha had been dragged along on this trip because it had to do with Thabo. Wherever the hell the goddess was.

Meanwhile, Molly had to get it together. "Yes Asha," she said, though it took two tries for her to get a word out. "My apologizes for the confusion." She was only now realizing that she might have died if Thabo hadn't intervened. Worse, if he hadn't gone half stone, he'd be dead too. And speaking of which, how was he managing to stand there while both rock and flesh? She knew it was a huge strain on him and he'd already done it once at the table with Uncle Sully.

Then she realized he wasn't managing it at all. Oh hell. Certainly, his chest had been solid rock. That's how the dagger had gone *thunk* and not *splat* right through his chest. But he'd turned back to human now as he pulled the weapon out of his shoulder. Blood seeped from the would into his tee, and Molly cried out in alarm.

"Frank! Get the first aid kit!" she cried to the cook. He'd peered his head over the counter the moment Thabo had called for Zeva and now bobbed his head before disappearing. Meanwhile, Molly grabbed a wad of napkins.

"It's fine," Thabo said as he tried to take the napkins from her. She wasn't having any of it as she tugged up his tee. Let bitch Asha see the gaping hole she'd made in all that glorious chest. And then Molly was going to put an equally big hole in her.

"Tsk tsk," a voice came from behind her. "You haven't been a very good curator, have you?"

Molly looked over her shoulder at a booth that had been empty a second ago. And there she was, the crazy woman from three days ago. The one who had reattached Thabo's arms. Oh hell. So this was Zeva. And why hadn't she realized that three seconds ago? Though, in her defense, Thabo had said the woman could change her appearance at will.

"What? Nothing to say for yourself?" the looney taunted.

Oh shit. Not looney. The woman was a goddess and Molly had to get some brainpower going fast. "Um, hello Goddess Zeva. I greet you with all due respect." She did her best not to stammer her words, which were way more formal than anything she usually said. But Thabo had insisted that deference was the only way to start. Problem was, the woman didn't look all that intimidating what with her fly-away gray hair and the bright blue overalls. She looked more like a homeless person after a bath. Not so bad, but not so great either.

Then she remembered something, and the words popped out of her mouth before she could stop them.

"Where's your tiara?"

Suddenly it appeared in Molly's hand, the weight of the glowing gold beyond heavy. Molly dropped it, of course. She couldn't have lifted that in a million years. So when it slipped from her fingers and hit the floor with a dull thud, Molly couldn't do more than gape. Especially when the soft gold distorted from the impact.

Oh shit. "Um, sorry? I didn't know you were—"

"Do you like it?" Zeva asked, her voice impatient.

"Uh, yeah. It's…" Dented. "Really pretty."

"I could give it to you. You could have it and immortality." The woman's voice had taken on a sing-song quality that dazed Molly. "Just pick it up and say you'll serve me forever and a day."

So compelling was the voice that Molly was already bending down. It was a pretty tiara, even broken. And she'd love to live forever and a day. She'd just closed her fingers around the edges when Thabo spoke, his voice sharp.

"Molly! You have a job!"

It wasn't his words that penetrated her foggy brain. It was his tone, sharp with alarm. That, plus the fact that she couldn't pick up the tiara no matter how much she tried. It was too heavy. So with a single grunt of effort, the tiara slipped through her fingers and she felt Thabo's hand tighten on her arm. He swung her around so that she looked directly into his chocolate eyes.

"Molly, do you remember?"

She blinked, her mind centering on his face. His mouth. Oh hell. What had she been about to do? Meanwhile, the crazy woman's voice came at her, the words feeling like stone against her skin. She actually flinched from the impact.

"You're his curator. Have you forgotten so quickly?"

"N-no," she stammered, still wincing from the impacts. "I remember. I take care of Thabo." Her voice grew stronger with each word merely because Thabo was smiling at her. Silently encouraging her.

"Then you of course remember the Rules." It wasn't a question.

"Actually, the Rules got lost." She lifted her chin. "Problem with my uncle." She didn't actually want to throw Uncle Sully under the goddess bus, but it was the truth. And something about conversing with Zeva had her mouth working when she really ought to be more circumspect.

"Not my problem," Zeva said as she pushed out of the booth. She stood up, her blue coveralls becoming brighter and more flowy, more like a gown. Then the tiara disappeared from the floor to re-appear on her head in absolutely perfect shape. Molly was still staring at it when the goddess glided forward to loom over Molly, who would have slunk backwards except she ran into Asha who blocked her in.

"Rule number whatever, what happens to him, happens to you."

It took a moment to realize what that meant. Thabo had been stabbed, therefore…"But it was Asha who did it! She's your minion!"

"I know," Zeva said with a grin. "Isn't that fun?" Then she stabbed downward with a knife that hadn't been in her hand a second before. Thabo reacted quickly. Molly could see him dive forward in her peripheral vision, but he wasn't fast enough. And besides, if he took this blow for her, she'd just get stabbed again for that. Which were only a few of the very logical thoughts that flew right out of her mind when the weapon pierced her skin.

Ow! Pain flared sharp and hot in her shoulder. From the force of Zeva's down thrust, the weapon should have gone straight through Molly's chest and out the back, but it didn't. It pierced deep enough to make the point, but not so far as to kill her.

Shit. Ow and shit. Those were the two words echoing over and over in her brain as a way worse realization burst through her consciousness. She realized that everything they'd planned, everything she'd hoped to accomplish was impossible. Thabo had said Zeva was a goddess, but the word had never really encompassed the magnitude of her power. She and her slaves moved through walls. She created weapons out of thin air and turned people to stone. Compared to that, Molly was less than nothing. It was the height of arrogance to think that she could do anything against this bitch. Which meant she and Thabo were doomed. And that broke her heart as nothing else could. Worse, it crushed her spirit completely.

Molly sobbed, clutching at her bleeding shoulder as she wished she had left Thabo's statue at the bottom of the ocean. What a disaster this was! They'd never succeed. And now the man she loved was going to be punished for daring to hope that life could be different.

And while Molly's hope died, Zeva straightened. The dagger disappeared from her hand and she spun around like a child. Thabo had been coming to Molly's side, but Zeva stopped him. She pushed him backward with the very tip of her finger, then she clapped her hands like an excited toddler.

"And now," she said in a booming voice, "I'm ready for *something spectacular!*"

CHAPTER 13

Thabo saw the moment when terror took hold of Molly. Her eyes went bleak and her body trembled, and not from the pain of her shoulder wound. He'd seen that very response in new recruits. Minutes into an encounter with Zeva, understanding hit. The goddess had absolute power and the whims of a child who liked to destroy things. At that moment, every recruit broke. Even the strongest crumpled for a time and Thabo, himself, had crawled into a tiny hole in his mind and had not emerged for years. That it had happened to Molly now was not surprising, but it broke him in a way wholly new. He ached in his heart for her, and he resolved to end this as quickly as possible. To ease her pain. And no matter the cost to him, he would count it well spent.

So he slipped into his showman mode. He was the jester of her army, after all, and Zeva loved to laugh at bloody displays. Especially, if they came with loud bangs and dazzling sleight of hand. He grabbed a gun out of the closest man's hand, flinging it up in the air as he began to juggle, quickly adding in a knife and a full cup of coffee. The drink spilled, of course, all over Uncle Sully, who sputtered in anger. That elicited Zeva's first real smile and gave Thabo a bit of petty revenge on the man.

He kept the items spinning in the air as he stepped around a table toward Bobby, in back. His hands felt nimble. Almost as good as before he'd lost his arms. He'd been healing and that was a good thing. So he added another gun, ripped from the other thug's hand, and when the idiot tried to grab it back, Thabo slammed the knife straight into his palm. The man screamed and Zeva leaned back against the edge of a booth as she watched. She did love it when blood flowed.

But now Thabo had a problem. The puppy was prowling up to Molly. She was still in the grips of panic, her breath coming in jerking pants, and the wolf would make the situation worse. He had to think of something fast to turn the animal away. Thankfully, Thabo was confident in his speed.

He threw the cup and two pistols high in the air as he leaped over a table toward Asha. She'd been watching Molly with narrowed eyes and Thabo didn't like it. Asha hadn't turned evil so much as sour, and she'd been known to hurt people around Thabo just to get a rise out of him. If she turned her attention to Molly, he wouldn't be able to control his fury. So, best to distract both the wolf and his ex-lover at the same time.

He kept the two pistols in the air and threw the cup of coffee right at Asha. She expected it, of course. Of all people, she'd studied his moves the most. But when she deflected the cup straight at Molly, he was prepared. Grabbing one of the pistols, he shot the thing, shattering it before it hit Molly. And just as he'd hoped, the shards sliced the wolf's nose. The creature jumped back, still too young to have been trained to attack whatever hurt it. Not bad, but it wasn't a perfect maneuver. Molly's cheeks sprouted a couple red slices of blood which she wiped away with a shaking hand. At least she wasn't frozen in terror.

"Nice," Zeva drawled, "but hardly spectacular."

"Kuk," he cursed under his breath. The goddess was more impatient than usual. He grabbed a full plate, adding it to the whirling things in the air. The pancakes flew past him to land in front of the puppy who gobbled it up in a single bite. And—extra bonus—the syrup made the plate sticky which helped him grab hold of things better. But Zeva was hard to impress, so he grabbed two more plates, one that gave a biscuit to the puppy and another that splattered eggs on Asha. She blocked the move, of course, but there was no way to deflect eggs without getting slimed, and she now had greasy yolk on her forearms.

And right here was where Molly was supposed to help out. Zeva sometimes enjoyed food, especially if the poison was subtle. It didn't affect the goddess in Idola, but Thabo had never seen her take it on Earth. It was a small hope, but perhaps the poison Molly had given the cook would be enough to harm Zeva. Enough that he could kill the bitch. Perhaps, but one look at her told him that Molly was too terrified to try. Her eyes were wide and she kept swallowing as if trying to choke down her fear. She was trying, and he loved her for it, but facing Zeva calmly was something people didn't manage for years.

That left things up to him.

"You know," he drawled as he spilled another cup of coffee, this time in a wide splattering display. "Molly told me this restaurant serves the best pancakes in the world. Would you like to try?"

Zeva curled her lips. "What is a pancake?"

There were a thousand answers to that. He could describe it or just tell her that people prized it as part of a great feast. Instead, he grinned. "It is spectacular."

The goddess arched a brow. "Then I will try it. And you will pay if it is not."

Yes, he knew. He hadn't realized how monotonous the goddess's threats were when he had something—or someone—other than himself to worry about. *I'll hurt her. I'll hurt you.* He grabbed a phrase he'd learned from Molly and murmured it beneath his breath.

"Blah, blah, blah."

He started to move toward the kitchen. He'd been keeping up a modest display of juggling throughout as a way to entertain the goddess. He'd even picked up a few knives to add flash, but the moment he turned toward the kitchen, Asha struck.

Leaping forward, she snatched a knife out of the air, spun, and threw it at Molly. Thabo panicked, losing a plate in the process. He hadn't been prepared for that and he had no way to protect Molly from the weapon.

Thunk.

The knife sliced across Molly's shoulder to embed in a large poster just behind her. In fact, the blade landed in the photograph right between the eyes of a boy about to eat an ice cream sundae. Molly flinched and slapped a hand on her arm. Then she drew it back and stared at the bright red blood that coated her fingers.

"You fucking bitch," she muttered. Then her eyes narrowed and she looked up at the room at large. "Fucking, steaming, doggie shit pile of bitchface!"

Everyone stared, Thabo included. And Zeva smiled.

"I love a woman who wakes so articulate."

Molly shrank back from the goddess. Understandable, but it guaranteed that the woman saw her as a victim. So Thabo stepped forward, struggling with now sweaty palms to catch Molly's eye. He succeeded, though he had to step nearly on top of her to do it. And then—finally—she looked straight at him.

It was a moment he'd never forget. In one glance she sent him so many emotions and he felt every single one as if it were his own. Panic and fear were there, but not for herself. She was terrified she was going to let him down. That she wouldn't be able to save him from his fate. Which was ludicrous. They'd never had any hope to begin with. It had only been her heart that had refused to face reality.

"There was never any escape for me," he said softly.

It took a second for that message to penetrate her awareness. That he had never had any real hope, but had been caught up in her enthusiasm.

"I accept it," he said.

"I don't," Molly retorted. Then she straightened. "Because it's bull-fucking-shit."

"Goodness, what a mouth you have," Zeva drawled.

"Yeah, I can curse like a sailor. Comes from working the night shift serving the best damn pancakes in the world to drunks and bitches alike," Molly returned. Then she glared at Zeva, her chin firming against the tremor that cursed her hands. "Frank!" she called loudly to the cook. "A pecan stack with the *special* sauce."

The poison.

Which meant the game was set. Zeva would eat the poison and be harmed or not, so Molly's part in this was done. So he moved forward.

"I will serve her," he said. He wanted Molly as far away from Zeva as possible.

But his hands were slick now. The syrup was gone and the sweat was taking its toll, making everything slimy. His muscles burned and his coordination was going. The first mistake came when he stubbed his toe on chair leg. He hated juggling in tight spaces where every step could spell disaster. Worse, he was moving quickly, trying to adjust for a bad throw, so the pain in his foot stole his breath and a coffee cup fell, shattering close enough to Zeva to splash a dark stain onto her skirt.

Everything came down around him in a deafening crash. It included the stack of banana pancakes that had been waiting for Molly to serve her uncle. The plate had been on the counter, but as Thabo stumbled, he knocked it to the floor.

Far from being frightened, the puppy dove for the food, knocking over tables and chairs in its haste. Sully and his man jumped back, climbing onto their seats to get away from the mayhem. And in all that, Zeva just leaned back and laughed. It was a high trilling sound that made her sound like a delighted child.

"Well, well," she said as she clapped her hands over the disaster. "You have certainly not been spectacular, but this has been fun."

Everyone stared at her. What else could they do? And in the middle of this silence, Frank banged the bell.

Ding!

Zeva's food was ready. A steaming stack of pecan pancakes covered in enough poison to kill a rhino. Zeva gestured to Thabo and he nodded already aware of what she wanted.

He stepped over the puppy, the mess of broken plates, and a puddle of spilled coffee to pick up the pancakes and carefully set it before her.

Zeva looked down, her eyes sparkling. She picked up her fork, carefully cut off a piece, and lifted it to her lips. But she didn't eat. Instead, she arched a brow at Molly.

To Molly's credit, she kept her face mostly blank. Mostly. And perhaps that was what gave them away. Or perhaps Zeva could smell the poison. Thabo didn't know but at that moment, he saw their doom.

"Care to have a bite?" Zeva trilled.

"I-I wouldn't dare presume," Molly stammered.

"Is that because you know I don't share with anyone? Or because you've poisoned the food?"

Molly blanched a sickening white. "What?" she whispered.

"Did you think I haven't been watching my favorite juggler? Do you think my entire court hasn't seen what you two have done together? Lessons and all. It has been our greatest amusement, hasn't it Asha?"

Thabo turned, his heart squeezing tight in his throat. Beautiful Asha, the woman he had betrayed, kept her expression hard but her eyes shimmered with tears. "We saw everything," she said coldly. "We even heard your plan to poison Zeva."

No. No, no, no, no! He rushed forward and dropped to his knees before Zeva. "It was my idea," he lied. "Spare her and I will do anything you want."

"Spare her? No, no. I'm simply going to let her *serve* these pancakes. That is her job, isn't it?"

She grinned then waved her fingers. Suddenly Uncle Sully jumped down from his perch on the booth bench. He stiff-walked forward, his face a mask of horror.

"Stop it!" he bellowed, but he was abruptly pushed to sit down at Zeva's table. That was bad enough, but then another strangled moan came from the back of the restaurant. Thabo didn't even have to look to know it was Bobby. The boy was being magically dragged forward. And soon, he too was sitting at Zeva's table.

"Goddess please," Thabo begged, though he knew it was useless.

"Please? Please make it fair? Very well." She waved her hand and suddenly three plates appeared on the counter, all looking identical to the poisoned one.

"See?" Zeva continued, gesturing to the empty space before her. "One of those lovely stacks of pancakes is the one meant to poison me. The other two are just pancakes." She looked hard at Molly. "Serve us."

"No," Molly whispered. "No. I can't."

"You can, my dear. Or I'll simply kill you all."

Her gaze cut to Zeva and Thabo was struck by the brittle sheen to her eyes. Hard like diamonds, but so fragile. If she accidentally killed Bobby, it would destroy her. He stepped forward to distract the goddess. No sacrifice was too great. He couldn't stop Zeva's game, but at least he could take the burden from Molly.

"I will do it," he said gruffly, but Zeva stopped him with a slow purr.

"You could," she said with a malicious grin. "But I want her instead."

"Goddess, I beg you—" he began, but Molly held up her hand to stop him.

It took her two tries to speak, but she got the words out with surprising power.

"You want me to serve you the pancakes? Instead of Thabo?" She stomped over to the tray. "Fine."

Bobby choked out a sob but it was her uncle who growled. "Moll—" Her name was choked off by another casual wave from Zeva's hand.

Didn't matter what the man was going to say. Molly wasn't listening. With fury boiling in her eyes, she grabbed one of the plates and slapped it down in front of Zeva. She even brought new utensils wrapped tight in a napkin and slammed that down as well. All right in front of Zeva.

"There. I've served in Thabo's stead," she snapped.

"And now the others—" Zeva began, but a sound overrode her words.

A bell reverberated, growing stronger with every second it filled the air. Thabo's hands became clumsy blocks that he couldn't move as sudden weakness filled his body. He collapsed, dropping to the floor.

So loud. So sweet. It echoed in every cell of his body.

He fought hard to remain conscious. His head throbbed and his vision dulled. But bit by bit, his breath flowed in and out, his hands tingled and stabilized. And that sweet sound slowly faded.

"Lie!" screamed Zeva as she pointed a single finger at him. He tensed, waiting for whatever blast would end him, but nothing came. Another voice, female and filled with humor, filled the room.

"Well played," she said as she clapped her hands. "I believe, sister dear, that Thabo's escape clause has been triggered."

Thabo raised his head and saw the other goddess. The one who had once been the cruelest but was softer somehow. Older too. She appeared now as a plain woman in soft jeans and a tee shirt that said, *I saw that.–Karma* Her name was Alethia and she stood between him and her sister's shaking finger.

"It's not true!" Zeva screeched.

Molly moved a step toward him. "It is true," she said and even from his place on his knees, Thabo could hear the smirk in her voice. "Thabo is free because I served you in his stead."

"You have not sworn yourself to me," the goddess hissed.

"And why does everyone make things so complicated?" Molly asked, glee in her voice. "I served you pancakes instead of Thabo. Your exact words. That plus Asha's sacrifice makes two." Then she stepped toward to Asha. "Can you make this moment even more spectacular?"

Thabo lifted his head to see Asha who stood with her jaw slack. But as everyone's attention shifted to her, she stiffened and snapped her mouth shut. Then Molly spoke, her eyes soft and her voice gentle.

"Thabo told me about you. About how you gave everything up to be with him and even served by his side for two centuries. He's what your heart most desires, isn't he?"

Thabo pushed to his feet, though he felt clumsy and slow. "I have apologized for what I did to you—"

"She doesn't want your apology," Molly interrupted.

At that moment, Asha straightened, her eyes bleak as she looked at Molly. "Do you love him?"

"Yes," Molly answered. "With all my heart."

Asha turned to him, pain flaring hot in her eyes. "And you. You love her? She is nothing. She squealed like a pig when we appeared. She cannot fight or steal." Asha held up Uncle Sully's wallet for proof. "She is not even that pretty."

"She is beautiful in every way," Thabo answered. "And I love her beyond what I thought possible." The words flowed easily from his lips. Reaching out, he took Molly's hand and pressed his mouth to her fingers.

"Then I give you to her," Asha said, her voice breaking. "I release you from your promise to stay with me forever. I give you up."

A second chime sounded, mixing clearly with Zeva's scream. This time Thabo understood that it was the breaking of a stoneman curse. The first was his, and this second was Asha's. They were free, stonemen no more.

And by the sound of Zeva's howl, they were all about to die. Especially as fireballs appeared in her hands.

Kuk. Fucking, shit-Kuk. Zeva was going to incinerate them all.

Nowhere to run from fireballs. Not here and not when thrown by the goddess of War. But before he could do more than shove himself between Zeva and Molly, Alethia spoke, her voice dry and her tone hard.

"I'm pretty sure that Dad would notice if a burning crater suddenly appeared in the middle of a Florida IHOP. Aren't you the one constantly telling us to be good losers? Isn't that what Dad likes most about you?"

Zeva's hands clenched, extinguishing the fireballs, but her hair burst into flame instead. "Do you seek to school me, sister?"

Alethia shrugged, but her eyes were hard. "Sisters!" she called. "Am I schooling Zeva?"

One by one the goddesses appeared until six stood looking about them, though one appeared not to have any eyes and another was more dragon than woman. The one in the business suit peered at him from over her glasses.

"Are we making stonemen today?"

"Freeing them," Alethia said.

"Then why did you call us?"

"Because Zeva is thinking about being a bad loser."

The dragon released a smoking puff of air. "I don't think she's thinking at all. Look at her. How can she think when her hair's on fire?"

There were other comments as well, none that he could comprehend. One started laughing as she flicked beetles off her clothing and into Zeva's flaming hair. And bit by bit, the tension rose in the room.

As quietly as he could, he tucked Molly behind him. They were trapped on all sides by the puppy, Alethia, and a booth. Nowhere to run, no way to survive. Not from a goddess battle. But he would do whatever he could to save her. He felt her tremble behind him, but she silently refused to cower. Instead, she turned so she stood back to back with him. He faced Zeva while Molly protected him from the goddess with purple scales for skin and no eyes. Throughout the room, the humans ducked as best they could. All except for Asha who shot him a last look before escaping outside.

At least he'd saved Asha.

"If she's going to blow, then she should get to it," said the goddess in a business suit. "I think I want a pedicure."

"But if she burns them, then Daddy will ice us and fry us up for dinner."

"I'd quite like to be iced and fried," said the dragon. "Sort of like that Mexican ice cream, right?"

And then, right in the middle of it all, the puppy let out a high whine. It was a loud keen, clearly voicing distress. The sound cut through all the discussion. The conversation stuttered to a halt as everyone stared at the wolf. What was wrong with it?

The huge creature belched.

Three goddesses stepped back, coughing at the smell. Which is when the puppy added a fart before he flopped onto his belly and sank his muzzle onto his paws.

"Ew! What have you been feeding him?" Alethia asked.

Pancakes and stale coffee, but Thabo didn't risk saying that out loud.

"You have poisoned Fluffy!" Zeva screamed.

"Fluffy?" Molly muttered from behind him. "Seriously?"

"I hate you all!" Zeva cried, then she scooped down, picked up her wolf, and disappeared in a puff of acrid smoke.

Gone.

From across the room, the goddess in a business suit rolled her eyes. "Like that's news. Pedicure time!" Then she disappeared. The rest followed. They vanished in puffs of scented smoke, each smell distinctive, all nauseating.

And all of them gone.

Thabo looked around, unable to believe it was possible. He saw only humans in the IHOP. He felt Molly's heat at his back, solid and clear. And he knew something else too.

Aches. A lack thereof. A dimming somehow. He'd lost his stoneman superiority, he realized. His body wasn't what it used to be. But he didn't care. He didn't care the tiniest bit because he was free.

Free.

"Is it over?" Molly whispered. "Is it done?"

"Not yet," Thabo answered, awed by how normal it all felt. And how absolutely bizarre. "There's one more thing to do."

CHAPTER 14

M olly felt her knees go out from under her. "I don't think I can take much more," she said, feeling adrenaline at war with terror in her blood. Which meant that every cell in her body felt tired. And jittery. And very overwhelmed.

Thabo cupped her elbow, his large hand steadying her as nothing else could. He guided her to the nearest chair and she dropped into it with an "umph." Then he squatted down before her, his chocolate eyes patient until she held his gaze.

"What?" she asked.

He kissed her, long and sweet. And with every caress of his tongue and lips, she felt such things. Gratitude, admiration, and most of all, love. She wasn't sure if she felt it from him or from her own heart, but it glowed so bright inside her. And when he pulled back, she flashed him her mischievous smile.

"Well, if that's the one thing left to do, then I say we get to it."

He grinned back at her, the white of his teeth so bright that she had to blink. "I love you, Molly Parker. Please let me spend the rest of my life showing you how much."

Oh, how sweet the moment. She hadn't even known she'd been waiting for him to say that. Hell, she hadn't known her own heart would sing with the words. So she pressed her lips to his but didn't deepen the kiss. Instead, she whispered her words straight into his heart. "I love you, too."

"And you're both crazy," said Uncle Sully behind them. Molly jolted. Trust her uncle to ruin the romantic moment. Meanwhile Thabo shot to his feet just as Uncle Sully slapped a piece of paper down on the table. It was the one with the coordinates for another of Zeva's stonemen. "Don't want this. Can't figure out why I ever did. And if you two play with those bitches, then I wash my hands of you both."

"We just want to be left alone," Molly said. Then she looked at her brother who was hovering a few tables back, his habitually sulky expression now one of embarrassment. "And for Bobby to get his head on straight."

Uncle Sully raised his hands as he headed for the door. "I wash my hands of you all." His two other men scrambled to follow, hitting the front door a half second behind their boss. The last thing she heard was Sully barking an order. "Drive me to the nearest bar. And if either of you say the word 'pancake' again, I will shoot you dead."

Meanwhile, Bobby stepped forward, his expression wary as he stepped over spilled coffee. "I…um…I think I'm going back to school. I'm not ready for the real world just yet." Then before Molly could say anything, he held up his hands. "I'll get a job and pay the tuition myself. I swear."

She studied her brother closely, seeing a change in him that hadn't been there before. There was a resolve in his eyes. Something in tonight's confrontation had changed Bobby for the better.

"It's not going to be easy, Bobby."

"I know. But I'll find a way."

"Maybe I can help," Thabo said, his voice low. And when Molly looked at him in confusion, he shrugged. "I wasn't the only thing buried when my ship went down.

There is more under the water if you can help me retrieve it."

She straightened. "There wasn't a whole lot of the ship left, Thabo. It's been nearly two hundred years."

"I can find it. The captain's box. It has coins that should help pay any teacher."

"How many coins?" Bobby asked.

Thabo shrugged. "Enough to pay for a full cargo of tobacco and cotton."

Suddenly excited, Molly squeezed his hand. "Two hundred year-old coins? Thabo, that would be worth a fortune."

He smiled. "And if I gave you every one, it still would not come close to what I owe you for my freedom."

"You don't owe me a thing, Thabo. Just love me—"

"I love you." He spoke over her words, clearly knowing what she wanted. What they both needed. And when he smiled at her, she knew that while she might have helped him gain his freedom, he was giving her something much more important: a future filled with adventure, magic, and his love. Nothing could be better than that.

CHAPTER 15

Molly groaned in ecstasy as Thabo expertly massaged her feet. Her shift at the IHOP had been brutal, but it was totally worth it when Thabo did whatever he was doing to her arches. It was a couple months past the showdown in the restaurant. Bobby was in classes and doing great. He'd moved back home and had been an enormous help in getting Thabo up to speed on the way the modern world worked. Which meant that Thabo also helped keep Bobby on the straight and narrow because he saw things in her brother that she'd never noticed. Thabo could curb wild ideas with a single hard stare. Plus, the two men spent many hours discussing life while they repaired her garage.

It was heartwarming, to say the least. And if her heart weren't already overflowing with love for Thabo, she'd have fallen just as hard from the way he was with her brother. He was going to make a great father someday. He was a kind and patient man, used to hard work, and grateful for the smallest bit of kindness. It ached to see how deeply his heart had been hurt, but she was all too happy to shower him with love. He returned it a hundred fold, and they'd managed to master lesson number eighteen too, which was a ton of fun.

They'd also recovered the captain's box. It contained a couple million in old coins, but selling them took time. So she'd stayed with IHOP as a way to cover their bills, of which there were many. But that too was worth it, so long as she came home to one of Thabo's foot rubs.

She was just about to suggest working on lesson nineteen when the doorbell rang. Molly rolled her eyes. If Bobby had forgotten his keys again, she was going to pierce them into his skin.

"I'll get it," Thabo said as he pressed a quick kiss to her lips. Then he rose, looking like an ebony god in his jean shorts and light tank. Bobby was also giving the man style tips. Not the most ideal tutor, but the clothing always came off easily so Molly didn't really mind.

Then Thabo opened the door and Molly was startled to hear a female voice instead of her brother. "Hello. Are you Thabo Conteh?"

Molly rolled to her feet, ignoring the wince in her arches as she rushed forward. She was disturbingly possessive of her man, even when a strange woman wasn't doing anything more than saying hello.

"That is my name," Thabo answered as Molly made it to his side.

Once there, she saw it wasn't just a woman, but a man as well who managed to look distinguished, even in casual khaki pants and a polo. And it was the man who spoke, his voice low.

"You were one of War's stonemen, now freed?"

Thabo stiffened and he abruptly switched on the outside light, flooding the front porch with stark clarity. "Kane?" he whispered.

Molly watched as both men greeted each other. It wasn't in words or even a gesture, but a connection of gazes that transmitted shared experiences and quiet shock all in the blink of an eye. Meanwhile, the woman looked to Molly.

"Hi. I'm Jacqueline and you must be Molly. We've been emailing."

Molly immediately placed the woman as the owner of the website about the stonemen. The one who was determined to free all the goddess's slaves. So she swung the door fully open. "Come on in. I think our conversation needs to be done inside. And probably with alcohol."

Kane flashed her a big grin at that, but Thabo hadn't moved. He stood solidly in the doorway, a massive man facing off against another large man.

"Thabo?" Molly said, touching his rigid arm.

"How did you get free?" he rasped, his gaze hard on Kane.

"Same way you did. Escape clause." Then he looked with warmth to the woman beside him "And *Jacqueline*." There were nuances in that one name. Layers of love and adoration that Molly recognized. It was the same way Thabo spoke her name, and it was enough to convince her that she wanted to hear the tale.

"I've been emailing with them," she said to Thabo as she tugged him out of the way. He went easily enough, but she could tell that the shock of seeing someone from his old life was significant.

It took a bit to get settled with beer, cheese, and crackers all around. It wasn't fancy fare, but it was what she had and the others seemed to take it happily. And then Jacqueline leaned forward.

"Look, we can get to our stories soon. Believe me, I want to hear every detail of how you stuck it to War. But first let me cut to the chase. We're here to offer you two a job."

Molly blinked. That was the last thing she expected. Meanwhile Kane leaned forward, his gaze on Thabo.

"We got free, and hallelujah, but there are others who haven't been so lucky."

Jacqueline nodded. "Plus the bitch thinks she's about to win. That doesn't bode well for humanity."

"Yes," Thabo rasped. "War is ready to end the game."

"By ending Earth," Jacqueline continued. "We know."

So did Molly and Thabo, and frankly that worried her. But she hadn't known what she could do about it. "What exactly do you think we can do?"

"Help us," said Kane. "Help us free more stonemen." He set down his beer. "You were closer to War than I was, in her court all the time. You probably know more of her plans than I ever heard."

Thabo nodded slowly. "I will share whatever I know."

"Excellent," Jacqueline said. "But we want more than just information. We need people who understand what's going on. Who will help free—"

"Yes." That was Thabo, his voice clear as a bell. "Yes. Whatever I can do, I will help."

"Good," Kane said. "We can pay expenses and a salary."

Really? That was interesting. "How many—"

And right like that, Jacqueline shifted to stone. Right where she sat, she stiffened and froze, her skin marble white.

Thabo leapt up from his seat, grabbing a baseball bat that he had nearby. It was the only weapon Molly had let him have in the house. Meanwhile, Kane jumped up in reaction to Thabo, but he held out his hands in a stop motion.

"Wait, wait. Listen! She's a stoneman to Alethia. She's charged with unmaking War's stonemen."

Thabo stood still, his body vibrating with tension. But he didn't attack, though his eyes had narrowed to slits as he glared at Jacqueline. They waited a moment. A moment more. And then, she came back to life. Her skin turned golden again, and her face contorted into a grimace. And then—as soon as she was supple—she fell backward against the couch.

"Ugh, I hate that," she groaned. Then she frowned as she took in the two tense men around them. "What happened?"

Kane chuckled. "You alarmed us, love. A warning next time would be more helpful."

"Hmm? Oh. Sorry. I had to ask for money." Then she leaned forward and scribbled out an account number on the back of a nearby envelope. "There's money in this account in your name."

"What?" Molly said with a jolt. "How?"

Jacqueline waved her hand in a dismissive gesture. "Like I can understand how they do it. But they can freeze time and turn people to stone. Hacking a modern bank would be child's play. Here's what we can pay you for a year's work."

She scribbled another number on the paper, large enough to make Molly's jaw drop.

"You're kidding, right?"

"Completely serious," said Kane. "My family will handle the paperwork."

"Trust me," Jacqueline put in. "His family is powerful enough to manage this without blinking an eye."

"But only if you help us."

Molly looked at Thabo, who was slowly returning to stand beside her. He touched her shoulder while she gripped his hand, and together they decided. No words. Just a quiet gratitude for a purpose that they both desperately wanted.

Then Molly spoke for them both. "Yes," she said. "And Thabo knows of an abandoned statue. We tried to get my uncle to deal with it, but he refused. I've been thinking of retrieving it to see what we can do to help there."

Jacqueline clapped her hands in delight as Kane dropped onto the couch beside her. "Great! Tell us more."

And so they did. It began with words and progressed quickly to plans. Before long, Molly had a very exciting and magical future laid out in front of her. She clasped Thabo's hand and his eyes danced in a mirror of her own happiness. They could do this. They could free stonemen and stick it to those bitch goddesses one slave at a time.

"I love you," she whispered to him.

"As I love you," he answered.

Then together, they made a grand and glorious adventure out of their future.

The End

HEART OF STONE

The Stone Men Series

Anna Argent

CHAPTER 1

H er work was flawless. It had to be. Her brother's life depended on it.

Sure, Benjamin had gotten them both into this mess, but he was still her flesh and blood, and she couldn't turn her back on him.

Even if it got her killed.

She'd spent the last several days doing nothing but the criminals' dirty work, and if she didn't return to her paying art restoration jobs soon, she wasn't sure how she was going to make rent this month.

Of course, not making rent wouldn't be a big deal if she failed in her task and the assholes killed her.

She eyed the small drilled hole in the bottom of the statue where scraps of wadded up newspaper were barely visible. The mystery of what was inside poked at her, urging her to pull out the contents and see what they were smuggling, but she refused to give into curiosity's annoying demands. No matter how curious she was, it was safer not to look—for both her and her brother.

Just as she adjusted the light to a better angle to begin plugging the hole, a knock sounded on her door. It was late—well past time for her clients to be stopping by. Her brother had already promised to leave her alone until she was no longer angry at him, and all of her friends knew she was working on a rush job.

That left the list of possible visitors a little too short for comfort.

Her hands went clammy as anxiety ricocheted through her system. She'd told the asshole criminals she wouldn't be done until tomorrow. She probably should have padded her timeline, but the guns they had tucked under their jackets warned her that lying to them might not be the healthiest course of action.

She briefly thought about pretending she wasn't home, but her music was playing in the background, and her curtains were thin enough that someone could easily see her moving around inside.

She had no option but to face the assholes and deal with more backlash from her brother's poor life choices.

Bethany wiped the grit from her hands on her jeans and answered the door. Instead of the two armed thugs she expected, there was a young couple standing on her welcome mat.

"We're sorry to bother you, ma'am," the man said. He had a muscular, corn-fed farm boy kind of build, and blue eyes that hardly left the pretty woman at his side. "But we heard you are the best at restoring old statues, and we have a bit of an emergency."

Bethany stood there, trying to figure out what a statue emergency might look like when the woman spoke. "I'm Sue Sullivan. This is Dalton Thatcher. We've come all the way from Nebraska to see you. I know it's late, but can we come in?"

The drive from Nebraska to Florida was long enough to pique Bethany's interest. That, combined with their *statue emergency*, made her positively curious.

Manners had Bethany backing away from the threshold so they could pass. "Sure," she said. "But I'm really busy, so you'll have to be quick."

The couple shared a silent look filled with concern and more than a little fear.

Instantly, Bethany wished she'd told them to go away. The last thing she needed was another set of someone else's problems to deal with. Her brother's were more than enough.

The couple looked around the space that served as both her living room and restoration studio. It was an open, airy room, painted a pale yellow that made the most of the natural Florida sunlight. During the day this room was almost as bright as the outdoors. Now, it was filled with artificial light and warm shadows.

The windows were covered with gauzy sheers that hid her neighbors rundown crap-shacks and swayed on the cool winter breeze. She wasn't close enough to the Gulf to see it, but she could smell just a faint hint of salt and surf and hear the cries of seagulls.

One corner of the room she'd set aside as a space to relax and watch sappy movies. The ancient, boxy TV and beanbag chair didn't look like much, but she didn't need anything more. Every penny she saved went into growing her business and reputation. That was far more valuable than any fifty-five-inch flat screen could ever be.

One day she would have that dream studio on the beach, but for now, this small, sunny house was all she needed.

The rest of the space was filled with tables holding sculptures and ornate picture frames in need of repair. A few pieces were in progress, including the trio of small statues hiding drugs—or whatever—in them.

Bethany shifted in front of them so the couple wouldn't look too closely.

"What can I do for you?" she asked.

The two shared another one of those secretive looks that made Bethany wonder if she should have taken that gun her brother had offered her after all. She wasn't altogether sure she could use the thing on another living creature, but unfortunately, she also wasn't sure if she might actually find herself needing to.

Sue's hand tightened around Dalton's arm. He covered her fingers, patting them in an effort to comfort her. "We have this statue. It's very dear to us. We'd like you to restore it."

"I'd be happy to do so. I'll get the paperwork for you to fill out and get started on it next month. Did you bring it with you?"

"We did. But, we were hoping you could do the job right away. We were planning to stay in town so we could take him home as soon as you're done."

Him? Not it? The statue really was dear to them.

"I'd love to help you, but I'm booked up for several weeks. I promise I'll call as soon as it's done, though."

"I'm afraid it can't wait. It's an emergency."

Bethany waited for them to explain, but they said nothing. "I don't understand."

The woman swallowed nervously. "My uncle is dying. He wants to see the statue repaired before he passes. I'm afraid he doesn't have much time left."

Dalton seemed surprised by Sue's story, which told Bethany that it was a pile of lies. No way was she getting involved in anything else sketchy. "I'm sorry. I wish I could help. There are other restorers I could recommend."

"We'll pay you well," Sue said. "Whatever it takes."

"That's right," Dalton added. "Whatever it takes. We can sell the house if we have to."

"But you love that house," Sue said. "You built it with your own hands."

"I can't think about that. Tristan needs our help."

She nodded at the man and they faced Bethany as a united front, worry obvious in the tense lines between their brows.

The couple was willing to sell their house to gain her help? How in the world could she turn them down? Maybe it was just a statue, but it seemed so much more important to them, and Bethany was a sucker for someone in need.

Which was precisely how she ended up helping bad men smuggle drugs or counterfeit money or whatever was in those damn statues.

Still, she knew that if she didn't at least try to help the couple, she'd spend the next year feeling guilty. "Let me see the job. Then I'll decide."

Dalton perked up with excitement. "I'll be right back."

If he was going to carry it by himself, at least it couldn't be that large. Maybe she could sneak it in before she started back to work on her other jobs. Right after the assholes took their secrets and left her the hell alone.

Dalton came back through the door carrying a life-sized statue covered in a white sheet. Bethany had no idea how he managed so much weight without help. It made her wonder what kind of material she'd be working with. Certainly not metal or stone. Lightweight plaster, maybe?

He set it down with a heavy thud. Dangling over his arm was a sack bulging with the angular lines of broken stone. "Did the statue lose an arm?"

"No," Sue said. "More like a chunk from his side."

"How did that happen?"

"Shotgun," Dalton said.

Bethany waited for the laugh to come indicating that he was joking. When she was still waiting several seconds later, she realized he was serious. "Someone shot your statue?"

"It's a long story," Sue hurried to say. "All we need to know is if you can fix him and how long it will take."

Bethany lifted the sheet slowly so as not to snag any fragile pieces. The first thing she noticed was that the statue was definitely stone. Solid, dense stone. The second thing she noticed was that it had no base. Its feet were its only support. The third thing she noticed was that there was a dull, rusty stain covering the surface—one that looked suspiciously like dried blood.

She pulled the sheet all the way off and was met with the face of agony. There was, indeed, a large section of stone missing from the statue's side. Imbedded just beneath the surface were several metallic bits she assumed were some kind of shot. A thousand tiny chips were gouged across the surface of the body, along with a few hairline cracks. She could see damage from both the elements and, if she wasn't mistaken, fire.

The statue's naked body was a work of art. Thick, muscular limbs depicting human perfection, and a package that would make any red-blooded woman swoon. Raw male power was evident in every line, down to the tiny striations in the muscle fiber. But it was his face that spoke to her. So much pain. So much misery and loneliness.

She had no idea how the sculptor had captured such potent emotion, but she felt the echoes of his pain as if the model were alive and standing right in front of her.

When she reached up to touch his cheek, her hand was shaking. "Where did you find this?"

"He's a family heirloom," said Dalton.

She stroked the face and swore she could almost hear a silent scream for help. All she wanted to do was drop everything and fix this work of art. "You keep referring to him as a man. I see why now."

"We call him Tristan," Sue said. "Can you repair him?"

Bethany tore her gaze away from Tristan's face long enough to inspect the major damage to his side. "How many pieces do you have?"

"Most of them," Dalton said. "There were a few crushed bits I wasn't able to recover—dust, really."

"Will you help him?" Sue asked.

"Yes." There was no other answer. She couldn't possibly send this work of art to anyone else. She had to know the repairs were done right. She didn't understand why that need burned in her so fiercely, but she couldn't deny it. "I'll start working on it next week."

"That's not soon enough. My uncle may not have that long."

"I want to help," said Bethany, "but I'm in the middle of another rush job."

She tore her eyes away from Tristan and glanced at the couple just long enough to see them sharing another one of those looks.

Dalton patted Sue's hand again. "We really need him to be whole as soon as possible. Can you at least repair the wound in his side?"

Bethany looked inside the sack with the shattered stone pieces. There were a lot of them. "It's probably going to take me about a hundred hours of work to do the major repair. If you want all the surface chips restored, it'll probably be twice that long."

A look of sheer terror crossed Sue's face as she looked up at Dalton. "That's way too long. What if he…?"

"We just have to hope Thyra leaves him alone. She doesn't want to lose him either."

Bethany almost asked who Thyra was, but decided it was none of her business. Over the past few months, she'd learned that the less she knew, the better.

Sue nodded and looked at Bethany, her warm brown eyes pleading. "Please fix him as soon as you can. He means a lot to us."

"We should go and let her get back to work," Dalton said. He wrote their contact information on the paperwork. "Thank you, Bethany. We'll be in town for at least a few days. Call if anything…happens."

"Happens?"

"You know," said Sue after jabbing an elbow in his side, "if your schedule changes or the work goes faster than you think."

The couple was definitely hiding something, but right now, Bethany couldn't bring herself to care. All she could think about was getting her hands on Tristan.

CHAPTER 2

Tristan watched Bethany. The sight of her eased some of the searing pain he endured, though he had no idea why.

It was probably another sick joke his twisted mistress played on him.

His body was ravaged and broken. He was frozen inside that moment of torment when lead shot had ripped into him. If he hadn't acted on instinct and turned to stone the instant before the blow hit him, the shot would have hit flesh instead of rock, and he would have died.

Over and over he'd cursed himself for his fast reflexes. If he'd hesitated for even a split second, he would have died as any normal man would have. But no, his instincts had saved his life and forced him to remain locked in his shell of pain—alive and aware of every tormented nerve ending.

Death was the only freedom a killer like him could ever hope to find.

But now, watching Bethany work, something in him quieted, allowing space for a portion of the rage he endured to trickle away.

She sat bent over her workbench, her long, graceful fingers working with efficient skill. He recognized the pieces of himself laid out like a puzzle before her, but as separated as he was from them, he couldn't feel her touch.

Her black hair stood out from her head in a bouncy array of tight curls that made his fingers itch to touch. Her skin was darker than the stone she pieced together, lending her bare arms a network of shadows that highlighted her supple strength. The tight shirt she wore hugged curves that would make even the most beautiful sculptors of Idola envious, but it was her eyes that he could not seem to forget.

Even though she wasn't looking at him now, he remembered exactly what it had felt like when she'd gazed into his dead eyes. She'd been close enough to him he could smell her skin, like some kind of dark magic meant to sooth his raging soul. She'd looked right into him, and the warm honey gaze had given him something he hadn't felt in a long, long time.

Hope.

He'd been so long without it, he'd almost forgotten what it felt like—pure and potent, with the kind of magic powerful enough to reach a soul as lost as his.

The hours slid by as he watched her. She rarely rose from her seat, and then only for a few moments. Her focus was absolute. He wasn't even sure she was aware that an entire day had passed since she'd begun assembling his broken pieces.

All she did was work to repair him. She hadn't even stopped to eat. Whatever the important job she'd spoken of was, it sat forgotten.

As the sun was setting on the second day of her tireless efforts, Tristan began to get upset. She wasn't taking care of herself. She was going to work herself sick if she didn't stop.

He had collected days of time off from his captor—time he'd never found a reason to use. Until now.

But if he were to turn to his flesh form and demand she eat and rest, he'd bleed out in seconds. Until the wound in his side was sealed, he was trapped in silence, forced to watch her work herself into exhaustion.

At one point, she laid her head down next to his pieces. She was still and might have slept for a few minutes, but it wasn't nearly long enough. The music that seemed to be her constant companion played on. Tristan was helpless to do more than stare and wish he could tuck her safely in her bed.

It was then that he realized how strange his thoughts had become. Normally, he was too consumed by pain to do more than plot his mistress's death. He'd become her slave a small handful of years after Jesus had been crucified. Since that time, Tristan had lived a life of violent service to his mistress Thyra. She'd caused him endless years of torment, and he'd spent most of them fantasizing about ways to kill her. After all, killing *was* what he did best.

Sadly, at some point during the past two thousand years, he'd realized that an entity as powerful as Thyra couldn't be slain. She could, however, wish for death.

Tristan had spent the last few centuries imagining how he could finally make that happen.

But now, those familiar thoughts of suffering, and all the rage connected to them, seemed a waste of this precious time. There was no way to know how long he'd be here, in this bright, clean place, with the sound of music in his ears and the scent of Bethany's light, magical fragrance surrounding him.

Soon he'd be back in his burned-out home, staring at charred, rotting beams and breathing in the stench of burned flesh and bone.

For as long as he was here, he wanted to languish in this place, in the presence of the woman whose artistic touch shone through everywhere he looked.

Someone pounded on the door. With his back facing that direction, he couldn't see who it was. What he could see was the way Bethany's body went instantly tense. Her tall, willowy frame tightened, and her dark hands began to shake.

She grabbed a cloth to cover the pieces she'd been working on, and hurried to answer the door.

"You done yet?" asked a man with a deep, gravelly voice.

"Almost. I just need a few more days."

"Days?" His voice radiated irritation. "You said that the last time I was here."

"It's a complex task. It's going to take as long as it takes. If I hurry, there's no way the work will pass through customs."

"The shipment goes out day after tomorrow. I'll be back in twenty-four hours to pick up the statues. If you're not done by then, my next call will be to your baby brother."

"No. Please. I'll get them done. Just leave him alone."

"He's a good kid," the man said. "The boss has just the right job set aside for him. I think he's almost hoping you fail to get the work done on time. Benny would be an asset to the team. And once he's in that deep, the only way out is feet first."

It took Tristan a second to realize that the man meant Benny would be dead.

"I won't fail," she promised. "And if you so much as text my brother, the next call I make will be to the cops."

"Are you threatening me?" asked the man in a calm, quiet voice.

Bethany backed up until Tristan could just see her from the corner of his eye. She held her hands up in front of her as if trying to ward the man away.

"I'm not afraid of you," she said, but the quiver of fear in her voice gave away her lie.

"No?" he asked. "Guess I need to step up my game then." He lunged, picking up Bethany by her arms and shoving her back into the wall so hard a nearby picture frame fell.

Glass shattered. She let out a terrified squeak.

Tristan felt the telltale shimmer of power at the base of his spine. It wasn't until he'd already begun the transformation to flesh that he realized what he was doing and stopped before he killed himself.

"You're going to sit that sweet ass down and finish the job tonight," the man said. "Or tomorrow, Baby Brother Benjamin and I are going out for a midnight stroll. And once he sees the operation the boss wants him to help with, there's no going back. Benny will be ours."

"I'll get it done," Bethany said. "Just promise me that Benjamin stays off limits."

The man shrugged, and the move was powerful enough it actually lifted Bethany a little higher off the ground. "You do the work. Then we'll talk."

He let her go and stalked out, slamming the door behind him.

Bethany slid down the wall and hugged herself. Silent tears streamed over her cheeks.

Tristan ached to go to her and promise to kill the man who had touched her. He was good at killing, and he couldn't think of a better target for his anger than someone who'd lay his hands on a woman as rare and beautiful as she was.

As soon as her breathing evened out, she pushed to her feet. But rather than going to work on whatever it was the dead man wanted from her, she came to stand in front of Tristan.

She was tall enough that without his base, she was only a few inches shorter than he was. From this distance, he could see straight into her honey-colored eyes.

There was so much sadness there—so much fear.

She cupped his cheek, giving him the living heat of her body. He felt it sink into his stone, driving away some of the pain his damaged shell inflicted upon him.

"I'm sorry, Tristan," she said. "I really wanted to finish putting you back together tonight. I was so close. Guess I have to take a little break to deal with my brother's bad choices."

Tristan didn't know what that meant, but it hardly mattered. She was speaking to him as if he were a real man, and that kind of attention had a potent effect. He was so used to being alone and unseen, he wasn't sure how to deal with the swell of need that arose in him.

He needed to touch her, thank her, let her know what her gift meant to him.

Sadly, all he could do was bleed on her floor and give her a dead body to explain to the authorities. It was not the kind of repayment for her gift he had in mind.

She let out a sad sigh before turning away and going to work on a small statue next to the fragmented pieces of his body.

Her movements were hurried. She didn't have that same slow, careful grace she'd used before. In fact, as he watched her, it almost seemed like she resented her skill.

As the hole that had previously been in the small statue became a seamless patch, her eyes kept straying to him.

Every time her honeyed gaze hit him, he felt it like a physical touch. The sheer warmth of her expression, the sympathy she had when she looked on him, was enough to make even stone squirm.

"That needs to dry anyway," she said. "Let's give you a test fit, shall we?"

She was talking to him, and the music of her voice was far sweeter than anything flowing from the speakers nearby.

Bethany carefully carried a section of broken stone she'd glued together. He knew that it had been gravel only a couple of days ago, but he couldn't see a single seam or crack in her work. It was as if she'd knitted his flesh together again, as good as new.

The piece grated against his wound, making pain flare to life. He snarled at it to shove it back where it belonged, but the effort took a large bite out of his dwindling reserves of willpower.

"Perfect." Her voice pulled him back up from the bleak depths of his pain. He wrapped himself in it, letting the soothing sound comfort him.

"There are still some metal fragments that need to come out, but I think it's safe to start putting you back together."

She smiled up at him. "I'm as crazy as Sue and Dalton, talking to you like this. Guess I really need to get some sleep."

She left him for a minute or two, and then returned. The stone piece went back into place, only this time it was a frigid pain, rather than the searing agony he'd felt before. Whatever glue she had used felt like an ice-cold blow torch welding his flesh together.

She took a long strip of cloth and bound him around the middle, using several layers to hold the mended piece in place.

"That'll set tonight, and tomorrow I can start working on all the surface damage." With that, she went back to work on the little statue, leaving Tristan aching for her touch.

He knew that what she'd do to him tomorrow would probably hurt like hell, but he didn't mind. He didn't care how much it hurt as long as she touched him.

CHAPTER 3

Bethany barely slept, and when she did, she dreamed of Tristan and about a dozen ways he could have ended up so wrecked. After one more nightmare where someone used him as a battering ram to break down her door, she finally gave up on sleep and shuffled back out into her studio.

The sun wasn't quite up yet, but it would be soon. The best light would hit Tristan right after dawn, and that's when she needed to be ready to work on digging out those metal bits so she could patch him up properly.

She grabbed a quick cup of coffee and gathered her tools. A few minutes later, she was perched on a rolling stool, which put her right on eye level with his manly bits.

Most of the statues she'd seen—at least the ones that weren't some kind of fertility god—had been more modest in their assets. Hair, leaves and other artistic flourishes were all used to conceal the goods. Not so with Tristan. His sculptor let it all hang out, and there wasn't a thing Bethany could have done not to notice or appreciate the view.

She pulled on a pair of lighted magnifiers to inspect the work she'd done so far. The seam was barely visible, and in the few places she could see it, there was still some fill work to be done.

The sun rose as her focus became complete. She didn't always reach this level of concentration, when the world fell away and nothing mattered but what was right in front of her. But with Tristan, she seemed to be unable to do anything but give him her rapt attention.

The sunlight changed. Her stomach growled. She couldn't remember the last time she'd eaten, but she couldn't stop working now. She pulled the last bit of metal from him and was almost ready to start filling in the gouges.

She used a clean cloth to wipe away yet another smear of rust-colored staining. It came off too easy to be oxidation. From what she could see it was merely on the surface. Just as if it were blood.

Freaky.

Her mind went to a dark place where that sweet couple hunted humans in a garden filled with life-sized statues. Maybe that's how Tristan had been shot—they'd been aiming for some poor person and it was his blood that had gotten splattered all over the statue.

A shiver passed through Bethany, and she tried to remind herself that it was none of her business. Curiosity was not her friend.

She'd just finished patching the largest chips on his abdomen when someone knocked on her door.

Her whole body went tense as she realized who it was. She hadn't been paying attention to the time, but the light had moved through the room, telling her most of the day had passed.

The assholes were here for their statues.

She pulled in a fortifying breath, and then answered her door.

The man standing there looked like he had his nose pressed flat against a piece of glass. It canted wildly to his right, obviously broken at least a couple of times. His bushy brows hung over his narrow eyes, matching the untamed thatch of chest hair that was working to escape from his overly tight shirt.

Several of his fingers sported heavy gold rings, and her guess was they were more functional than decorative. There were probably a few men who were wearing the reverse imprint from the jewelry on their faces. She wondered how many of them had been fed to the alligators.

He moved inside without an invitation, forcing her to back up or let him touch her.

Bethany scurried inside, more than ready to be done with this exchange. "The statues are done."

"That's good. My arm's tired from workin' all day."

No way was she going to ask what kind of work. Pounding skulls was all a man like him was good for.

"I'll get them wrapped up. It'll just take a minute." Less if she could manage it.

"No rush. Bobby's unloading the next job for you to start on."

Bethany froze in the act of tearing off a section of newsprint from the roll. "Next job?"

"Yeah. The boss says he's got one more job for you."

She'd been dreading this. She should have known that working with men who didn't know the meaning of honor was only going to end badly.

Her throat went dry with anxiety, but she had no choice. She had to stop this now, before it was too late. "I'm sorry, but I can't do any more jobs for you. We had a deal."

The man tilted his head, studying her from beneath those bushy brows. "The deal changed. It's just one more job. Baby Brother Benny is worth that much, isn't he?"

Her natural protective instincts rose up, unleashing a growl in her chest. "You leave him alone. I mean it."

The man stretched his fingers as if limbering them up. His knuckles cracked and popped. "Whether we do or we don't is up to you."

"I already did my part. It's over. I'm through."

"That's too bad for Benny." He shrugged. "Then again, it's no skin off my nose. I always liked working with him."

"You can't. You promised me that if I did this job you'd leave him alone." If these criminals approached Benjamin, offering him another job, he'd cave. He was too weak to resist the lure of power and money these men cast out.

False apology laced his tone. "I really want to help you, but the boss has his heart set on you doing this last job."

She knew if she said yes, they'd come back. There would always be one more job. She couldn't show weakness or fear. These men fed on it.

It took all her courage, but she crossed her arms over her chest and gave him an even stare. "I don't work with men who go back on their word. I'm sorry, but you're just going to have to uphold our original bargain."

One second she was standing on her own two feet. The next, she was dangling in the air with pain radiating up from his crushing grip on her arms. "You saying I'm a liar?"

Fear cascaded through her system, making it hard to breathe. She couldn't find the air to speak. All she could do was squeak in terror.

So much for pretending she wasn't afraid.

He gave her a shake so hard she could see her black curls bouncing around her face. "Answer me!"

"You said before that this was the last job. Now there's one more. You tell me if that makes you a liar."

She landed hard on her feet. The back of his hand hit her face, stunning her. She'd never been hit before, and she was still struggling with the concept when she saw a blur of motion from her left.

The statue moved.

Maybe she'd been hit harder than she thought. Statues couldn't move. And yet Tristan kept coming closer, his face a mask of fury.

Something in her expression must have given away his approach, because the man holding her let go and spun around.

"You hit her," said Tristan, his voice quiet with the promise of lethal violence.

"What the fuck?" the man asked, mirroring her own *WTF* moment.

"I'm going to hit you once as payback for your offense. If you survive, you will leave."

The man squared up to face Tristan, clearly comfortable with the threat of bodily harm. He lifted his chin and relaxed his shoulders. "*If* I survive? Someone's sure of himself."

He swung, slamming his fist right into Tristan's jaw.

Bethany gasped at the power of the blow, but his head merely snapped to this side before he looked at the man again. "My turn."

Tristan's blow plowed into Asshole Number One's gut. He flew back into the wall, hitting hard enough to leave a dent. Drywall dust fell on the floor. He gagged and wheezed as he scrambled to regain his feet. His face turned purple, and he looked like he might get sick.

"You will not defile her home with your vomit." Tristan picked him up by one arm and half carried, half marched him out the door just as Asshole Number Two was coming in with an armload of statues in boxes.

"Later," choked the man. "I'll be back."

"And I'll be waiting," said Tristan as he shoved the man out and closed the door.

The whole thing had taken only a few seconds, and Bethany still couldn't get her mind around what had happened.

She stared at Tristan, speechless.

Blood trickled from every shallow cut on his body. She'd studied him long enough to see that the marks in his flesh matched up exactly with the ones that had been in the statue.

The only area of his body that wasn't bleeding was where she'd done her repairs. There were faint lines of scarring where she'd fit the pieces together, but somehow, the work she'd done to the stone had healed his skin.

She glanced over to where Tristan's stone form had been standing. It was gone. She hadn't imagined that part.

"You're alive?" she asked.

"Thanks to you." He crossed the space between them in a few long strides. He was still gloriously naked, but every one of his wounds cried out to her, diluting the thrill she would have normally had at seeing such a prime male subject.

She'd never been much of an artist, but every fiber in her being ached to draw, paint or sculpt him.

He knelt in front of her, and it was only then she realized that she was on the floor. He reached toward her face. As soon as she saw the blood and scars covering his hand, she flinched in sympathy.

He had to be in terrible pain. Assuming this wasn't all some vivid hallucination brought on by a blow to her head.

He saw her flinch and his hand stilled midair. "Did he hurt you?"

Her cheek stung, but she barely noticed anymore. She shook her head. "How can you be real?"

"I'm not. You just hit your head."

"Then who beat the hell out of Asshole Number One?"

"You should go rest now. You've been working too hard."

"Do hallucinations normally order people around?"

He managed to look uncomfortable at her question. He'd faced down an armed asshole wearing nothing more than his own blood, and yet her question upset him?

"I'll help you to your room. You'll feel better after you sleep." He held out his hand to her, then saw his blood and let his hand fall.

He'd saved her ass. A little blood wasn't going to bother her.

Bethany grabbed his hand and let him pull her to her feet. He was careful with his hold, but she'd shaken enough hands to know controlled power when she felt it, and his control was absolute.

Tristan was freakin' strong. She'd seen it with her own eyes.

Then again, she was also seeing a statue walking around, which didn't exactly make her a fantastic witness right now.

Through the curtains on the front of the house, she could see that the two assholes were still out there. Her guess was they were gearing up to come back in for round two.

"They won't leave until they have what they came for," she said.

Her gait was a bit wobbly, but she managed to finish packing up the statues she'd repaired.

"I'll take those," said Tristan. "Stay here."

He picked up all three boxes at once—more than two hundred pounds. The ease with which he carried them made it look like twenty.

He set the boxes outside her door, gave the men one last glare, then shut and locked them inside.

A moment later, they drove off, leaving her alone with a bleeding statue.

The shock of the whole situation was still floating on the surface, not yet sinking in. She knew she should be more upset or afraid, but what point was there in being afraid or upset by something that couldn't possibly be real.

"How the hell is this happening?" she asked.

"I wish I could tell you. I cannot."

"Because you don't know or because you can't say?"

"My mistress has bound my tongue."

Bethany had no idea what that meant, but the idea of some corseted, black-booted, fishnet stocking-clad bimbo taking a whip to him didn't sit well with her at all. "Mistress?"

He looked past her, shame lowering his gaze. "I cannot say."

Even with the blood smeared across his cheeks and forehead, he was gorgeous. She'd seen the structure of his face within the stone, but it gave her no clue as the color of his eyes or the supple softness of his mouth. She'd never seen eyes so black before, and the way the light glittered within them seemed unnaturally bright.

Then again, everything about a statue coming to life was unnatural.

"You can rest now," he said. "If they come back, I will defend you." His deep voice sent a trickle of feminine awareness through her. As did his nearness and the fact that she was alone with him.

"Defend me? How is that even possible?"

He didn't answer. All he did was stare, his glittering, black gaze trailing down her body and back up. When he met her eyes again, his jaw was tense and color stained his cheeks. With gentle care he cupped her chin and tilted her head to the side. His touch was cool against the swelling heat in her cheek.

"He marked you."

"It'll fade."

His thumb swept over her cheek in a caress too delicate for a man his size. The resulting shiver that danced down her spine was completely beyond her control. It was as if the parts of her that were all soft and feminine had suddenly decided to hijack the rest of her and throw a wild house party. Whatever good sense and sound judgment she'd had a few minutes ago was already blitzed on Jell-O shots, dancing on the coffee table.

He was the kind of man that made a woman forget she'd ever known what good judgment looked like.

Tristan's gaze slid from the injury to her mouth and settled there. "I should have killed him for touching you."

"I'm glad you didn't. We'd be dealing with a body right now, rather than…chatting."

He blinked twice and it seemed to break whatever had held his gaze fixed on her mouth. "I must go now. Where would you like me?"

In my bed was the first thought that came to mind. Sure he was bleeding, but she could fix that. A gallon of Neosporin, a few hundred band aids, and he'd be good as new. And after a few minutes, neither one of them would be thinking much about all those cuts.

She must have been silent too long because he moved to the spot where his statue had been standing. "Is this good?"

She already missed the feel of his fingers on her face, but said nothing. She merely nodded.

A wave of warmth passed through the room like a summer breeze. As soon as it was gone, Tristan the statue was back. His blood was smeared across the stone, and all the little chips, nicks and cracks were back in place.

She raced to him and took his face in her hands. "How the hell did you do that?" she nearly screamed.

She got the answer she expected: silence.

After washing her hands, putting a bag of frozen peas on her cheek, and pouring herself a glass of wine, she found the number that Dalton had written down.

She dialed the phone. When Sue answered, Bethany said, "You know that *something* you guys thought might happen? Well it did. Big time."

CHAPTER 4

Tristan felt his essence being pulled from his stone form the instant he solidified. He would have known that wrenching, clawing feeling anywhere.

His mistress Thyra had summoned him to Idola— the realm where she lived.

He braced himself just as his surroundings formed around him. Thyra's love for chaos and mayhem was something he'd lived with for more than two millennia, and yet he still never knew what to expect.

Today, she was holding court with a dozen of her slaves, all of whom were dressed as different animals. They sat at a giant table set for tea. Thyra herself was huge—easily twice the size of anyone here—and while she always appeared different, in this moment, she was a blond child in braids. Her tri-colored eyes were the same as always—each one with segmented pie-shaped pieces in red, silver and purple. Her flouncy dress was fluffed with layers of petticoats, patterned with bright red cherries on a yellow background. Her giant feet were bare, and there were blades of grass sticking from between her toes.

The surrounding garden stretched out for a few yards in every direction before it dissolved into a shimmering, foggy mist.

Tristan, like the other stonemen held hostage to Thyra's will, was trapped on the island of chaos with his mistress until she decided to send his spirit back to his shell.

"So good of you to come," she said in a child's voice.

As if he had a choice. Years of punishment kept him from spouting his first thought. All he wanted now was to get out of here and back to his stone shell where he could make sure those men didn't come back and hurt Bethany again.

Just the idea was enough to have his blood pumping. He could feel it trickle over his skin, leaking from his ravaged flesh.

Thyra could have imagined him whole and uninjured, but she had always preferred to see him suffer.

"You've been a naughty boy down there, turning to flesh without asking."

"I have built up many days of freedom from your rule, have I not?"

She waved a chubby hand. "Details. You should know better than that. Where are your manners?"

He stood in silence, knowing anything he said would only make her angry.

"You haven't even bowed to me, your queen."

"My warden, you mean."

She shoved the table away with a thrust so powerful it sent several of the stonemen seated flying. Dishes crashed into one another, shattering on contact.

Thrya's form changed, morphing into a tall, black-haired sorceress. The childish dress melted into a gown designed for sin, revealing far more of his mistress than he cared to see. It didn't matter how beautiful she might appear, inside the woman was all rotted soul and filth.

She stalked to where he stood, towering over him by a good foot. Spittle flew from her lips as she leaned over, ranting at him. "I've kept you alive for far longer than you deserve, you ungrateful weasel. I could have slain you at any moment, and yet you live by my grace alone. You show no respect for a superior being. You show no fear for one far more powerful than you are even capable of imagining. Why should I not simply kill you where you stand?"

Tristan lifted his gaze, refusing to be cowed by her ire. "Because the only thing you value more than your petulant whims is having more stonemen than your crazy sisters. If you kill me, you'll have one less toy to lord over them. That—and that alone—is why I still live."

She shrank slightly with his calmly-offered response. "You're not worth the trouble you cause."

"Then kill me." Normally, his words would have been given with absolute indifference. Today, however, he was not nearly so stoic. Those men could come back to Bethany's house at any moment. If he wasn't there to stop them, harm could come to her.

That, he could not allow.

Thyra grinned, showing sharp white teeth. "Something has changed." She pulled in a deep breath. "I can smell it."

Tristan said nothing. He picked a point in the distant fog and focused on it.

Her finger trailed over his brow, and the salt from her skin burned like acid in his open wounds. "It has something to do with your recent moment of freedom, doesn't it?"

Silence.

She twisted her finger against a larger gouge in his flesh, then licked his blood from her finger. "It must be a woman. Is she beautiful?"

Bethany's image flared in his mind, bright as the sun. Her smooth, dark skin. Those soft, springy curls that framed her beautiful face. Her honey-colored eyes that warmed when he touched her cheek.

"She *is* beautiful," Thyra said with a pout. "Perhaps I should send one of my other slaves to end her so she will no longer be a distraction."

"No!" said Tristan, before he could stop the word from exploding from his mouth.

Thyra smiled, showing his blood on her pointy teeth. "It's like that, is it? Wonderful." She clapped her hands together, her form melting into that of the blond child again. "I propose a game."

"I'm not interested."

"I understand." She glanced across the clearing to one of the men dressed as a mouse. "Abraham, you will go to Earth and slay Tristan's pretty human."

Tristan grabbed Thyra's arm. "No. You can't."

Thick spikes sprouted from her skin, impaling his hand and sending a riot of pain up his arm. He tried to pull away, but he was caught in place, unable to move.

Thyra grew taller, forcing him to go up on his toes to keep from ripping his flesh. "I can do whatever I like. That's the rule. But if you don't want me to kill her, then you will play my game."

He gritted his teeth. "What game?"

"If your curator agrees to release you, then the pretty human can take care of you."

She was going to let Bethany become his curator? He'd be able to live in her home, protect her and her family. She'd always be close and he'd always know she was safe. It seemed too good to be true.

Which meant it was.

He had to work hard not to let his excitement show on his face. "My curator hates me. She wants nothing to do with me. Convincing her to release her responsibilities will be easy."

"You're not the one who must convince her. Your pretty human woman must do that job. While you watch."

No. There was no way he could let Bethany go anywhere near that woman. If she did, she'd find out what he'd done. Bethany looked at him with such trust, he couldn't stand the thought of that trust being slain.

And if she knew about his past, that trust would definitely die a swift, ugly death.

"I won't let her do it," he said.

"Before you decide, you should know what I plan to do with you if you don't talk her into playing my game."

"It doesn't matter what you do. Torture me. Kill me. I can take it."

"Really?" She morphed back into the shape of the child she'd been when he'd first arrived. The spike through his hand slowly receded, its barbed surface taking little bites of his skin with it as it went. "You really think that torture and death are the only tools in my box?"

He tried not to wince, and put the image of Bethany's face firmly in his mind. "It doesn't matter."

She gave him a confident smile. "If you don't convince your pretty human to play my game, then you shall have two choices: One, you may spend the next hundred years in Idola, kneeling at my feet, your head bowed in reverent worship of my power and beauty. The only words you will be allowed to utter will be in highest praise of me. You will do all of this of your own free will, without the compulsion of my power."

"I'd rather die than do that."

"Or," she continued, "Two, you may watch as I torture and kill your pretty new girlfriend and everyone she loves. It will probably take me a while. You might want to pack a lunch."

He choked down the urge to vomit. "Your father would never allow you to do something like that."

She shrugged. "What Daddy doesn't know..."

He tried a different approach. "I barely know this woman. She means nothing to me."

"Then you won't mind watching her die. Excellent! I'll put you down for option number two."

"I won't participate in your games, Thyra."

"Yes, you will. Now choose." Her words were filled with power, forcing his obedience. "Play my game, worship at my feet, or watch a woman you barely know die. Which will it be?"

He had no choice but to pick an option as they were laid out before him. Thyra was too powerful for him to break the compulsion she had over him, or he would have done it centuries ago.

If he accepted her game, all that would change. He'd be choosing to break the last little piece of humanity he had that remained.

Even though he was a slave to her will, he'd still maintained a tiny sliver of himself. He'd protected it from her taint. That alone had allowed him to hold his head high. He'd never once bowed to her of his own free will, though he *had* been forced to bow. How could he lose that last scrap of himself?

"I can't," he said, his voice a weak echo of its usual strength. "I won't."

"Then the human woman can die." She shrugged. "It's all fun for me. Abraham?"

"No! Wait."

"Second thoughts?" asked Thyra, looking sweet and innocent inside the shell of a child.

"If Bethany convinces my curator to release me, you'll leave her alone? She'll be safe?"

"As safe as any breakable bag of aging skin and bones can be. There are so many delightful diseases. So many accidents." She sighed in bliss and spun, making her flouncy skirt twirl.

"Promise you'll stay away from her. No diseases, no accidents. You won't even look at her."

"So you *do* want to play."

"No, I don't, but if it's the only way to keep Bethany safe, then I will. There's just one more thing."

"What?"

"Until the game is over, I get to stay with her. In the flesh. No turning me to stone, no bringing me here. That way I know she's safe."

Thyra rolled her eyes. "Fine. Whatever. Just don't be too long. You know how bored I get. Once the game stops amusing me, I'll find another way to have my fun."

At his or Bethany's expense, no doubt.

"I choose the game," he shoved out between clenched teeth.

It took all his willpower to reach his bleeding hand toward the woman who'd destroyed his life and made his suffering last for eternity. "We have a deal."

CHAPTER 5

Bethany was on the verge of freaking out. The shock from the blow she'd been dealt, and from seeing a statue come to life had worn off, taking with it the blissful numbness that had allowed her to function.

Now that reality had set in, she wasn't ready to face it.

Sue and Dalton were on their way over. She didn't know why that would make her feel better—considering they'd been the ones to drop the statue in her living room—but it did. And right now, she was willing to take any bit of feeling better she could find.

To that end, she gathered up some soapy water and a cloth and started cleaning the blood from Tristan. Once that was gone, she mixed up some patching compound and began filling in the worst of the holes in him. She didn't know how much her efforts would help, but she had to do something.

Time fell away as she worked. An hour or a day could have passed. She really had no idea how long it had been when she heard the knock at her door. All she knew was that it was dark, and she'd managed to repair nearly every crack and pit larger than a chip.

The work was flawless—her best ever. Even she had a hard time telling which was original stone and which was patching compound.

She wiped her hands and answered the door. Sue and Dalton stood there, hand-in-hand. The sight was so sweet it made her realize just how alone she really was.

When was the last time she'd gone on a date? Before Benjamin's troubles? Longer?

It didn't matter now. All she cared about was finding some sense in the chaos that had visited her tonight.

"Thanks for coming," Bethany said. She led them to the kitchen were there were enough chairs for them to sit. While she could imagine the couple all cuddled up together in her bean bag chair, she really didn't want to remember the sight every time she sat there alone.

"We're glad you called," Sue said. "I know how scary this whole thing must have been."

"I kinda doubt that," Bethany replied.

Dalton held out a chair for her. "Actually, she does know. She was faced with the same kind of…surprise not long ago."

Sue swatted his arm. "Hush. We can't talk about it."

"*You* can't talk about it because *you* swore an oath of secrecy. I did no such thing."

Right. Dalton was the guy who was going to spill. Good to know.

"I saw Tristan come to life," said Bethany. "Tell me I'm not crazy."

"You're not crazy," Dalton said.

"Did he hurt you?" Sue asked.

Bethany frowned, confused. "No. He scared away some bad guys before they could hurt me…much."

The two shared one of those looks that carried an entire conversation—the ones only tight couples could manage. At the end of it, Dalton patted Sue's shoulder.

"Tristan is dangerous," he said.

"No kidding. He drove off armed men without breaking a sweat."

"No, I mean dangerous to *you*."

She instantly rejected the idea. "You're wrong. He saved me. Said he'd come back if I needed him again. How the hell is that even possible, by the way?"

"It's a long story," said Dalton. "The important part is that you can't get in his way. Think of him like a speeding train. He has no way of putting on the brakes."

"I don't understand."

"Men like him are trapped. Slaves. They have to do what they're told. Period. And if he's told to do something and you get in his way, he'll flatten you. He may feel bad about it, but that won't change what he does to you."

"I don't believe that. He was so careful with me."

"Do you think he used his free time?" Sue asked Dalton.

"She's not his curator—who he would have been able to protect, the way I did you. Without using some of his free time, I don't see how else he could have become flesh."

"How much free time does Tristan have?" Sue asked.

Dalton shrugged. "No idea. But if he saw the threat, it would have made sense that he acted so that Bethany could keep repairing him."

Bethany held up her hands. "Wait. Slow down. What's this about free time and curators?"

Sue stood. "It's probably best if I don't hear you spill the beans, Dalton. It comes way too close to me not protecting the secrets I swore to keep."

He nodded and waited for Sue to leave the kitchen. As soon as she was gone, he turned to Bethany. "Tristan is what's called a *stoneman*. He's bound by a contract he made with a powerful woman. She's not human. She's...I don't know what you'd call her, but there are seven of them, all sisters. They collect men like Tristan the way some people collect coins. Whichever sister has the most stonemen, the most beautiful ones, the most rare ones—she wins."

"This is all a game?"

He gave a grave nod. "To them it is. To the humans whose lives they ruin, it's anything but. These women love to make deals, offer contracts. They lure you in with something you desperately want, then tie so many strings to it you're trapped. Sometimes forever."

"You seem to know a whole lot about these men."

"And women. Mostly men, though. The sisters enjoy their man-candy as much as any female."

"You evaded my question nicely there. How about you try again. How do you know so much about these stonemen?"

"Because I used to be one of them."

"Wow. Okay. Not exactly what I'd thought you'd say."

"I spent decades trapped in stone the way Tristan is. I had no choice but to obey the will of my mistress, who usually forgot I existed. I spent a lot of years in utter boredom. Tristan hasn't been so lucky. He's been used to hurt people. To kill. That kind of thing changes a man, no matter how good that man was when he turned to stone."

"Are you saying I should get rid of him?"

"No. He's in bad shape. I saw you repaired most of his major wounds, but every little cut in his stone form will always make him bleed when he turns to flesh. Until you heal his statue, he'll be doomed to pain, every day, for the rest of his long, long life."

"He's your friend, isn't he?"

"Not even close. He tried to kill me not long ago. But I don't hold it against him. He was acting under orders, and I owe it to him to see that he's given the best care I can find him. That's you."

"That's why you wanted me to rush. You don't want him to suffer."

"No, I wanted you to rush so he wouldn't bleed to death when he was forced to turn to flesh for some mission his sculptor demanded of him. With that chunk blown out of his side, he would have died within seconds of animating."

Bethany's stomach lurched at the idea, and she had to take several deep breaths to calm her nerves. "What happens after I finish the job of repairing him?"

"I'll take him back to my home for as long as I can. No one seems to know where his base is, so that's the best I can do."

"His base?"

"A stone block that's like his home. He'll eventually be compelled to return to it. Judging from the condition he's in, wherever that is isn't a healthy environment. His curator deserves a good beating for letting him get this bad."

"You've mentioned a curator a couple of times. Does he live in some kind of museum?"

"No, his curator is the person who's sworn to protect him. That's what Sue was to me before I beat the curse."

"Can Tristan beat his curse, too?"

Dalton shrugged. "I don't know. I didn't even know I *had* an escape clause, much less what it was. The sisters are tricky that way. They like to keep your contract a secret so you can't squirm your way out of it."

"I want to help him," she said. "He saved my life. Whatever I can do…."

"Just finish patching him up. That'll buy him some time for us to find his base and take him to a safer home."

"This is all so insane. It's hard to believe that any of it is real."

"I know. It's hard for everyone to believe when they first learn about it. But give it a bit. It'll sink in and you'll no longer feel quite so unsettled."

She let out an amused grunt. "Unsettled? Try freaked out of my mind."

He rose from his seat. "We can stay here tonight if it will make you feel better."

She peered through the doorway at the statue. Her fingers itched to get back to work. There was so much left to do still, and every cut she filled was a little pain Tristan wouldn't have to endure. "No, thanks. I'm just going to work. I'll call if I need you."

Dalton nodded. "Okay. If you're sure. Just remember what I said: stay out of his way. He will hurt you. He won't want to, but if you try to stop him it'll still hurt all the same. He could even kill you."

CHAPTER 6

Time meant nothing on Idola. The sadistic sisters could stretch it out or rip it to shreds at will so that seconds seemed like days or vice versa—whatever suited their whims. When Thyra finally returned Tristan to his stone prison on Earth, he realized that he'd been gone much longer than he'd expected.

His first clue was the fatigue hanging over Bethany. Her slender shoulders were slumped. The skin under her eyes was too dark. The bright honey color of her eyes was dulled with exhaustion. Her usually bouncy curls drooped. She was still wearing the same clothes she'd had on before, but they were wrinkled and stained with smears the same color as his stone.

However long he'd been gone, she hadn't stopped working on him. His skin no longer burned with the fire of a hundred cuts. There were a few places where she hadn't yet worked her magic, but those were merely minor annoyances.

The feeling of inhabiting a body relatively free of pain was so odd, he didn't know what to think.

Her fingers moved across his skin, leaving her warmth behind wherever she passed. Her caresses were both gentle and made with purpose. Each movement was filled with the grace of an artist and the care of a healer. Why she would spend such rare talent on him was a mystery. Her workbenches were laden with projects more beautiful than him, all awaiting her attention.

As much as he wanted to flow into his flesh and blood form, he knew that the moment he did, she'd stop touching him.

He wasn't ready for that yet. He wasn't sure he'd ever be.

Still, her exhaustion called to him. He had no idea when she'd last slept or eaten. If he were the cause of her falling ill, he'd never forgive himself.

In the end, there was only one choice.

Tristan let power gather at the base of his spine slowly. He urged it outward, letting it seep through him rather than rush. He didn't want to scare her with another sudden change, but he only had so much control.

As soon as his body began to warm, she gasped and moved her hands away from him. The loss of her touch made an ugly surge of possessiveness streak through him, but he managed to stop it before he lost control and forced her to put her hands where he wanted them.

She blinked a few times, shaking her head as if not sure she believed what she saw.

"Hello again," he said, keeping his voice quiet.

"You came back. I wasn't sure if you would."

How was he going to tell her about his need for her help? Hadn't she already done enough?

Only the certain knowledge that bowing at Thyra's feet would kill him, kept him from giving up the quest altogether.

"How long was I gone?" he asked.

She looked around as if the answer would be painted on one of the walls. "I don't know. A couple of days. Maybe three."

"You haven't slept in that time, have you?"

"I napped."

It wasn't nearly enough. "Were you afraid those men would come back?"

She frowned as if she didn't understand what he meant. Slowly, she caught up and shook her head slightly. "I couldn't leave you wounded like you were. Not when I knew you were alive and able to feel pain."

She'd tortured herself for him? The concept that someone would suffer for a slave like him was impossible to grasp. "I've been wounded for decades. A few more days would have been nothing."

"Not to me. I still remember your blood." She shuddered and hugged herself.

He looked down at his naked body. He saw three tiny scratches so small they'd already stopped bleeding. Other than that, he was whole. "You said this work would take you two hundred hours. You did it in just a few days."

"I was highly motivated. Besides, running my hands over you wasn't exactly a hardship." She grinned, then swayed as if even that small move was too much for her.

Tristan grabbed her by the arms, being careful not to crush her bones in his grip. Her skin was bare, smooth, and so deliciously warm he completely forgot why he was holding her and simply reveled in the feeling of her flesh under his hands.

"Tristan?"

It wasn't until he heard her questioning tone that he realized he was stroking her, sliding his palms along her arms from shoulder to elbow and back again.

He didn't know this woman. He certainly had no right to touch her like this.

"I apologize," he said, letting her go and stepping back.

"It's okay. Just not used to sexy, naked men I hardly know petting me."

His first thought was that he needed clothing so she'd be more comfortable. His second was the realization that she'd called him sexy.

Pride warmed his chest and made some dark, primal part of him sit up and take notice. He hadn't had a woman in a long, long time. Too long for him to even remember what decade it had been. All he knew was that he could not remember a single detail about her now, not while standing in front of Bethany. Even as tired and wilted as she was, she was beautiful. Enthralling.

He could think of at least a dozen ways he could ensure she slept, and every one of them started with his hands on her body.

The mere thought made him stir in ways he'd forgotten were possible. The tingling swell in his groin was an old but welcome sensation. It reminded him that he'd been a man once. Several lifetimes ago.

"Do you have something I can wear?" he asked.

"Yeah. Dalton left a bag of clothes in case you woke up again." She crossed to where a bag sat on the floor by the door. As she leaned down to pick it up, she started to pitch forward as if she'd lost her balance.

He was beside her in a split second, easing her into his arms.

She clung to him willingly, and every part of him roared in victory. In this moment she felt like his woman, and it was hard for him to remember that she wasn't.

"Sorry. Guess I shouldn't have skipped breakfast. Or lunch. Or eating yesterday."

Tristan set her down on a cushion before he no longer could. A woman as potent as Bethany went to a man's head, making him think impossible things were real.

"I will feed you. Then you will sleep."

Her gaze strayed to his naked groin, which was far too close to her face for propriety. She swallowed visibly. "Maybe pants should be step one."

He tipped his head in acceptance. "Of course."

With her comfortably seated where she couldn't fall over, he felt safe to move away. The borrowed clothes went on. He found the kitchen and an apple in a bowl on the counter. One of the drawers held a variety of knives, and he found one that fit his hand.

She was still sitting where he'd left her. He settled on the floor in front of her and cut a slice of apple.

She ate it, and her stomach rumbled with gratitude. "Yeah. Definitely forgot to eat for a while. You're one heck of an engrossing project."

"I thank you for your efforts, but I never would have wanted you to damage yourself."

She shrugged and took another slice. "I'm not damaged. Just tired."

"You'll sleep next."

Her dark brows lifted. "You've got a little bit of bossy in you, don't you?"

He had no clue what she meant. She must have seen his confusion, because she clarified. "I'm a grown woman. You can't tell me when to go to sleep. At least not in this century."

Of course. He'd overstepped his bounds. "I apologize. There are simply some things a man can't witness without working to correct. You wore yourself out helping me. It's my duty to make sure you rest now."

"Yeah? Well, let's just say that I'm headed for a little R&R whether or not it's what *you* want."

"When you wake, we will talk."

"There you go again, issuing orders. How about you try to ask a girl, rather than tell her?"

He wasn't used to her time or her ways, but he owed her too much to insult her. Plus, he still needed her help if he wasn't going to spend the next century bowing at Thyra's feet.

"I will try again," he said. "I would very much like to talk to you about something after you are rested."

"Okay. That's a good start. Now add the question."

"Will you speak with me?"

She beamed. "Sure. Be happy to."

He looked at the empty apple core. "What else would you like to eat?"

"Nothing right now. I need to sleep." She started to stand, so he helped her to her feet.

He could feel a fine tremor of fatigue running through her body. It made him wonder just how long it had been since she'd had a proper night's sleep.

"How do I get in touch with you once I wake up?" she asked.

"What do you mean?"

"Do I knock on your statue or something?"

"No. I will be flesh."

"Do you have a phone?"

"No."

"Then how do I reach you?"

He still didn't understand what she was trying to learn. "Simply stretch out your hand. I'll be right beside you, guarding your sleep."

"Um. No, you won't."

"I already spoke to my mistress. I will be flesh for at least a short time—long enough for you to rest."

"No, that's not what I mean."

"Please clarify."

"I mean that you're not going to be guarding my anything. No way am I sleeping with a stranger in my house."

"You want me to leave?" he asked, feeling the pangs of insult strike him. She didn't trust him, and for some reason, that hurt far more than any of the wounds she'd patched.

"Don't you have somewhere to go? Friends to visit or something?"

"Any family or friends I had are long dead."

Her face fell. "Oh. I'm sorry. I didn't realize. I figured Dalton was your friend."

"That's highly unlikely. I tried to kill him recently."

They were past her bedroom door now. She pulled away from his touch and backed up toward her bed. "He said as much, but until now I really didn't believe him."

Her apprehension made him replay his words. Only then did he realize how they would sound to her. "I didn't want to kill him. I was acting under my mistress's compulsion."

"Do you do that a lot?"

"Try to kill people or act under compulsion?" he asked. "Never mind. It doesn't matter. The answer to both is the same."

"What's the answer?"

"In the past two hundred years, the only time I've ever been flesh is in order to inflict violence."

She moved around her bed so that it was standing as a barrier between them. "You're flesh now. Who do you want to hurt?"

"This time is different. My mistress has offered me a bargain." He realized that wasn't exactly true. "Actually, she gave me little choice, but the bargain has given me a brief respite from my stone form."

"What bargain?"

"You're too tired to discuss it."

"I'll tell you what I'm too tired to do: sleep under the same roof as a man who just told me he goes around hurting people."

"Not by choice."

"Doesn't really make it better. I think you should go." She was trembling, and he didn't believe it was only because she was so tired.

He'd frightened her.

"I would never hurt you," he said.

"If you're compelled to do things against your will, then how can you be sure?"

She had a point. If Thyra ordered him to kill Bethany, he knew he would. He'd have no other choice. When his mistress took control of his will, she could make him do anything he wanted.

Tristan bowed his head in regret. "You're right. I'll leave. You need to feel safe so you can sleep."

He turned away before he could cause her any more fear or discomfort. After what she'd done for him, he owed her more than that.

It wasn't terribly cold here, wherever he was. He had weathered colder nights and survived, though his stone form had granted him some small measure of protection.

Still, he was a tough man. The elements were a minor thing to suffer now that he was whole and well.

Tristan took up a position outside her little house. He stood where bushes would hide him from nosy neighbors while still ensuring he had a clear view of anyone who might approach. If those men came back, he would be ready. Bethany would sleep safely. He would make sure of it.

CHAPTER 7

Bethany fell into bed as soon as she made sure the doors were locked. Exhaustion sucked her in and held on tight. When she finally opened her eyes, nearly twenty hours had passed. The sun was just starting to set, and her stomach was demanding attention.

She showered and shuffled to the kitchen.

Western light splashed across the window over her sink, along with the shadow of a man.

Her heart squeezed out a healthy dose of adrenaline, making her need for coffee irrelevant.

Someone was standing right outside her house. Someone big. It was pouring down rain and even though the Florida winters were mild, it was still too cold to be lingering out there. But he wasn't taking cover.

She picked up the crowbar she used to pry open crates and opened her front door just wide enough to peer out.

Tristan stood with his feet braced apart and his hands fisted at his sides. He was inside some overgrown bushes, hidden from the road, but not from her front porch. Rain plastered his clothes to his body, showing off the muscular contours of his chest and shoulders. His dark hair dripped into his eyes, but he didn't even blink. His gaze was vigilant and unwavering as he stared down the length of her driveway.

As soon as light from inside splashed across the front porch, he looked her way. Those black, glittering eyes fixed on her, stealing her breath. The stark lines of his face were set in a hard mask, rosy from the cold rain.

"What are you doing out here?" she asked, sounding more than a little perturbed.

"Standing guard. As I said I would."

"Have you been out here the whole time I was asleep?"

"Yes," he said, as if her question were ridiculous, as if there were no other possible answer. "Are you feeling well now?"

She had been, right up until she'd realized she'd made the poor man stand out in the rain while she was all warm and cozy in her bed. "Get inside. You're going to make yourself sick."

She pushed the door open wider so he could pass. The move put him so close she could smell the scent of rain and ocean on his skin.

Her nervous system went into overdrive, turning the adrenaline from her scare into something else—something quivering with feminine excitement and possibility.

Down, girl. Nothing here to see. Move along.

Her libido ignored her, instead choosing to admire the way he looked soaking wet with his clothes plastered against all those delicious muscles.

He paused just inside the door and began stripping.

"What are you doing?" she asked, unsure if she was more excited or outraged.

"I don't want to ruin your home. You've seen me naked before, but if my nudity offends you, I'll stand here until I dry."

He meant it. There was no humor or impatience in his tone.

"You'd really stand there for a few hours while you dry out?"

Now he frowned, pulling in a deep breath as if seeking patience. "I'm not clear what you want, Bethany. Please tell me. Shall I drip on your floor, strip naked, or stand here until I dry?"

Naked won the vote in a landslide victory, but as much as she wanted to see him flaunting his impressive wares around her house, it seemed like a great way to forget her good intentions. "Just hang on. Let me get you a towel."

She came back with the biggest towel she owned and handed it to him. "I'll go make us some coffee while you put this on." She slipped away before she could get a peek at the show.

A minute later, he came into the kitchen. His hair was still wet. The damp towel was tucked around his waist, covering him. And either fortunately or unfortunately—depending on how she looked at it—the terry cloth was so thin it clung to him just enough to remind her of all he had to offer.

Normally, the sight of naked flesh did nothing for her. She was more aroused by words and deeds than appearance. However, she'd never exactly been faced with a man as striking and intense as Tristan. If she didn't get his clothes dry and back on his body, she didn't think she could rightfully be held responsible for anything she might decide to do with him.

While he sat in her kitchen, she picked up his soggy clothes and put them on the fastest wash cycle her machine had to offer. She only hoped it was fast enough.

"How do you like your coffee?" she asked. Her voice quivered, giving away his potent effect on her.

"Hot."

Just like him.

She poured a mug for him and set it down in front of him, rather than risk an accidental brush of his hand on hers. For as long as he was only one little tug away from naked, she needed to keep her hands to herself.

She filled her own mug and sat as far across the table from him as possible. "So. You just hung out here? For a whole day?"

"I have nowhere else to go."

The simple statement given so casually nearly broke her heart. She reached for him before she could remember her no touching rule. Her hand covered his and she felt just how chilled to the bone he was. "Would you like a hot shower?"

"Very much, but there's something we must discuss first."

"Sounds important."

"It is."

"Okay." She leaned back in her chair, out of reach. "Hit me."

His horrified look told her how appalled he was at her statement. "I would never willingly choose to do such a thing."

"No," she hurried to say, "I mean tell me. It's just an expression."

"An atrocious one."

"Sorry. I really didn't mean to upset you. Go ahead."

He looked at his coffee, at the table, at the wall behind her—everywhere but at her. "My mistress enjoys games."

"Who doesn't?"

"Not like this. She thrives on striking deals, and on creating chaos wherever she goes."

"Ah, a very dedicated agent of entropy, is she?"

He frowned. "I suppose. This latest game of hers involves you."

"How is that possible? I don't even know her."

"Count yourself lucky. Still, she is aware of you and what you've done for me." His gaze met hers then, and nearly drove the breath from her body with its force. He wasn't doing anything special, just looking at her, but with him and those black, glittering eyes, that was enough.

"I want you to be my curator," he said.

Dalton had mentioned something about that, but she still wasn't clear what it meant. "Your curator?"

"It's a great burden, but there are some benefits as well."

"Start with the burden part."

"You and your lineage would be responsible for my care when I'm in my stone form. My statue's base would be moved here. You would protect me from theft and damage."

"Like a priceless work of art. That's not such a burden."
Especially if she got to look at him whenever she liked.

"It would be when I'm sent on one of my mistress's
errands. Anyone who gets in my way could be hurt. Even
killed."

He wasn't kidding. "Dalton warned me about not getting
in your way. I guess it's true. So, what's the upside?"

"Absolute and complete protection for you and your
family. Anyone who comes through your door intending to
do you harm, I will stop. By whatever means necessary."

"Beats the pants off ADT."

"I don't understand."

She waved the comment away. "So, that's it? You want to
park your statue here in my place and be my one man
army?"

"I do."

Bethany thought about it for a minute, staring at her coffee
so his dark good looks couldn't sway her decision.

The man had nowhere to go. Whoever was supposed to
take care of him must have been dead, because he'd been in
horrible shape—the kind that only decades of neglect could
create. She'd always been a sucker for someone in need,
even when that someone wasn't half as hot as Tristan.

On the other hand, having him around wouldn't be like
having a roommate. She couldn't talk to him or ask him to
empty the trash. And having him around might even get in
the way of her love life—if she found one. What man would
want to come over to a place where he had to compete with
someone like Tristan? There would be no contest.

"How long would the job last?" she asked.

"It's not the kind of position from which you resign. The
fact that Thyra is allowing me to find a replacement is more
than a little surprising."

"Why?"

"Because being a curator is a family commitment. It's
handed down from one generation to the next. Children are
trained to respect the responsibility and honor the agreement
made by their ancestors."

"So you're not just asking me to do a job. You're asking me to force any kids I might have to take over when I'm too old."

"Exactly."

"Then why the hell were you in such bad shape? Did the last of your curator's line die?"

He looked down, shame tinting his cheeks. "No. One is alive."

"So where is she? Why isn't she taking care of you?"

"She chooses not to."

"It sounds like there's something you're not telling me."

He rose from the table. "Would you like some more coffee?"

He was definitely avoiding her question. "Okay. Keep your secrets. The bottom line is whether or not I want to do the job, right?"

His big hand froze as it gripped the handle of the coffee pot. "It is."

His back was to her. She could see his chest expand as he breathed, but there was nothing to give away how much this meant to him. She was sure it had to be a big deal, but he wasn't pushing. Yet.

"Let's pretend I say yes. Then what?"

"You and I would travel to my curator's home and ask for her to relinquish her duties to you."

"And if she refuses?"

"She won't. She hates me. Getting rid of me is all she's ever wanted to do."

"Did you hurt her?"

His shoulders fell, and he slowly turned around to face her. There was regret painted across his features. "Not in the way you mean. I never laid a hand on her."

"Then why does she hate you?"

"I refuse to say." He set down his mug and stalked from the kitchen into the laundry room.

Bethany followed right behind him. "Hey. Where are you going?"

"I never should have asked for your help." He opened the washer door and pulled out a soggy mass of clothes. Water dripped all over the floor, so he dropped his towel to soak up the mess as he began pulling on a soapy pair of jeans.

"What the hell are you doing?" she asked.

"Leaving. Before I change my mind."

"About what? I haven't even finished answering your question about being your curator."

"I revoke my request. The position isn't right for you."

"How do you know? You don't even know me."

He pulled a dripping T-shirt over his head and stared at her. "You spent days going without sleep or food to heal me, some of that effort was made before you even knew I was a real man. That's all I need to know about you."

"I don't understand. Doesn't that mean I'd be good at the job of looking after your statue?"

"Too good." He started to leave the small room, but she grabbed his arm, stopping him.

"So what's the problem?"

He looked at her hand, then into her eyes. "You're a good woman. You care. You suffer for the sake of others."

He made it sound like a bigger deal than it was, but she decided that was an argument for another time. "So what?"

"My mistress is not a good woman. She cares only about herself, and would sooner see others suffer than to feel any sort of discomfort whatsoever."

"I get it. You don't think we're alike. That's fine. I'm not asking her to move in with me."

"No, but where I go, she follows." He covered her hand, his tone going soft. "And you, sweet Bethany…she would eat you alive."

CHAPTER 8

Tristan had been a fool to ask for Bethany's help. He'd realized the idiocy of his request too late, and now she was on the offensive, preparing to charge headfirst into battle to win a prize she didn't even yet know she would despise.

But he knew. He'd found his sense of reason late in the game, but not too late to stop the damage from being done.

"You don't know that she'd eat me alive," she said. "I'm not a wimp. I can hold my own with anyone."

"Not Thyra." He had to get out of here. Every second he spent here was another step closer to him begging for Bethany's help.

She deserved better.

He was dripping wet and chilled to the bone from the hours he'd stood outside. He couldn't even remember the last time he'd been warm, and the lure of her home and the heat of her touch were almost more than he could resist.

She stepped in front of him, blocking his path from the laundry room. "I'm not letting you go. Not wearing soaking wet clothes and shivering. Now strip the hell down and let me finish doing the laundry."

"I'll be fine. I've been colder and wetter than this for a lot longer before and survived."

"I just patched up your ass from that exposure. Do you think I'm going to let you go out in the cold and mess up my work?" She crossed her arms over her chest, which pressed her breasts up on glorious display.

Tristan's gaze dropped and held fast, completely drawn to the smooth curves of flesh he was dying to touch.

It was that distraction that was his undoing. He knew that if he stayed just a little longer, not only could he get warm and dry, but he also might get another glimpse of feminine perfection.

That alone was worth whatever price he had to pay.

"Get naked," she ordered, her words far too tempting for him to ignore.

His wet clothes went back into the machine. She took him by the arm and marched him through her house into her bathroom. He let her lead him around and waited quietly while she started the shower and fetched him a clean, dry towel.

"You get warm. I'll make us food. Then we're going to sit down and talk about this curator thing. Understood?"

Tristan was used to following orders. He wasn't, however, used to doing so without being compelled. The fact that he had a choice now was thrilling to him. He was free to do as he pleased.

And making Bethany happy pleased him very much.

Odd.

Still, his desire was strong enough that he didn't over-think it. He simply acted.

Once he was ensconced behind the waterproof curtain, she seemed satisfied enough to leave him on his own.

The hot water was a welcome luxury. He lingered beneath the spray, wondering what it would be like to be a normal man who enjoyed such pleasures every day.

The soap smelled like Bethany's skin. He ran it over his body, trying to fight off the intense physical reaction he had at knowing that the sweetly scented bar had recently touched every part of her. In the end, he lost the battle. His soapy fist stroked over his hard cock as he pictured the shadowy cleft that led down between her breasts. As slick as he was now, her breasts would glide over him easily, sliding up and down on his erection until he found release.

His hand moved faster. It wasn't nearly as soft as her flesh would be, but it was all he was going to get. Her scent, her image, his hand. It all melded together until he was on the brink of orgasm.

"Tristan?" came her soft voice from the other side of the curtain.

He tried to speak, but his throat was closed off by the grip of lust.

"You've been in there a long time. Is everything all right?" she asked.

All that came out was a strangled sound of air locked in his lungs.

Panic tightened her tone. "Are you okay?" She ripped back the curtain and found him, erection in hand, on the verge of release.

Her honey-colored eyes went wide and her full lips parted in shock. She seemed frozen in place, her stare fixed right on his dark, throbbing cock. "Oh my."

He caught her gaze, watched her eyes dilate and darken to a smoky bronze color. Her pulse quickened and her breathing sped.

He tried to unlock his fingers, but they refused to obey. He was only a few strokes away. It had been years—decades—since he'd come. "I'll stop." He wasn't sure how, but for her, he'd find a way.

She licked her lips. "No. Don't."

Tristan's control broke. He grabbed her by the back of her neck and pulled her toward him. His mouth covered hers, feeling her melt against him. His tongue plunged forward, stealing a taste from behind her lips. Her fingers gripped his shoulder, and that single touch was all it took.

His orgasm ripped through him, coming all the way from his toes. He groaned into her mouth, refusing to break contact with her. Her sweet taste filled his head as his body clenched, forcing his seed from his body.

She pulled away from him long enough to watch his semen splash against the shower wall. Her fingers tightened, and her small whimper echoed in the small space.

When it was over, and all that was left was the last few shudders of relief, he let his head fall until their foreheads touched. Spray from the shower misted in her hair. Their breath mingled, connecting them in a way that was far more intimate than proper.

She stared into his eyes, unblinking. "I shouldn't have interrupted you. I'm sorry."

"I'm not."

His damp hand still tethered her to him. He couldn't seem to let go, even though he was dripping water on her shirt. He wanted to drag her into the tub with him and take her right there, against the wall. Even his orgasm, as powerful as it had been, wasn't enough to keep him from wanting her.

"I should let you finish. Showering, I mean."

"And I should let you go. But I can't."

"No?" she asked, her voice wavering. The pace of her breathing increased, and the unmistakable stain of arousal flushed her cheeks.

He was going to kiss her again. Her mouth was only inches away, and no amount of water or mess could stop him from taking advantage of that.

He leaned forward, tugging on her neck as he went so she had no choice but to angle her head to his liking. This kiss was softer. Sweeter. But no less potent. She tasted like wild fantasies, enticing enough to make him wish he still had a soul to sell for her.

His tongue played with hers, coaxing her inside his mouth so he could angle her for an even deeper kiss.

A riot of need marched down his spine, making his recent orgasm irrelevant. He had decades of desire stored away—more than enough to stay hard and take her over and over again.

As soon as the image flared to life, it couldn't be slain. It was a living, breathing thing that demanded he obey.

"I need you," he said. "Naked. I need to be inside you. Fill you with my cock."

She swayed slightly, grabbing his body to steady herself. The move put her directly under the spray, which was swiftly going cold.

She shivered and stared at him as if making up her mind.

He couldn't allow her to suffer, so he pried his hands away and turned off the water.

The only sound in the room was that of dripping water. She continued to stare at him, and he could see the fine tremor streaking through her limbs.

He'd aroused her, upset her, or both.

Cool air hit his skin, taking with it some of the heat raging inside of him. It was then that he realized that he'd let his lust rule him. No matter how much he wanted to fuck her, a gentleman didn't say the things he had just said.

Perhaps it was a good way to scare her off. Make her realize that being his curator was a bad idea.

So he could spend the next century kneeling at Thyra's feet?

That thought washed away enough lust to allow him to think clearly.

"I'm sorry," he said. "None of that should have happened. And I certainly shouldn't have said that."

She backed away a couple of shuffling paces.

He stepped out from the tub and handed her his towel. When she didn't take it, he draped it over her head to absorb the droplets of water clinging to her springy black hair.

Her shirt was soaked, giving him a clear view of the lacy bra she wore beneath. Her nipples were erect beneath the layers, drawing his complete attention.

What he wouldn't give to know how those stiff, little peaks would feel against his lips. How she'd sound when he drew them deep into his mouth or feathered his tongue across them. Maybe used his teeth on them, so very gently.

She cleared her throat. "I should, um, go."

Before he could stop her, she turned and fled.

He sat on the edge of the tub and took several deep breaths. He'd made such a mess of things. She'd been so kind to him, and he'd practically forced her to watch him pleasure himself.

Sadly, the release had given him little relief. His body still craved hers. Perhaps even more so now that he knew how she tasted, how she sounded when aroused.

He found another towel and dried off, covering himself securely before leaving the room.

The smell of food made his stomach rumble with greed. He had no idea what she had prepared, but he couldn't remember the last time he'd eaten. Thyra's curse on him sustained his flesh outside of his stone form. Inside his stone form, he didn't grow hungry or thirsty. He stayed as he was, not changing unless his statue changed.

Bethany stood at the stove, dishing food onto plates. She'd changed her shirt to a dry one—one he could no longer see through. The curve of her body was obscured by the loose garment, but it hardly mattered. He'd felt her body before and knew its shape. Perhaps not as well as he would like, but no amount of clothing could change the fact that his hands were the perfect size to fit her hips, holding them so he could drive into her from behind.

He tried to shatter the image his mind conjured, but it was no use. One kiss from her and she'd worked her way under his skin. There was no cure for a woman like her. All he could do was hope he could move on with as much of himself left intact as possible.

As soon as he walked in, she looked up and said the four most terrifying words in the English language. "We need to talk."

CHAPTER 9

Bethany set the food out, searching for a place to begin. The problem was, she didn't know which direction she wanted to take.

One way led her away from Tristan, but left her alone to deal with armed criminals when they showed up.

Which they would. It was only a matter of time.

The other way led her toward Tristan. She could become his curator, move him into her house to act as her personal security detail for as long as she lived. But with that lovely benefit came a price: she would spend the rest of her life living with a man she would always want, but could never truly have.

She wanted some kind of life for herself. A family...children. She wanted to fall in love and marry. How in the world was she ever going to find herself a husband if she couldn't stop thinking about the giant statue staring at her, day after day? And what man would want to be in the same house where comparison to a living statue would leave him lacking? Because there sure as hell weren't very many men out there who could measure up to Tristan physically.

She hadn't fallen for him yet. Her heart was still safe, even if the walls around her girly parts were a little wobbly.

She definitely wanted him, but she'd wanted men she couldn't have before and survived. She'd survive this irritating case of lust poisoning, too. Somehow.

But what about him? Every minute she was with him, she grew closer to him. He could never have a real life. He'd never marry. Never have children—at least not ones he could raise himself.

He belonged to some magical bitch who controlled him. How in the world could Bethany move on with her life, build a family and rub her happiness in his face?

She didn't think she had it in her to be that cruel.

He sat down to eat, moving as if he was certain the plate was filled with poison. "I apologize for what happened in the shower. You should never have had to see me like that."

She wasn't sure if she should thank him or scold him for that. "Let's pretend it never happened. I'm more concerned about this curator business."

He gave her a look like he was waiting for the catch, but when none came, he picked up his fork and started eating. "There's nothing for you to be concerned about. It's already settled."

"You asked for my help. I haven't decided whether or not to give it yet, so I'd say it's far from settled."

"I rescinded my request. I was wrong to ask."

She opened her mouth to tell him that he couldn't just rescind requests like that, but before she could get the first word out, there was a flash of light. When she opened her eyes, she was no longer in her kitchen. She was…somewhere else.

The whole place was white. So white she couldn't tell where the walls stopped and the floor and ceiling began. There was no source of light, but the place was bright all the same.

In the center of the area stood a table and two chairs— also completely white.

Bethany stifled a scream of surprise. While there didn't seem to be any kind of threat here, she had no experience handling her sudden teleportation—or whatever had happened. It took her a minute to calm her frantic pulse and steady her breathing.

A second later, a woman appeared, sitting in one of the chairs. She wore a white T-shirt and jeans. Her brown hair fell around a face pretty enough she didn't need makeup. She looked up at Bethany, waving to the empty chair. "Please sit."

"Where am I?" asked Bethany.

"Idola. My home. It really is better if we don't take too much time. If Thyra learns I've brought you here, she might summon Tristan, just to cause a ruckus."

Bethany knew from Tristan that this Thyra chick was a bitch. And a ruckus was definitely not something anyone needed right now. "Why am I here?"

"Because you need to know what's at stake."

"I don't understand."

"Sit, Bethany. Please."

She did as the woman asked, but it didn't make her feel any better. The floor was spongy under her feet, absorbing any noise she might have made.

"My name is Alethia. Thyra is my sister."

"I'm sorry," came out automatically.

Alethia gave a faint smile. "Thank you. Apparently you've heard about her."

"Only a little."

"Count yourself fortunate. Poor Tristan isn't so lucky."

"Is this about him?"

"It is. You've seen what Thrya let happen to him?"

"You mean all the damage?"

Alethia nodded. "She could have repaired him or removed him from his curator's care at any time, but instead has chosen to let him suffer in order to teach him a lesson."

"What lesson?"

"That her will is absolute. That Tristan should bow to her and thank her for the privilege."

"Yeah. Bowing doesn't sound like him."

"He's a proud man. His refusal to kneel before her has always been a thorn in her side. One that tickles me."

"What does any of this have to do with me?"

"More than is healthy or enjoyable for you, I'm afraid. You see, Thyra has offered Tristan a bargain. She will allow you to become his new curator and care for his statue if you can convince his old curator to free him. I brought you here to ensure that happens."

"He was just now telling me that he wasn't going to let me go through with asking her."

"That's unfortunate."

"Why?"

"Because the other part of the bargain was that if you failed or refused, he must spend the next century kneeling at Thyra's feet."

"Have you met Tristan? Kneeling doesn't really seem to be his thing."

"It's not, but he agreed to the terms. He will honor them. No matter how difficult it will be on him or what it might do to his spirit."

The image of Tristan on his knees in front of a beautiful woman popped into Bethany's head, fully formed. His naked body was tense, his muscles straining against the urge to stand. Sweat trickled down his temple and along his spine. Raw, potent hatred poured from him, visible in his clenched teeth and tight fists.

The woman smiled down at him, her lush mouth as wide as a shark's. Glee danced in her tri-colored eyes, and triumph held her head high.

She lifted a stiletto heel and shoved it against Tristan's back. Her strength made him topple forward, onto his hands and knees. She kept her foot there, holding him down in a pose of utter victory.

Tristan's head sagged down in defeat.

"A hundred years," Alethia said. "Of this."

As the image of Tristan's defeat faded, Bethany had to choke back tears. "It will kill him."

"Then we agree. This outcome must be stopped. *You* must stop it."

"Okay. I agree we can't let this happen. But how? If this crazy chick is powerful enough to send a man as strong as Tristan to his hands and knees, what chance do I have of stopping her?"

"You must find a way."

Bethany thought about it for a minute. "Do you know where I can find the curator?"

"I do."

"Then I'll just go there. I won't have to ask Tristan to tell me where she is."

Alethia tilted her head in thought. "This could work. I'm certain I can find a way to entice him to come along."

"He doesn't need to go with me, does he?"

Her gaze slipped away. "I think it would be best if he did."

As much as the idea of spending time with Tristan appealed to her, she wasn't sure how smart it was. She was too drawn to him. And after seeing him in the shower…"I should go alone."

"These men who want your help with their illegal works? Who are they to you?"

"A nuisance. My brother got involved with them to pay off some debt. I knew that if he kept working for them the best-case scenario would be me be visiting him in prison before his thirtieth birthday. The worst case…I'd be visiting his grave. I couldn't let that happen, so I made a bad decision in the hopes of counteracting *his* bad decision."

"Did this plan work?"

"Not as well as I'd hoped."

"Will they hurt you?"

"If they think it's the only way to get what they want, yes."

"I can work with that."

And with that cryptic statement, Bethany was once again back in her house, sitting at her kitchen table. The world stood still for a moment, as if she were catching up to it. A second later, everything started spinning as normal.

"What the hell was that?" she asked.

Tristan frowned. "What?"

"You didn't see me disappear?"

He shook his head, but his expression hardened with suspicion. He looked around, and stood, bracing his feet as if expecting attack. "Thyra summoned you, didn't she?"

"No, actually it was her sister."

"Which one? She has six."

"Alethia."

"The deceiver." He pulled a knife from the caddy on the counter and came back to stand in front of Bethany.

"What's going on?" she asked.

"The sisters like to play games. They've just involved you in one. Whatever you do, you can't play along."

"There was no game."

"She wanted something, didn't she?"

"She wanted me to help you."

"She lies. She always has. I've heard rumors that she's changed her ways, but only a fool would believe someone so skilled at deception." He wrapped his fingers around Bethany's arm, which made every nerve ending below her shoulder light up with giddy excitement.

This man's touch was far too potent for her own good.

"She seemed perfectly nice," said Bethany.

"I'm certain that's what she wanted you to think."

Someone pounded on her front door hard enough to shake the silverware on the table.

Tristan gave her a hard stare. "Stay here. Stay quiet."

She probably should have told him that it was her door and she'd go see who was there, but honestly, she'd had enough surprises for one day.

He left, gripping the knife, wearing only a towel. Still, even without the benefit of armor and real weapons, he looked like a warrior going into battle.

She heard the door open. Heard a man's harsh voice. Tristan's rumbled response. She couldn't make out the words, but the tone was growing tenser by the second.

She was just about to go out and see what was happening when someone grabbed her from behind. A rough hand closed over her mouth and nose, cutting off her air and sending panic skittering through her system.

"You really should lock your doors," said Asshole Number One, who'd visited a few days earlier. "But you didn't, which is going to make my job a whole lot easier."

Bethany tried to kick, but he simply lifted her off the ground, and pinned her legs with one of his own.

"You want to do this the hard way? Fine with me. I like a woman who has a little fight in her."

Her air was running out fast. Panic sped her heart and made her lungs ache for oxygen. No matter how hard she clawed at him, he held fast, his tough hands seemingly impervious to her short fingernails.

Just when stars started dancing in her vision, he eased up enough to let her suck in a gasping breath through her nose. As soon as she breathed in, he blocked her airway again.

"Can't have you passing out. Not before you get the boss's message. He says you've got until the end of the week to do the job he wants done. Shipment leaves Saturday night. If you refuse, not only is baby brother going to have himself a new job, you're also going to have a new home. Inside a 'gator's belly. Nod if you understand."

Bethany nodded frantically.

"Good girl. We'll leave the statues outside. Don't take long. We'll be watching."

He dropped her like a hot rock and slipped back out the way he'd come in. She fell to her hands and knees, gasping for air.

She'd involved herself with the wrong people. It didn't matter that she'd done it for a good reason. All that mattered now was that if she didn't do what they wanted, both she and her brother were dead.

CHAPTER 10

Tristan found Bethany on her kitchen floor. Tears streamed down her cheeks. There was a trickle of blood spilling from the corner of her mouth. She was shaking so hard he could see it from across the room.

He was already riding the edge of rage, and seeing her like this shoved him right over. "What happened?"

Her voice shook harder than her body. "Back door was unlocked. He found me."

Tristan didn't stop to think. He simply scooped her up and carried her away from the scene of her assault.

She curled into him, clinging to his neck as if seeking refuge.

No other woman had ever done that with him before, and it gave him the strangest sensation. He felt needed. Important.

Wanted.

He held her tighter as he carried her into her bedroom, sat on the bed, and settled her in his lap. She shifted lower until her cheek was over his heart and her fingers curled against his chest. He stroked her back, giving her a minute for her fear to settle.

"Tell me what happened." His anger was still riding him, but he maintained enough control to keep it out of his voice.

"You answered the door. The other guy came in the back way. He grabbed me. Cut off my air. He told me that if I didn't do the job, he'd kill me and ruin my brother's life." She shuddered inside his embrace. "I can't let that happen."

"It won't. I will hunt them and kill them."

She nearly slammed her head into his chin, sitting up as fast as she did. "You can't do that. I won't let you."

"It's not your decision. It's mine."

"It's my problem. I should be the one to deal with it."

"No. This is not the kind of problem that you're equipped to handle. I, however, am."

"Let's say you do handle it. Let's say you find them and kill them tonight. It won't matter. Their boss will send two more, and two more after that. There are always men who will be willing to do the dirty work of another for the right price."

"This is what you fear will happen to your brother, isn't it—that he will become an evil man's tool?"

"Benjamin made a bad choice once. If they try to lure him back in, I know he'll go. He's not strong enough to resist the temptation to make a lot of money. And if he does go back to work for them, his life will be over. Even if he doesn't get caught and spend the rest of his years in prison, he'll still be ruined. We were raised with morals. A life of crime will kill him from the inside out."

"So what do you propose?"

She let out a slow breath, deflating as she did. "I don't have a choice. I do the job they want me to do and hope this time really is the last."

"And if it's not?"

"I can't think about that right now. Benjamin needs me to do this to protect him. Maybe if he leaves town he'll be safe."

"And what about you? Who will keep *you* safe?"

"I'll be fine. If I have to move, then that's what I'll do."

He couldn't let her be run out of her home. She'd made a life for herself here. She was skilled at what she did. In order to go into hiding, she'd have to find a new career, and he couldn't imagine her doing anything else. She had been born to restore artifacts. He was walking proof of that.

"You'll become my curator," he said. "When those men come back, I'll stand ready to defend you."

"Just like that?" she asked. "What happened to the matter being settled?"

"You don't want to be my curator?"

"No, I do. But I have to do this job first."

"We shouldn't wait to take advantage of Thyra's offer. She could change her mind or decide I've taken too long to perform the task. She could summon me away at any moment. The only true protection you have is if I'm here, standing guard when those men return."

"This whole thing seems a little crazy. I normally live a nice, quiet life. There's no organized crime, no armed assholes, no statues turning into hot dudes." She looked up at him, her honey-colored eyes shimmering with tears. "I really want my quiet life back."

"Then you will have it. But first we're going to have to make some noise." He held out his hand. "Will you come with me?"

She stared at his hand. "What about Benjamin?"

"When you are my curator, those men will stop bothering you. I'll see to it, even if I have to use every hour of free time I've saved to make it happen. I will hunt them down like the animals they are and feel no remorse for ending their lives. Whatever it takes, Bethany. I swear it."

She nodded slowly and put her slender hand in his. "I'll pack a bag. We'll leave as soon as your clothes are dry. We can't drive to Tennessee with you wearing only a towel."

He stilled, his instincts raging. "How did you know where we're going?"

"You told me."

"No, I didn't." He was certain he hadn't.

"Lucky guess?"

"Try again."

"Alethia told me where to find your curator," she admitted. "Or at least she wanted me to know, and now, apparently, I do. Not sure how it happened, exactly, since I don't remember her speaking the words, but it did. I can see your curator's house as plain as day." She tapped her temple.

"Nice trick."

"Something tells me she's got plenty of them."

She moved away from him and began pulling things from her drawers. He saw a lacy scrap of fabric that made him wonder what she had on under the clothes she wore now. And whether or not she'd let him find out if he kissed her again.

Her physical response to him had been unmistakable. He'd seen the signs of arousal in her skin, her eyes, her body. Maybe if he kissed her again, he wouldn't stop this time.

Just the thought was enough to make him need to tighten his towel around his hips to hide his growing erection.

"I'll go put my clothes in the dryer."

"You know how to do that?" she asked. "You seem to be a bit out of your element, technology-wise."

"I spent an entire year stealing single socks from dryers all over the world, compliments of Thyra's twisted sense of humor."

Bethany stopped packing and stared at him. "So that's where they go."

"Mystery solved. She likes creating chaos, and missing socks are her idea of a good time."

"What does she do with them?"

He shrugged. "I never asked. Some things are better left a mystery."

They packed up what they'd need for the drive. Tristan pulled on his warm, dry clothes and waited for Bethany by the front door.

"I think we're set," she said.

"Just one more thing." He stepped onto the front porch where the box of three small statues was waiting. He picked up the first one and crushed it in his grip.

She grabbed his arm in a panic. "What are you doing?"

"Sending a message."

"You're going to get Benjamin killed. Or me."

"I won't let that happen." He picked up the second one and destroyed it as well. A small bag fell onto the pile of gravel and dust. Through the dirty plastic, he could see something sparkle.

"Diamonds," she said, as if solving a great mystery.

He crushed the last statue without stopping to investigate further. "They're worth too much to leave sitting here, unguarded. My guess is the men will be nearby, probably watching."

"We should go. The damage is done. Running seems like a good idea."

He brushed off his hands, and then picked up her suitcase. "I just crushed stone in my bare hand. If they come after us without taking a moment to pause and consider that, then they're too stupid to live."

"Let's not test that theory. We don't have time to hide any bodies right now."

CHAPTER 11

Bethany drove until she could no longer keep her eyes open. "We have to stop. There's not enough coffee in the world for me to drive safely anymore."

Tristan turned around and looked behind them, as he'd been doing every few minutes for the past ten hours.

"What are you looking for?" she asked.

"Signs that we're being followed."

The reminder made her shoulders creep up toward her ears as her neck tensed. "Have you seen any?"

"Not so far. That doesn't mean we're alone."

"Lovely. Just what a girl needs to help her get a good night's sleep—dreams of armed criminals lurking behind her."

"I won't let them hurt you," he said. "It's safe to stop for a while. I saw a sign for a hotel up ahead."

"That would be lovely, but I can't afford a room. Unless you have some magical stash of cash you're able to hide when naked, we're sleeping in my car."

She could tell he didn't like that idea by the way he went silent, but there really wasn't a lot she could do about it. After watching Benjamin fall into a spiral of debt, she'd chopped up every credit card she had. Her debit card would get them a room, but not when her account was so empty it echoed when she dropped in a few pennies.

Tristan was just going to have to find a way to deal with their less than ideal sleeping quarters.

She turned off at a rest stop and parked at the opposite end from where two truckers were also parked. As soon as she opened the door, a harsh, cold wind swept through her SUV, taking away all the heat she'd built up with it.

It didn't take long for her to lay the back seats flat and spread out blankets for a couple of pallets, but by the time she had, she was shivering—probably as much from nerves as from cold.

"I'm going to go wash up in the bathroom. Be right back," Bethany told Tristan.

She made quick work of brushing her teeth and hair, washing her face. A comfy pair of jammies would have been great right now, but that was a luxury for people who weren't sleeping in their cars, running from armed criminals and avoiding the notice of crazy, magical sisters. For now she was better off being ready to go at the first sign of trouble.

When she came out of the bathroom, she saw Tristan standing guard right outside the door. His gaze scanned the surrounding area as if expecting trouble.

Bethany huddled deeper inside her coat and hugged herself.

As soon as he saw her, he offered her his arm in a move so smooth it was clearly natural for him.

Men didn't do that anymore, which only served to highlight just how out of place he was. This wasn't his world—not really. He lived in it, but it didn't leave a mark on him in the same way it did people who weren't made of stone.

In that moment she realized how different they were, and how—no matter what happened—he could never be a part of her life in any normal way.

She settled her fingers on his arm, letting herself pretend that their differences didn't matter. Their lives might not intersect in the way she would have liked, but if this plan for her to become his curator worked, their lives would definitely intersect. It was in her best interests to make nice with him—the man who would protect her and her family from harm.

She crawled in back and burrowed under her blankets. Tristan followed her in, but laid atop his pallet. The space was small, and they both had to bend their knees a little to fit, but at least this way they didn't have to sleep sitting upright. It was about as comfortable as they were going to get without more cash.

There was a two-inch space between their pallets—a clear neutral zone that she'd left on purpose so that she remembered where the boundaries were.

He curled his arm under his head and used it as a pillow. Even beneath his shirt and jacket she could see the bulging outline of his biceps.

"Do you sleep?" she asked.

"I can. But I won't. Not tonight."

"Why not?"

"We're too vulnerable here. Besides, I don't get to spend a lot of time in my flesh form. I'd rather not waste it in sleep."

"Won't you get tired?"

"Not for several days. I regenerate when I turn to stone— injuries, fatigue—it all goes away quickly."

"But every time you've turned to flesh, you were bleeding."

"Because my stone form was injured. Whatever is done to my statue will be inflicted on my body when I turn. It's the reason we have curators—to protect our stone form from harm."

"Your last curator sucked balls at her job."

His gaze jerked away, and she saw a flash of guilt in his eyes a second before it did.

"Something happened, didn't it?" she asked. "Something bad."

"Try to sleep. We should get moving again as soon as possible."

Obviously he didn't want to talk about it. Part of her wanted to push, but she was too worn out to fight him. Plus, he was right. She needed to sleep so they could keep moving. The longer they stayed here, the more likely it was that Benjamin's bad decisions were going to catch up with her and Tristan.

She closed her eyes and tried to clear her mind. Instead, her head did an instant replay of the last few days, forcing her to linger over everything that had happened.

The image of his battered statue was still too fresh in her mind. She could remember every rough patch, chip and gouge her fingers had found between smooth swaths of stone. She'd spent hours touching him, and her body had already begun to think of him as hers.

Especially after watching him come in the shower.

Every detail of that moment lingered in her memory without blurring or fading. She could still see the way his muscles strained, the way his pulse pounded, and taste the kiss he'd given her while he growled out his release.

The connection hadn't been planned, and she should have turned away, but a sight so potently masculine was far too powerful for her to resist. Ever since that moment, a small part of her wanted to know what it would feel like for him to be even more connected to her in that moment. Not just through eye contact or a kiss, but him moving inside her as deep as a man could go.

Her body started to warm at the fantasy. Soon, she was too hot to sleep, so she stripped out of her coat and folded it up so Tristan could use it as a pillow.

He took the gift, pressing his nose into it and breathing deeply. He let the breath out on a moan. "Smells like you."

She wasn't entirely sure if that was a good thing or not until he looked at her again. There was no mistaking this expression for anything other than stark desire.

Bethany swallowed and tried to think of something clever to say to break the tension. No way was she sleeping with the memory of that look on his face haunting her. She wasn't the kind of girl would could witness such a deep level of need and not respond in some way.

She reached out and stroked his cheek, hoping it would smooth his features enough that she could pretend she hadn't seen what she'd seen.

Instead, her touch made his black eyes glitter with excitement. Color washed over his cheeks, and the cords in his neck stood out as they had right before he'd come.

With one powerful shift of his body, he came over her, holding himself up on thick, muscular arms.

"You look at me like I'm something good to eat," he said. "How am I supposed to keep my distance when I can't think about anything but letting you take a bite?"

"I'm more of a licking kind of girl."

That was so the wrong thing to say, judging by the way he moved closer—almost close enough to kiss her.

"I would let you lick me wherever you like. But only if I get to go first."

Her stomach clenched and a slow, steady heat built low in her abdomen. She tried to tighten her thighs together to help ease the ache, but all it did was make her acutely aware of how slick she'd become in such a short time.

"After all," he said, "You got to watch me find my pleasure. It seems only fair that I get to watch you find yours." A crooked smile did devastating things to his mouth—things too irresistible for her to ignore.

"What about the danger?" she asked.

"I'm not easy to damage. With me on top of you, nothing those men do can hurt you."

Oh man. She could see it now. The image had flared to life in her head, fully formed. His beautiful naked body on top of her. Inside her. Even the idea was nearly powerful enough to push her right to the brink of orgasm. It wasn't going to take much to shove her over the edge.

Maybe a little release wasn't such a bad idea. She was strung too tightly. She couldn't sleep, even though that's really what she needed. She didn't have to have full-blown sex with him. A little touching, a little kissing—that's all she was going to need to get her there.

That was not, however, all that his hot gaze promised to give her.

She tried to tell him they shouldn't, but something shorted out on the path between her brain and her vocal cords. Her mouth opened, but nothing came out.

Tristan took it as an invitation, covered her lips with his and plunged his tongue inside with clear intent.

He tasted so good. Earthy and clean, with a hefty dose of heated determination.

His arms bent slowly, giving her his weight a little at a time. She couldn't feel his muscular contours through the layers of blankets between them, but she knew they were there. She'd run her hands over his statue enough to have memorized every one of them.

His kiss stole her breath and robbed her of any thought she might have had. She knew there'd been something she'd been about to say, but for the life of her, couldn't remember what it was. All that mattered was the solid feel of his weight on top of her, and the sweet, consuming kisses that left her delightfully dizzy.

He stripped the blankets away, but the cool air didn't touch her. All she felt was his hard heat getting closer, urging her thighs apart so there was room for him to settle between them.

Tristan broke the kiss long enough to lift his head and look down at her. "Unbutton your shirt."

With shaking hands, she reached up and did as he demanded. As each button slipped from its hole, his mouth moved down, kissing every inch of bare flesh as it was revealed.

When she'd managed to free the last button, his hand splayed across her chest, right above her breasts. His skin was lighter than hers and easy to see in the shadowy confines of the SUV.

"I can feel your heart speeding," he said with a satisfied smile.

His pinky and thumb inched just below each lacy cup of her bra. Her instant nipple erection was so fast it hurt. She gasped at the tiny bite of pain, wishing he would kiss away the sting.

He slid his finger along her skin, just beyond where she really wanted him to touch. She arched her back, but it did nothing to work his hand further beneath the barrier of her bra.

"You should take this off. It's such a pretty thing. I'd hate to shred it."

She wasn't sure she'd hate to have it ripped off, not when it was done by a man like Tristan. Still, she had packed light, and new lingerie wasn't exactly in the budget.

Bethany reached behind her, inadvertently thrusting her breasts at him while she worked the clasp. He let out a low, animalistic growl and dove down, taking her covered nipple between his teeth.

The sharp sensation winged through her, settling in a hot jumble of need in her belly. The bra came loose, and she wasted no time shoving it up so there was no barrier between them.

His mouth covered her, drawing her nipple deep and hard. There was no warm-up, no slow buildup of pressure. He just took what he wanted, and left her reeling.

His hand slid between her legs, cupping her sex. She was wet enough to soak through her panties and jeans, but couldn't find the strength to care. The heel of his hand pressed against her clit, rubbing her just right. Between that and the tugging pulls of his mouth on her nipple, she was already fighting her orgasm.

She didn't want this sweet pleasure to end. Not yet. It had taken him only seconds to get her here, and she needed the ride to last a little longer.

Her body had other ideas. It went where Tristan led, careening off madly into the throes of orgasm. Each gripping contraction tightened her body, shoving out mewling sounds that filled the dark space.

She gripped his shoulders, holding on for dear life. By the time it was over, she was panting and trembling. She couldn't seem to catch her breath. Maybe because his mouth was on hers again, kissing her like he'd die if she made him stop.

No chance of that happening. She liked him right where he was, consuming her like she was the most delicious substance on the planet.

He'd magically managed to unfasten her jeans while she was distracted. A moment later his hot hand was inside her panties, stroking her with expert skill.

He let out a harsh groan. "So wet."

Her body's answer to his rough praise was another rush of heated liquid spilling over his fingers. She couldn't control her response to this man, not even if she wanted to. It didn't matter that he'd made her come only moments ago. She needed him inside her, right where he belonged.

But first, there was something she was dying to do—something she'd been thinking about since the first time she'd knelt in front of him to repair his battered body.

"Take off your pants," she panted. "I want that glorious cock in my mouth."

CHAPTER 12

Tristan's entire body tightened against the sudden spurt of lust Bethany caused. He was barely able to unclench his body long enough to roll aside so he could do as she demanded.

Through the fog lining the inside of the windows, headlights splashed over his face. The van entering the rest stop headed right for them. As it passed under a light, he saw a man open the side door and lean out.

There was a gun in his hand.

Tristan rolled over Bethany's body just as bullets ripped through glass and steel. He felt the punch of hot metal slam into his back three times before the gunfire ended in a squealing screech of tires.

Pain splintered his concentration even as rage bound his will into a tight bundle.

He lifted his head. The van's tail lights glowed red as it merged back onto the highway. Nearby, a truck driver peered out of his window while another one made his way away from flying bullets.

Tristan lifted up, checking Bethany for damage. "Are you hurt?"

She gave a tight shake of her head. All the sweet desire that had been glowing in her eyes a second ago was gone now, leaving only fear.

The one truck driver who'd stayed was on the phone now, probably calling the authorities.

Blood seeped down Tristan's side. If police came, they might force him to go to the hospital. That was not something he was willing to do—not when those armed gunmen were still out there, drawing breath as if they hadn't just tried to kill Bethany.

Tristan was going to enjoy killing them.

She trembled beneath him. Bits of glass clung to her hair. He tried to brush it away, but the movement caused a lightning strike of pain to streak across his back.

The last trucker pulled away, leaving the rest stop empty.

"We need to go before police arrive," he said. "Can you drive?"

She swallowed hard. "I think so. I'm sure as hell not tired anymore."

"Good. Let's get moving. We'll stop when we put a few miles between us and the scene of the crime."

He rolled away enough to give her room to pass, but that was as far as he could go. The bullets were still in him, impeding his movement somehow.

Bethany opened the back door of the SUV to crawl out. As soon as she realized he wasn't coming with her, she turned around.

The dome light shone down on him, and from the look of horror on her face, there must have been a lot of blood.

"You're shot."

"I'll be fine."

"Three times," she said. "Getting shot three times is not fine."

He pitched his voice low and calm. "I'm going to turn to stone now. Just for a little while. It'll stop the bleeding and help me heal fast. I need you to drive, Bethany. Anywhere. Just get some miles behind us, okay?"

She nodded, causing chunks of glass to fall from her springy curls. "I'll drive. You heal. It's a plan."

Tristan waited as long as he could before giving into the need to turn to stone. The added weight of that form was going to slow her down, but there was nothing he could do about that. He had to be ready to fight if those men showed up again, and right now, he was too damaged to even stand up on his own.

The weakness grated on him, and finally, as she took an obscure exit off the interstate, he let go and allowed his body to harden. He felt the bullets get shoved out as his cells closed ranks. All the heat left him. The fire she'd built in his belly with her kisses disappeared as if it had never been.

Glass crunched under his body as his statue swayed with each turn she made.

He wasn't sure how far she drove before she came to a stop. He couldn't see much from his low vantage point, especially through the shattered window. There were no signs of street lights out here. The stars were bright in the sky, as visible as they'd been when he was a child.

She scrambled into the back, brushing away chunks of glass as she went. Her hands cupped his face as she leaned over him, tears visible in her golden eyes. "I wish you could tell me you're okay."

She stroked his face with shaky hands. Every few seconds she looked around as if worried the gunmen would find her.

Tristan needed to be with her as a man. He needed to hold her, warm her, reassure her. But the burn of his wounds was still too fresh. He needed more time to heal before giving into the needs of his flesh. If he came back to her, bleeding and wounded, he wouldn't be able to protect her.

She curled around him as if trying to keep him warm. The sweet scent of her skin filled the air, tinged with a hint of fear.

Her blouse was still open, her bra loose. While his stone form still wore the clothes he'd had on, he desperately wished he'd stripped bare before solidifying. It would have been so much nicer to feel her skin on his—even his stone skin.

"We're just going to hide here for a while," she told him. "We're out in the country on a deserted back road. The trees are thick here. No one will find us."

He hoped she was right.

The minutes moved by too slowly. He could do nothing but wait as the healing process took as much time as it took, knitting his body back together.

He was vulnerable like this. Not just to attack, but also to Thyra's whim. If she summoned him away now, there would have been nothing he could do to stop it. His essence would be forced from his shell, leaving Bethany alone to defend herself.

And she wouldn't even know he was gone.

In the dim light of the car, he could barely see her sweet face. Her eyes were huge with worry, her mouth drawn tight. He ached to smooth the lines of tension from her brow with the tip of his finger. Every second he had to resist the urge to retake his flesh form.

A few minutes slid by. The heat from her body seeped into him. Her breathing was too fast, but the rhythmic sound of it eased something deep inside of him. She was safe. Scared, but safe.

Headlights splashed across the springy curls on her head. She lifted her gaze, and in those honeyed depths he could see her pupils shrink with fear.

"They're here," she whispered, terror straining the sound. "I don't know how, but they found us."

CHAPTER 13

Bethany was not equipped to handle the violence that was about to go down. She was unarmed, unarmored, completely outclassed. The bullet holes in the side of her car were proof that there was no shelter to be found here.

And Tristan was way too heavy for her to even think about moving.

As the van crunched over the gravel road, drawing closer, she saw the side door open and the barrel of a weapon come out.

She scrambled into the front seat and started the car. The engine took half of forever to engage, but once it did, she hammered down the accelerator and careened down the rocky back road.

Her tires spun, working to gain momentum with the weight of Tristan's statue in back. She had plenty of traction, but no power. The four cylinders running her car were supposed to have horsepower, but instead it was more like geriatric hamster power.

One of the assholes fired. She heard the bullet pierce through the back quarter panel and ping off something hard.

Tristan.

He was a sitting duck back there.

She spun the wheel, turning the car onto an unmarked road. The chain barring her path snapped as she powered through it. A few yards in, she realized her mistake.

This wasn't a road at all. It was an unpaved access to a farmer's field, and there was nowhere for her to go.

The back end of her car sunk into something soft. She hit a muddy spot in the low ground causing the tires to spin and slosh sideways. A few seconds later, the back of the car sunk even lower. She heard Tristan roll and thud against something.

She was no longer moving forward. Mud spewed out from her back tires, but she didn't budge an inch.

Bethany was stuck.

The assholes in the van saw her predicament and stopped. Two armed men peered from around the far side of the vehicle.

"Get out of the car," shouted one of them. "Boss wants to see you."

If she stepped foot outside her vehicle, she knew she was dead. Maybe not in the next two minutes—the way she would be if she held her ground—but either way, this wasn't looking like the beginning of a long and happy life.

"If he wants to see me," she called through the busted glass, "then why are you shooting at me?"

"Nothing personal. That guy you're with had to go. No witnesses, and all that, you know."

"Gee. I feel so much better knowing you weren't aiming for me." *Asshole.*

"Get out of the car. It's time to go."

What choice did she have? If she went peacefully, then Tristan at least had a chance to heal and get away. It seemed like the asshole thought he was dead since he hadn't shown his face.

Bethany slowly lifted her hands. "I'm getting out. Don't shoot. You don't need to kill anyone else."

She left the car, and even though the thin sheet metal and fiberglass had been no armor at all, she still felt vulnerable out in the open like she was now.

The closest man shoved his gun in a holster under his jacket and grabbed her arm in a rough grip. Her skin crawled at the contact, but she didn't dare try to shrug him off.

Behind her, the shocks on her car squeaked. She had no idea why. Then glass and metal shrieked as the side of her car exploded and she knew exactly what had happened.

Tristan was back in his flesh form. And he was pissed.

He erupted from the vehicle, his face blank and empty of all mercy. His clothes were partially torn from his body. The skin below was bloody, and beneath that was all powerful male charging in for the kill.

The man holding her let go and reached for his gun. Behind him, the other man fired, missing.

Bethany dove to the ground, getting out of the way of the violence speeding toward her.

Tristan hit the man who'd grabbed her. The blow was so hard, he flew back into the van, making it rock on its wheels. He slid to the wet, cold ground and didn't get back up.

The second man fired a steady stream of bullets in Tristan's direction, but he was moving so fast that not a single shot landed.

The man's gun clicked as it went empty. He kept pulling the trigger, not yet realizing there was no help coming from the weapon now.

Tristan grabbed the asshole's gun as he closed into range. One hard squeeze, and the man started screaming as his hand broke around the butt of the weapon.

The damage didn't end there. The gun actually bent inside his grip, the metal letting out a faint squeak as it skewed—barely audible between the man's shrieks of pain.

Tristan picked the guy up over his head in a show of blatant strength, and flung him into the trees. Then he turned and looked at Bethany, his black eyes too calm for the violence he'd just done. He reached out his hand toward her and took a step closer.

She backed away with Dalton's and Sue's warning screaming through her brain. She was unsure if Tristan might be coming for her next. Without a look of anger dissipating from his expression, she had no clue if he was still in a lethal mood, or if he was all done hurting people for the moment.

His hand fell. He planted his feet where he stood. His tattered clothes were wet with blood. His chest rose and fell evenly, as if he hadn't just tossed a couple of armed men around like stuffed animals. He wasn't even winded.

"Are you hurt?" he asked.

She shook her head. Little chips of glass fell from where they were clinging to her curls.

"You're afraid of me." It wasn't a question.

She went still, wondering if her fear might set him off. All the warnings Sue and Dalton had given her to not get in his way were starting to set in. Hard.

"I'm not going to hurt you," he said.

She wanted to believe him. Her nervous system was on overload. Her pulse was a terrified little bunny doing frantic laps through her veins. She could feel herself shaking, hovering on the edge of running. The only question was whether she should be running away from him or getting closer, where nothing bad could reach her before he killed it.

His expression shifted, going from the blank mask of violence to something warmer, darker. "I'm going to touch you now," he warned her. "Please try not to run. I'm not sure what would happen if you make me chase you."

She wasn't sure either, and for that reason alone, she held her ground.

In the distance, the brush rustled as the injured man began limping away. She was glad to see him go, but once he was gone, there were no witnesses. The other man was still slumped, unconscious against the van.

Tristan moved in slowly, his pace steady so that she could predict exactly when he'd reach her. By the time he stood in front of her, she was as ready for him as she was ever going to be.

He lifted his hands and touched her face with the barest tips of his fingers. The heat from his skin sank into her, driving away the numb chill that had gripped her until now. With careful, slow movements, he ran his hands along her arms, checking for damage. His eyes were on her face, gauging her expression for any sign of discomfort.

Each touch of his hands melted away a little more of her terror. By the time he reached her fingertips, she was on the verge of a relieved sob.

"You're not used to violence," he said. "I'm sorry you had to see that."

"I'm sorry you had to do it. That can't be a good time for you." She hoped.

"I do what I must and spend little time thinking about how I feel about it. It's the only way to survive a life like mine."

She didn't want to think about that. All she wanted was to be back at home, consumed by her work where no thoughts of criminals or inhumanly strong, impossibly intriguing men could reach her.

"It's over now," he said. "You're safe."

Was she? If so, her body hadn't yet caught up with the news.

"You did well. Kept your wits about you. Your delay tactics gave me the time I needed to finish healing."

"You're kind of a mess, again."

He shrugged, and the movement was so powerful it made her body rock slightly. That's when she realized he was still touching her. He hadn't let go. Her quivering hands were tight in his grip, protected from the chill of the night air.

"The damage is minor. I'll heal as soon as I know you're calm and settled."

"I'm not sure if I'll ever be calm again. My brain is spinning through an infinite loop of gunfire and violence."

"Then I will stop the spin." He pulled a few bits of glass from her hair, then plunged his fingers deep against her scalp.

He was going to kiss her.

Instantly, all that fear and shock melted away, leaving only a heady kind of excitement behind. She wasn't ready for this man—not even close—but she wanted to be.

Bethany held her ground as he closed in and covered her mouth with his. He caught her on a breath, and she pulled in the scent of him just as his tongue slipped behind her lips.

Sweet, merciful heaven. He tasted like sin, like midnight and whispered secrets. His whole body shook with restraint, his hands holding her just hard enough to make sure she couldn't get away.

Like she was going anywhere.

The kiss went on, and her nerves switched from fear to something far more fun, if no less intense. His hand curled into a fist against her scalp, leaving a delicious sting along her skin. She tried to get closer, letting her hands quest across his back and shoulders, but there was no closer for him to get. Every bit of his prime, male flesh was plastered against her, vibrating with tense control.

He pulled his mouth away. She tried to follow him up, but his hold on her hair held her back.

"We should go now. We're not as alone as I want to be for the things I want to do to you."

"Oh. My." She wasn't sure what he had in mind, but she was all for it.

Her knees weren't functioning properly. His kiss had made them go all soft and wobbly. If not for his arm around her waist, she wouldn't have been able to travel the short distance to the van.

He got her behind the wheel. "Do you know how to operate this vehicle?"

Bethany didn't see much choice. Her car was totaled, stuck in the mud, with a permanently gaping sunroof on one side. "I'll manage."

He went around the far side of the van and moved the unconscious man's body out of the way. She could barely see what he was doing in the dim light, but it looked like he might have taken the man's wallet.

A few seconds later, Tristan was sitting beside her, holding out a wad of cash. "Is this enough to rent us a room for the night?"

She stared at the stack of hundreds and nodded. "I can't believe you stole his money."

"I'm certain it wasn't rightfully his. And this is far less than the value of your car. I'm sorry I had to ruin it."

She took one last glance at it as she eased back onto the gravel road. "We're alive. We're free. My car is totally worth what it bought us. Besides, I'm insured." She wasn't sure exactly how she was going to explain what had happened to her insurance agent, but she'd think of something.

As she headed back to the main road, the same question kept turning over and over in her mind. "Why did you kiss me?"

"Two reasons. First, you appeared to be on the verge of emotional collapse. There wasn't time for that. I needed you alert and clear-headed enough to drive, since I don't know how. I thought that if I distracted you from your fear, you might be able to refocus your emotions elsewhere."

"Well, it worked like a charm. I was about to freak out."

"And now?"

"Better."

Another couple of miles passed before she realized he'd left something out. "You said there were two reasons you kissed me. What was the other one?"

"Because I wanted to."

"Oh. Well." She swallowed, trying to ease the tightening in her throat. "Good to know."

"I still want to," he said, glancing at her. "I think it's only fair to warn you of that."

Instantly, her nervous system lit up with excited little pulses. The tingle between her thighs had her clenching them together. The van slowed down as she let off the accelerator. It took her a minute to realize what had gone wrong.

She cleared her throat and tried to sound like a fully functioning adult. "I like it that you're a fair man."

"How long before we reach a place to rest?"

"I'm not sure. Maybe as much as an hour."

"I'll return to my stone form then. That will be enough time."

"For what?"

"To heal." He brushed her curls back behind her ear. "And to decide exactly what I'm going to do to you first."

CHAPTER 14

Tristan wasn't thinking clearly. Bethany's taste had gone to his head and twisted his thoughts around.

He wanted to fuck her. Needed it.

She was willing, or would be, with very little coaxing. He could see it in the way her honeyed eyes dilated when she looked at him, feel it in the way her breath caught every time he kissed her.

If he ever got his fingers between her lovely thighs, he knew she'd be wet and ready for him.

But what then? If he fucked her, things would go from complicated to impossibly so. Already he wasn't sure she would really go along with becoming his curator. Sex could make her run from him and never look back.

Then again, it could also bind her to him, urging her to make a commitment to him she might otherwise not make.

There was simply no way to know.

His healing went fast. By the time she'd pulled into a motel, his body was as strong and whole as it was going to get. Still, he stayed in his stone form, resisting the urge to be with her as a man.

He couldn't mess up his one chance to be rid of his current curator. He couldn't risk losing the opportunity to see Bethany every day for decades to come. She brightened his otherwise gloomy world, giving him something wholesome and rare to gaze upon. If he was forced to go back to that burned-out shell of a house, he wasn't sure how he'd stand it.

Even worse, his essence would be with Thyra, kneeling at her feet, which was far worse than suffering through the pain of his weathering stone shell.

A shudder of revulsion passed through him, leaving behind more than a hint of rage.

Bethany returned to the van, pulled it around to the back side of the motel and parked. "Are you in there?" she asked.

Tristan resisted the urge to animate and answer her. At the base of his spine he could feel the tingling pressure building, urging him to release himself from his stone prison, but he controlled it, maintaining his current form.

"I don't want to leave you out here alone," she said, touching his arm.

Her heat sank into him, calling to his flesh. Still, he resisted. He needed time to think—time away from her intoxicating scent.

She sat with him for a few more minutes. When she finally spoke, he could hear fatigue in her voice. "Okay. I have to sleep now. I'm going to our room. I'll leave you a key card so you can get in. Room one-seventeen."

He felt the thin strip of plastic slide just under his heavy thigh. Then she was gone.

Tristan let the power of his transformation sweep through him as he turned to flesh, ensuring Thrya couldn't summon him. He sat alone in the van for a while. He wasn't sure how long. For a statue, small increments of time had little meaning.

Cold seeped into the space. Her lingering scent dissipated, leaving him feeling lonely.

Why was he hesitating? Why wasn't he in there with her, enjoying every bit of time he could as a real man?

As he pondered the question, the answer came to him, as clear as it was disturbing.

He didn't want to hurt her. Didn't want to use her. She was soft, kind and gentle. He was anything but. As his desire for her built, he knew how close he was to giving into his baser urges.

Sex with a man like him might change her, and she was a rare and precious thing just as she was. He couldn't stand the idea of destroying even the slightest part of her. No matter how good it might feel.

Such sentimentality wasn't like him. Interacting with her was making him soft. And a man with a life like his couldn't afford to be soft.

Tristan pulled his self-control around him and hardened his resolve. Bethany was going to be his curator so that he didn't have to spend a century kneeling at Thyra's feet. That would have to be enough for him.

He slipped into the motel room and was greeted with her warm, magical scent. It hovered in the moist air, lingering in a cloud of steam that billowed from beneath the bathroom door.

He caught his reflection in the mirror over the sink. The bright fluorescent lights hid nothing, showing him every smear of blood—both his and his enemies'. His eyes were dark, wild. There was a hint of desperation lingering around his mouth, and more than a little pain.

He couldn't let her see him like that, so he splashed some water on a hand towel, soaped it up, stripped his shirt off, and scrubbed himself clean.

Her sweet voice lifted in some haunting melody as she showered. The siren song lured him toward her, impossible to resist. He pressed his hands against the wood and lowered his forehead until it touched the painted surface.

He wasn't nearly close enough.

The sound of running water taunted him. She was naked behind that door. Even locked, it would have taken little more than a twitch of his hand to bust through. His body was supernaturally strong, and he couldn't think of a single thing he wanted to do with that strength more than break down the door that stood between them.

Warmth pooled around his ankles. Behind the door the water turned off. Her singing stopped.

She would come out soon. Hot, damp. Perhaps, even naked.

A low groan of need erupted from him, vibrating the wooden door.

It flew open, revealing a dripping wet Bethany clothed only in a too-thin towel. She'd tossed it haphazardly around her body, barely hiding her assets. The soft swell of her breasts rose above the clinging fabric, making the need to groan again rise up in his throat.

Concern darkened her face. "I heard you moan in pain. Are you okay?"

He didn't answer. Couldn't. His voice was no longer his own.

Her concern deepened with his silence. "Tristan?" She reached for him. The towel slipped down, catching on the stiff tip of her nipple for a split second before it fell away.

She tried to grab the wayward fabric, but he was faster. He stepped closer, closing the distance between them.

Her hot skin met his. Soft breasts yielded to the hard contours of his muscles. Her tight nipples stabbed him in the sweetest way. Her honey-colored eyes darkened to a rich bronze as acute awareness of him flared in her gaze.

"Oh my," she squeaked.

"I think you mean, *oh mine*."

Her lips parted—maybe because of surprise, maybe she just needed more air. Either way his body took it as an invitation to take and taste.

He covered her mouth, thrusting his tongue in to conquer the space. Her body tensed for a fraction of a second before relaxing in one long, languid wave. Her hands slid over his shoulders, clinging to him. Delicious heat sank into him, reminding him that he was alive.

He tipped her head back, exploring the gift of her mouth. She gave him a pretty little moan that flew along his nerves, all the way to his toes. The taste of her intoxicated him, driving away what little self-control he might have had left.

Tristan had to possess this woman. He knew there were reasons why he shouldn't. Good ones. But not a single one of them came to mind now, while her hot, silky body was in his arms, giving him everything he'd ever wanted.

Her strong fingers dug into his muscles, holding on tight as if she never wanted to let him go. He reached around her, cupping her sweetly-rounded bottom in his palm. Her hips bucked toward him, and she breathed another delicious sigh of delight into his mouth.

One second he was standing in front of her, trying to remember how easy she would be to break if he wasn't careful. The next, she slid one of her sleek thighs up his leg, propping it against his hip.

Blinding patches of light burst against his retinas, and when his vision cleared, she was pinned against the wall high enough that her breasts were within easy reach of his mouth.

He flicked his tongue across one tight nipple. Her fingers curled along his scalp, and both of her legs locked around his hips. He could feel the damp heat of her core sinking through his jeans. With each tugging pull of his mouth, her hips rocked toward him, rubbing his erection.

Tristan's knees weakened—something a man as strong as him should never have experienced. He gathered all the tattered scraps of his concentration enough to remember how to walk the few feet it took to get her to the bed.

He laid her down, covering her body with his own. Not that she gave him much choice. Her strong legs were still locked around him, clinging to him.

Her damp hair spread out across the pillow. The rich golden color of her eyes sucked him in, refusing to let go. He'd never seen a woman more beautiful than her before, not in all the years he'd lived.

Bethany offered him a smile that was part sweet, part scalding. It stroked down his spine, making every cell in his body light up with interest.

"I like the way you feel on top of me," she told him.

"That's good. I plan to spend the next few hours that way."

"Hours?"

He kissed the tip of her nose. "I'm quite patient. Comes with the job."

She shivered, and he felt her nipples harden against his chest. "I'm not sure I'll survive it."

"You're the toughest woman I've ever met. You can take everything I have to give."

"I'd really like to test that theory."

Because he might never have this chance again, because not doing so would slay him, Tristan bent down and kissed her.

Her full lips parted under his, giving him the sweetest sigh of relief he'd ever heard. A moment later, that relief was swept away as she turned demanding.

Her fingers roamed over his back, tightening as she pulled him closer. Beneath him, her hips wiggled as she shifted to align their bodies. The air between them heated as their panting breaths came out faster and faster.

Lust prowled just beneath his skin, driving away whatever reservation he might have had. The only thing that mattered now was possessing this rare and delicate creature squirming beneath him.

He pulled away from her just long enough to strip off his jeans, then moved back to where he belonged.

When her soft body was back beneath his, Tristan slid one thick arm under the small of her back to tilt her hips to just the right angle. Her hot, slick sex lined up just right, and there wasn't a thing he could have done to stop what he had to do now.

The blunt tip of his cock was bathed in her juices, making it easy for him to slide in. Her body was snug, but accepted him eagerly as he eased in as far as possible.

Bethany went still, her frame tensing for a second before she melted beneath him. She pulled away from his kiss long enough to look up at him with hammered bronze eyes made dark with lust.

"So fucking beautiful," he managed to say. "So hot and wet. So mine."

Becoming possessive was a dangerous thing, but he couldn't seem to stop himself. Not now. Not with her. She created in him every forbidden hope and dream a man with a heart of stone should never feel.

A sultry smile was her only response as she arched her back and thrust her tight little nipples against his chest.

That wanton look was his undoing.

He let go of his inhibitions and control and began to move within her. Every heavy thrust was welcomed with sweet heat and a whimper of pleasure from her. His sex-starved body cut his brain out of the loop and took what it needed.

He was on the edge of climax far too soon. He'd hardly had time to warm her up when his orgasm ripped through him, stealing every bit of his self-control.

Tristan crushed her body against his as he came, buried deep within her softness as he found his release. The physical pleasure went on for miles before the rough grip of his orgasm finally loosened its hold and allowed him to breathe again.

He lowered his head next to hers, panting to find his breath. Her soft, slender fingers stroked his hair as the storm passed.

"I bet that's been a long time coming," she said. There was need quivering in her voice.

He hadn't satisfied her. There hadn't been time. His body's demands had left him unable to hold back even long enough to see to her needs.

That wasn't the kind of lover he'd ever been. And it sure as hell wasn't going to be the kind he was now. She deserved far better than that.

She moved to urge him off of her, but he held fast. "You're not going anywhere yet."

"It's okay," she said, as if certain their fun was over. "Really. It was kinda hot watching you lose control like that."

"I'm not accustomed to losing control. I assure you, it won't happen again." To punctuate his point, his hips surge forward, ensuring that she could feel he was still hard and ready. "We're not done here."

Her eyes rolled back into her head in pleasure. "You sure as hell don't feel done. But I know you came. No mistaking that."

His semen leaked out from around his cock, leaving her even slicker than she'd been before. "I've been without a woman for longer than you've been alive—several times over. Once isn't going to be enough. Not by a long shot. Now lie back and let me make you come."

CHAPTER 15

There was nothing Bethany could say to his dark order but, "Okay."

Her body was buzzing with need. The way he'd gone at her a minute ago, like he was starving for her, only served to heat her up to near combustible levels. When he'd gotten off and she'd thought it was over, she wasn't sure how she was going to walk way without bursting into flames.

The fact that she didn't have to gave her both a relief and a new level of desire she'd never felt before.

She shook with unspent lust as he pushed his torso up off hers. Sleek, powerful muscles flexed in his arms and chest, giving her a visual thrill. Her dark fingers slid over his gleaming skin, creating the kind of tactile treat few women ever experienced.

Then he began to move inside of her, and all she could feel was the sweet glide of his cock surging slow and deep.

Bethany closed her eyes and let him work his magic. It wasn't long before she was on the verge of orgasm. Her body coiled tight, her breathing sped, and a hot, sweaty flush covered her skin.

Just as she was about to let go, Tristan stopped.

She started to ask him what game he was playing when his big hands grabbed her hips and flipped her onto her stomach. A second later, her ass was in the air, and his thick cock was right back where she needed it, plunging deep and hard.

There was no steadying herself against his dizzying blitz to her nerves. All she could do was bury her face against the sheets and grip them tight while her body spiraled out of control.

He pressed one hand against the small of her back. "Arch for me, love."

She did as he asked, unable to think of one single reason why she shouldn't. Her reward was the glorious harmony of a whole new set of nerve endings singing as he conducted.

Semen dripped down the inside of her thighs. The wet slap of flesh on flesh filled her ears. The whole experience was raw and rough, not at all like the emotional, romantic sex she was used to having. And no matter how hard she tried, she couldn't find it in herself to care. This was too good. Too satisfying and compelling in the most primal of ways.

Thick, hot fingers found her clit and danced across it with expert precision.

She'd never flown this high before, or for this long. Now all that was left was the exhilarating fall waiting for her.

He lightly pinched her clit between his slippery fingers, launching her headfirst into her climax. Tristan's rough growl and the hot splash of semen inside her told her that she wasn't alone. He'd come along for the ride. And what a ride it was.

Her body burst into pure sensation, showering her brain in a waterfall of heat and light. She couldn't breathe, couldn't move. All she could do was ride out the kind of pleasure that stripped her down to her most basic animal parts and left her spent and quivering.

She'd never felt anything like it before—like falling and soaring all at the same time. She wasn't big enough to hold all the pleasure he gave her, and yet she instantly craved more.

So much more.

When the ride ended and she was lying on her side with his hot body holding hers, both of them gasping for air, she realized her mistake.

She'd never before felt anything like that, and doubted she would ever again. Which left her with the bleak knowledge that if she became Tristan's curator, she would look at him every day for the rest of her life and know what she was missing. This was not the kind of experience a woman ever forgot.

From this day on, a little piece of her would be his. If she became his curator, she'd see him every day and remember what they'd shared. It didn't matter if she moved on and dated other men. No man could compare to such perfection.

As her future stretched out in front of her, reality settled in.

Tristan would always be a giant, seven-foot reminder of this moment standing between her and her future.

He pulled on her shoulder until she rolled onto her back where he could see her face. "You're already regretting it, aren't you?"

She didn't want to lie to him, but she didn't want to hurt his feelings, either. Instead, she avoided the question completely. "We should get some sleep. I'm wiped out after that. Can we talk about it in a few hours?"

He stroked her ribs and abdomen, lingering below her navel. "Of course," he said. But his hurt look told her that he already knew the answer. "I will guard your sleep."

"You should rest, too."

"I will. Later."

When he was stone again.

She already missed him, but rather than dwell on a future she couldn't change, she simply nodded. "Okay. Wake me in a couple of hours and we'll get moving again."

He said nothing, but also made no move to get up.

"Is there something else?" she asked.

His hand stilled on her stomach, filling her skin with his living heat. His expression was guarded, and he hesitated, as if unsure how to proceed. Finally, after a moment, he asked, "Are you fertile?"

The blunt question sent a trickle of shock through her. "Probably something we should have discussed, before...but no. I'm on the pill." When he frowned in confusion, she clarified. "Birth control pills, so I can't get pregnant."

He fell silent again, his black gaze unreadable. "That's good. I don't think I could stand watching a child of mine grow up and be unable to be a part of his or her life."

She couldn't even imagine such a fate. And just like that, she realized how lonely he must be most of the time. Still, silent, unable to do anything other than watch the world around him. It had to be a slow kind of hell, even without all the chips and cracks his statue had sustained.

"We should have some fun while you're free," she suggested.

"Fun?"

"See a movie, drive bumper cars, ride roller coasters...whatever floats your boat."

He slid his hands into her hair and kissed her until she was unable to breathe. When he lifted his head, hers was spinning.

"You are the only fun I need, Bethany. Sleep now, before I decide to take you again."

The man had already gone a couple of rounds, but one glance at his groin told her that he was ready, willing and more than able to go again. She, however, was exhausted, despite the little quivers of interest that winged their way through her limbs.

"If you keep looking at me like that, I'll take the choice from you," he said.

Because she wasn't sure her poor heart could stand another climactic love-fest with this man, she scurried into the bathroom and made quick work of cleaning herself up. Once she was done, she slid under the sheets and rolled over so he was out of sight. Then, and only then, was she able to close her eyes.

Not that it did any good. Her dreams were still filled with him.

She dreamed of having him in her life—a constant, silent presence. She dreamed of him standing guard over a family he could never have for himself, watching her children grow. But mostly, she dreamed of the sadness she saw in the stone lines of his face. The emptiness in him grew year after year, and there wasn't a thing she could do to stop it.

Tristan was truly alone. All she could do was give him what little time he had now and make the memories sweet enough to last for a long, long time.

CHAPTER 16

Tristan was rarely nervous, but the closer he got to his curator's home, the more anxious he became. By the time he and Bethany pulled up the long gravel driveway and came to a stop at a modest farmhouse, he was actually shaking.

His statue's base was nearby, vibrating with enough power he could feel it in the air. The burned-out building wasn't in sight, but he never needed to see it again to know it down to the last charred, rotting knothole. He'd stared at the walls for decades, and the only thing that ever changed was how much decay had eaten the blackened structure. No matter how much wood nature reclaimed, the stone fireplace remained standing—a reminder of the man Tristan had killed.

Bethany laid her hand on his thigh to still the nervous twitch he'd developed. Her warm eyes met his. "It'll be okay."

"You don't know that." How could she? She'd never met Jillian Branch. She'd never seen how much his curator hated him.

What if that hostility rubbed off on Bethany? What if she sided with Jillian and hated him just as much?

It was no less than he deserved, but it would kill him to see Bethany's sweet face twist with loathing.

"Do you want me to go up there alone and talk to her about becoming your curator?" she asked.

"No. She's dangerous."

As he said the words, a scrawny, gray-haired lady shuffled out onto the front porch to investigate her visitors. She wore a bright muumuu in a garish Hawaiian floral print and fuzzy, pink house slippers. A sturdy cane held her steady, and a thick pair of glasses perched on her nose.

"She doesn't look all that dangerous," Bethany said.

"Try enraged and vindictive. She didn't have to lift a finger to hurt me. All she had to do to ensure my suffering was nothing. Nature did the rest."

"Why didn't Thyra stop her?"

"Because it amused her to know I suffered."

The old lady squinted against the sun and shielded her eyes from the glare bouncing off the windshield.

"Stay here," said Tristan. "This is likely to get ugly, and if she attacks, I don't want you in the line of fire."

"She can barely hold herself up, much less attack. Besides, aren't I supposed to be the one to convince her to let me take over her job?"

"Please. Just do as I ask and stay here. It's my duty to at least pave the way so you won't bear the brunt of her anger."

Bethany sighed, signaling her acquiescence. Only then did Tristan step out of the vehicle.

The instant he did, Jillian saw him.

"What the hell are you doing here?" she demanded. "I was hoping you'd crumbled to dust by now."

"Sorry to disappoint you," he said. "We need to talk."

"I have nothing to say to you. Go, or my next call will be a bulldozer service to come over and bury the old house. You can sit under the ground and rot for all I care."

Bethany popped out of the vehicle before he could stop her. "Wait," she said. "Please. All we want to do is talk to you."

"I don't know who you are, little girl, but you should know that this man isn't what he seems."

"He's a stoneman. I know."

"Do you also know he's a killer?" Jillian asked.

Bethany lifted her hands and stepped closer. "He only does what Thyra commands him to do."

Jillian glanced at him with hatred shining in her eyes. "Is that what he told you? What about the rest? What about Andy? Did he tell you what he did to my husband? That he killed him in cold blood? He may be flesh right now, but that heart of his is solid stone."

And there it was, Tristan's second biggest regret—almost as bad as his first.

He'd killed his curator's husband.

He opened his mouth to apologize, knowing there was nothing he could say that would make a difference. But before he could utter the first word, he felt the telltale whooshing at the base of his skull as he was swept from one world to another.

Only this time, he didn't come to Idola alone as he had so many times before. Jillian was here, and so was Bethany.

Thyra jumped up and down, gleefully clapping her hands. She was dressed in a cheerleader's skirt made from the same garish Hawaiian print as Jillian's muumuu. Her hair was in high pigtails, bouncing as she jumped up and down. "I couldn't miss this," she said. "I'm so excited to get Tristan where he belongs, obediently worshiping at my feet."

He was driven to his knees, his clothing stripped away as if it had evaporated. Pressure built against the back of his head as Thrya tried to make him bow to her, but he fought it.

"He's not yours yet," Bethany said. "You haven't even given me a chance to change his curator's mind yet."

Jillian looked around in shock, wobbling on her cane. "Where the hell am I?"

"Idola," said another voice from behind Tristan. It was low, but unmistakably female.

"Zeva," Thyra said. "Who invited you?"

"I have as much right to be here as you do." The woman stepped into Tristan's line of sight.

She was six and a half feet tall, with spiky black hair and eyes the color of tarnished armor. She wore a full suit of plate mail that was speckled with something that looked suspiciously like blood. Sweat had dried along her brow, leaving glittering crystals behind.

"Leave us, sister," ordered Thyra, her appearance changing from that of a cheerleader to that of a small, iridescent dragon. She made a hissing sound as she moved, as dry scales slid against one another.

Zeva settled into an antique wooden folding chair as it materialized behind her. She drew her giant sword and laid it across her armored knees. "I'm staying. Deal with it or bring it on. You know you're no match for me in a fight."

Thyra huffed, letting out a little puff of smoke and flames from her snout. A moment later, she morphed back into a woman with tri-colored hair that exactly matched her eyes.

Those eyes landed on Bethany, and Tristan surged against his invisible bonds. It was no use. He was trapped. Immobile. Helpless.

"Fine," Thyra said. "If you want to chat with the woman who despises Tristan so deeply, then feel free. I'll enjoy the show."

Jillian shook her head as if to clear it. "Will someone please tell me what the hell is going on?"

"I will," said Bethany. "This…woman is toying with you. With all of us. She wants to hurt Tristan."

"Good. The bastard deserves everything he gets."

"Does he?" Bethany asked. "I saw the shape he was in— the thousand cuts and gouges in his skin. I saw his blood and his pain. He's been suffering for years. Isn't that enough?"

"He killed my Andy. Killed him and didn't even look back. There is no amount of suffering that will ever make up for that."

"I'm sure it wasn't his fault," Bethany said.

"You're *sure*?" Thyra asked. "Are you sure because you fucked him, or because you have some kind of magical proof? I mean, what do you really know about Tristan here? He's handsome, sure. But is that enough to forgive him all of his sins? Do you even know why he's here? Why he's a stoneman?"

Bethany's brow drew low as her eyes slid to him. Even from this distance, he could see suspicion clouding the honeyed depths. "We never talked about it. I didn't know he had to do something to become what he is."

"Well he did, sweet cheeks," said Thyra. The way she looked changed again. She took on the appearance of a business woman, complete with prim suit, hair in an elegant twist, leather planner in hand and classy black-rimmed glasses. She tapped a gold pen on a notepad inside her planner. "Let's see…" she flipped a few pages in the calendar, as if to refresh her memory—as if she hadn't been there when it happened, encouraging his grieving sister-in-law the whole time. "Ah, here it is. Tristan's birth as a stoneman. It says here that there was some kind of altercation…yada, yada, yada. He killed his brother. His sister-in-law cursed him in her grief and bingo! Here we are."

Thyra lifted her gaze over the rim of her glasses. "See, Bethany? This whole killing thing is a pattern with your sexy boy toy, here. Killing is all he's really good at." She turned her head to where Tristan knelt. "Isn't it, darling?"

Zeva rose from her chair, her chin thrust out in belligerence. "He should have been mine. He was born to serve in battle. Born to kill."

"You can't have him," said Thyra with a pout. "I was there first."

"But I was there second. We had a deal."

"Not now," growled Thyra and waved her hand, causing the air to crackle with power.

Zeva disappeared on a scream of rage as Thyra banished her.

Thyra beamed as she adjusted her glasses. "Now, where were we? Oh, yes. Bethany was just realizing that she'd had intimate, dirty relations with a killer." A microphone emblazoned with a local news station's logo appeared in her hand, which she thrust toward Bethany's mouth. In a tone all too serious, Thyra asked, "How does it feel knowing you had naughty carnal shenanigans with a murderer?"

Bethany shoved the microphone away and took a step toward Tristan. "Is any of this true? Did you kill your own brother before Thyra got her hands on you?"

The pressure caging Tristan's head dissipated, leaving him free to move and speak. There was no other answer to her question except the truth. "It's true."

"See," said Jillian, waving her arms so vigorously that it made her garish muumuu flutter. "I told you he was a killer."

"So," said Thyra to Bethany, "do you still want to be Tristan's keeper? Protecting him from all booboos?"

"That's why they came to my house?" Jillian asked. "*She* wants to be his curator?" She laughed and sarcasm filled her tone. "Oh, absolutely. He can have whatever curator he wants. Over my dead body."

A wave of power flowed through the space, changing the scenery as it went. Gone were the fluffy clouds and billowing fog, and in its place was a library stuffed to the gills with ancient books. "A bargain has been struck," said a woman seated at a nearby antique desk. A feathered quill was in her hand. She wore a neat black suit, an elegant updo, and an air of superiority. "As Keeper of All Contracts, I hereby decree that Mrs. Jillian Branch's offer has been accepted. As she has no living relatives, upon her death, the duty of curator to one Tristan Celeres shall be bequeathed to Miss Bethany Kinden or other suitable curator as Tristan so chooses." She scribbled something with a flourish and slammed shut the giant leather bound book in which she'd been writing.

Thyra's face twisted with rage as she grew three feet taller. "Who asked you to butt in, Lalia?"

"I'm merely doing my sworn duty, sister. I'd think you would thank me for such prompt service. I *am* a busy woman, you know."

Thyra loomed over the woman, growing fangs and six-inch claws. "Leave us!"

Lalia sighed. "Fine, fine. I have another appointment, anyway. Your new contract will be on file. If you'd like a copy, office hours are from two to two-fifteen, Eastern Standard Time, on the second full moon in any given May."

With that, she vanished as quickly as she'd come, taking her library with her.

"I don't know what just happened," said Bethany, "but I'd like to go home now."

"What about Tristan?" asked Thyra, shrinking to normal size. "Will you abandon him?"

Bethany looked at Tristan. "You kept telling me you weren't a good man. I didn't want to believe you, but maybe I should have."

"I never lied to you."

"Then tell me the truth now. When you killed your brother, were you compelled by outside forces?"

"No, it was my choice."

Bethany flinched. "Was it an accident? Some fit of rage?"

"No," he said. "I'd known for a while that I was going to kill him."

"Not just murder, but premeditated murder." She nodded, her sweet mouth twisted in disgust. "My brother has done a lot of shitty things to me over the years. He's lied to me, stolen from me. He even put my life in danger. But *never once* did I ever consider killing him." She sucked in a deep breath and shook her head. Black curls danced around her face. "I felt sorry for you, Tristan. I wanted to help. I guess I should have done my homework, huh?"

Thyra grinned. "I thought you were all fired up about saving him from the super-icky fate of bowing to me for the next century."

Bethany wiped a tear from her eyes. "I can't let that be my problem. Not now that I know the truth. You kept trying to tell me you weren't a good man. I guess I should have listened." She looked at Thrya. "If he wants a different curator, that's fine, but it's not going to be me. Please send me home."

Thyra flicked her fingers in dismissal and Bethany disappeared.

Tristan wanted to wail in fury and grief, but he was no longer able to move or speak. Thyra's control was back in place, unbreakable and absolute.

She changed attire in the blink of an eye, donning the regal gown of a queen. Gold threads shimmered within a deep purple velvet skirt, winking as the light hit them. Jewels dripped from her ears, circled her throat, and perched haughtily upon her head, nestled in a crown of thick gold filigree.

"Now then. Where were we?" Thyra asked. "Ah, yes. My prize. Bow to me, slave. Of your own free will."

CHAPTER 17

Bethany paced her house, hugging herself, struggling to find some comfort where there was none to be had.

What was it with her and bad men? Was she wearing some kind of sign only assholes could see? Natural Born Sucker. She'll Trust Anyone.

She could have loved Tristan. In fact, if she was being honest, part of her already did.

What the hell was wrong with her?

No matter how long she paced, she found no answers, only a pile of work waiting for her attention.

Her art restoration had always been her solace, so she sat down at the bench and began repairing an elaborate, centuries-old picture frame.

She had no idea how many hours had gone by when a knock on her door startled her. She jumped, nearly gouging the sweet cheek of a fragile cherub skirting the picture frame.

Asshole Number One stood there, his beady eyes darting nervously over his crooked nose. "Where's your boyfriend?"

Anger and frustration over this whole mess took over, leaving her no room for fear. "What the hell do you want now?"

"Boss says you're still going to do the job—fix what your boyfriend broke."

"And if I refuse?"

Asshole Number One hadn't been expecting that response. He blinked a couple of times before finding his tongue. "Then we'll have to have a little visit with your baby brother."

That threat made room for a twinge of fear to sink in. Still, she held her ground.

"What's the job?"

"Same as before. Only twice as many pieces this time."

"And I suppose you want them done yesterday?" she asked, tapping her foot in irritation.

He looked at her, confused. "Uh. Two days. You have two days."

She opened the door wide and stepped back. "Fine. Bring them in. Set them on the floor over by my workbench."

He scurried to obey, clearly uneasy with her uncharacteristic agreement.

"Do me a favor, will you?" she asked.

"Maybe I will, maybe I won't."

"I need some art supplies. Can I borrow your car for half an hour? Mine was all shot up by some violent assholes." She gave him a hard stare so he'd know she was fully aware of just who was responsible for that unfortunate circumstance.

"Uh, sure. I guess."

"Great. Thanks. Just make yourself at home." She waved to the comfy beanbag and her outdated, fat TV.

Once he was settled, she took his car and drove across town to her brother's house. On the way, she called the police and reported the diamond smuggling operation and the proof that was currently sitting in her living room. She warned the cops not to use sirens if they wanted one of the criminals to be there when they showed up.

They started to ask her a bunch of questions, but she hung up. There would be time for that later—likely more than she wanted. But right now she had an important task to complete—one that couldn't wait.

By the time she made it to Benjamin's place, she was seriously pissed. She didn't even wait for him to invite her inside when he opened the door. Instead, she simply barged in, shoving him back on his heels.

He had the same tall, lean build that she did, but with more muscle. His black hair was shaved close to his scalp, and every year he looked more like Dad.

"That's it," she told him. "I'm done cleaning up your messes. You want to be a criminal, be my guest. It'll break Mom's heart, but I'm tired of covering for you."

Benjamin peered outside his door as if worried she'd been followed, then hastily closed it. "I don't know what you're talking about."

"Yes, you do. Stop playing dumb. The only thing worse than a criminal is a stupid one."

"You're upset. You need to calm down so we can talk."

"I'm as calm as I'm going to get. And *we* don't need to talk. *I* do. You're going to shut up and listen."

When he opened his mouth as if to speak, she glared at him so hard he fell silent.

"You made friends with some bad people, hoping to make a quick buck. And, apparently, you told them about me. About what I do. How *could* you?" Anger prowled beneath her skin, making her sweat.

Benjamin held up his hands in innocence. "It wasn't like that."

"No? Then how was it that your *friends* decided to use you as leverage to get me to do illegal acts?"

"I never mentioned you. They found you on their own. It wasn't supposed to go down that way."

"But it did." She shoved him hard enough to send him sprawling to the couch. "But it's over now. I reported them to the police, like I should have from the very beginning. There's a good chance that you and I will be implicated in all of this, too. You might even go to jail. But at least it will be for a relatively minor infraction compared to what it could be once those assholes get their hooks into you."

"You can't do that," he said, fear putting the whites of his eyes on prominent display. "They'll kill you. And me."

"Too late. It's already done. I'll deal with the consequences of my actions as they come—the way we were raised to do. I guess you're going to have to do the same."

"That isn't fair. You can't take me down with you."

"You have already sunk to their level. You didn't need me to *take* you anywhere."

"I needed the work, Bethany. You don't know what it's like."

"The hell I don't. You know how hard I worked to get my business going, how many days I had to go without decent food just to make ends meet. But I never once thought it would be a good idea to take a shortcut and break the frickin' law." She grabbed a pillow from the couch and slammed it into the side of his head. "How could you be so stupid?"

"Not stupid. Desperate."

She stared at his giant flat screen TV and brand new gaming system. "You call living like this desperate?"

"Those were gifts."

"I just bet it was. All you had to give in return was your honor."

"Don't you judge me," he growled.

Sirens blared in the distance, growing louder. "The cops are on their way."

"You ratted me out?"

"No, they probably tracked my phone. I'm sure they're going to want to have a nice, long chat with me."

"And me?"

She shrugged. "Guess that's up to you. Do you step up and be a man, owning up to what you've done, or do you cower like a little boy who's afraid Mommy will find out he's been naughty?"

They stared at each other in silence, both seething mad.

"I just can't believe that you would do this, Ben. I'm your sister and you let them *hurt* me."

All his anger faded in a heartbeat. He went deathly still. "They hurt you?"

"Yeah. If not for a…friend, they might have done more than that."

He rose from the couch, his hand stretched out toward her. It was shaking. "They promised me they wouldn't lay a hand on you. They said you were too valuable to injure. I thought you were safe. I swear it."

"Well, I wasn't. Not even close."

"I'll make this right," he said, his tone clear and decisive. "I'll tell the cops everything I know—whatever it takes to pay those fuckers back for hurting you."

Relief filled her up like cool water, putting out all that smoldering anger. She gave Benjamin a hard hug as the police closed in and pounded on the door. "Now that's the baby brother I know and love."

He took her hand in his. "Let's go make this right."

CHAPTER 18

Tristan stared up at the creature he loathed, furious at himself for agreeing to her game.

"Are you going back on your word?" Thyra asked. "Will you not bow to me of your own free will as you promised?"

"What about Bethany? She isn't safe."

"That's hardly my problem. She's just one more rat scurrying through a maze." Thyra reached down and stroked his hair. "You're stalling."

"I want you to ensure her safety. You promised."

His aging curator still stood nearby, watching his humiliation play out with a look of glee glimmering in her eyes. "Since when are you worried about the safety of others? You're all killer and no kindness."

Tristan looked at Jillian. "If you want to be angry at someone, try focusing that rage on Thyra, where it belongs. It was her order I was following when I killed your husband."

Thrya tapped a bejeweled slipper. "I'm getting bored now. Get to the bowing already, will you?"

"Not until I know that Bethany is safe."

Thyra's gown turned into a black lace creation that looked far too much like ebony cobwebs for his peace of mind. Fanged spiders skittered across her hem, jumping ship and heading right for him.

"Are you trying to renegotiate our bargain?" she asked, her voice cracking with fury.

"I'm asking for you to find some speck of compassion in that black soul of yours and keep the woman you swept into your petty game safe."

She leaned down close, showing off her ample bosom. "What will you give me if I grant you this boon?"

"I have nothing left to give. You have everything now. My freedom, my honor."

"Honor," snorted Jillian, pointing her cane at him. "You wouldn't know honor if you sat on it."

"Silence!" bellowed Thyra. "Or I'll slay you where you stand."

"I'm not afraid of you, you high-and-mighty bitch. You're at least partly to blame for all the bad shit that's come down on me and my family. If you think I'm going to bow to you like killer here, then you're as crazy as those costumes you wear."

Tristan winced. "You'd better do what she says."

"Or what? She has no power over me."

"You think not?" asked Thrya, her voice deceptively sweet. "That's adorable. And dead wrong."

She waved her fingers and Jillian melted, leaving only a brightly colored pile of muumuu behind. Her cane clattered to the floor. A second later, something small and furry scurried out from the fabric.

A mouse. It made a beeline for the only refuge to be found in the vacant space: Tristan.

The air shifted, growing warm and moist. There was a faint scent of ocean breeze that reminded him of Bethany's cozy home nestled near the shoreline.

He could have been happy there—assuming the emotion was still left inside of him after all this time. Still, if there was ever a place that he could call home, her brightly lit abode was it.

"Thyra," said a woman who appeared at the edges of the white mist. "You know how Father feels about us toying with humans."

"Alethia. Who invited you?" said Thyra with a pout. She was back in her royal purple gown, straightening the crown on her head.

The mouse that had once been Jillian—the woman who'd left his stone form out in the elements, the woman who had tried to burn him to the ground, the woman who would have rather died than allow him to move on to another curator—ran up his leg and hid in the small space left open inside his fist.

There was nowhere else for her to hide, and he was certain that she had to be terrified. Anyone in their right mind would be, with Thrya tossing her power around like a water balloon.

In her white T-shirt and jeans, Alethia looked plain next to her glamorously-garbed sister. She wore no makeup, and there was nothing special about her common features. There was, however, a light of brilliant intellect gleaming in her brown eyes. "I'm only here to help."

Thyra laughed, but the sound was foul and rotten. "You can't have him. He's mine."

"Him?" asked Alethia, waving a hand at Tristan. "He's not my type. It's the woman you've transmuted that bothers me."

"She defied me," said Thyra as if it were all the explanation needed.

As she spoke, Tristan felt Jillian mouse try to crawl deeper into her hiding place.

It would have been so easy to kill her. Just one little squeeze of his hand and her tiny mouse back would snap like a toothpick. And then he'd be free to choose his own curator.

Bethany didn't want the job, but maybe he could still convince her. Maybe it wasn't too late….

She was down there alone, dealing with those armed criminals, and he wasn't there to scare them off. Even if they stayed away for a while, eventually they'd come back. Filth always did. And eventually she'd refuse to play nice with them, because she was too good to become a criminal. When that happened, they'd hurt her.

Maybe even kill her.

Tristan couldn't allow that. He had to find a way to be near her so he could protect her. But how?

The only thing he could think of was for her to be his curator. She might hate him, but at least when Thrya sent him away from Idola and back into his stone form, he'd be nearby. He'd be able to keep her safe.

To make that happen, all he had to do was kill his current curator—the little mouse in his hand.

Jillian had said *over her dead body*. The contract had been entered into whatever official records counted in this insane place. If he killed her, he'd be free to choose a new curator. And while Bethany might not want the job, he'd find some way to convince her it was the only way to keep herself and her brother safe. Surely she would realize it was the best option.

He stared down at his closed fist, feeling the tiny claws scratching at his tough skin as it tried to burrow deeper, seeking refuge. Bethany's life was worth far more than this rodent. Even the woman who might still be lurking inside the little furry creature was not nearly as precious as Bethany—to anyone. She had no family and was far too bitter to have any friends. No one would mourn her.

And Tristan would be free to be near Bethany. Even if she hated him, at least she'd be safe in her hatred. For a man like Tristan, that was the best he could ever hope for.

As the sisters squabbled over rules and what their father would say if he found out what they were doing, Tristan tightened his hold on the mouse so it couldn't get away.

One little squeeze. One tiny snap of broken bones.

He wanted to close his fist—wanted it so much that his whole body shook with the effort of resisting the urge to kill.

She was only a mouse. A nuisance. Something people killed every day as pests.

Sweat beaded on his brow and trickled along his temples. He'd killed before. Many times. But never like this.

All he was really good for was killing. He accepted that. Owned it. Why then, could he not bring himself to crush the thing that stood between him and what he wanted?

The creature—and the woman—was helpless. Vile, but helpless. She was an old lady in a dying shell filled with hate and bitterness. She'd caused him decades of torment. Cold, pain, loneliness…

But did that mean she deserved to die?

He'd taken something precious from her. Not by choice, but that didn't change the fact that he was the weapon used to kill her husband.

How would he have felt if someone killed the woman he loved?

Bethany's face bloomed in his mind, complete with the responding thrill he got every time he gazed upon her. She was so beautiful, brave and talented. So kind. How could he not love her?

He let that love fill him up. It grew and bloomed like a field of sweetly-scented wildflowers. It blinded him with its beauty and made him tremble with its power. As that love swelled, the strangest thing happened.

Somehow love washed away his need to kill. A man who was lucky enough to love a woman as precious as Bethany had to be a better man—even if he could never be with her. He had to rise above his baser nature and be what she'd want him to be. Not a killer, but a man of mercy and forgiveness. That was the only way he could stay connected to her goodness.

And he had to have some connection to her, even if he never saw her again.

Doing what she'd want was the only way to honor her, so Tristan opened his fist and let the little mouse scamper away.

Anna Argent

A deep gong sounded, but it was a feeling more than a sound. The noise reverberated in his skull until it was all he could think about.

Two seconds later, a rush of power flowed through the room like a storm front, bringing with it the chill of winter and the rustle of dead leaves.

Both sisters immediately stopped their bickering and turned to face the new arrival.

It was the giant woman covered in dented armor and flecks of blood.

"Zeva," said Thyra, hands on her hips in irritation. "Haven't you bothered me enough for one day?"

The warrior sheathed her bloody sword. "I was in the middle of something myself, but even I was paying enough attention to know what just happened. You two were so busy bitching at each other that you missed the big event."

Alethia frowned. "What event?"

Zeva pointed at Tristan. "Your boy here just activated his escape hatch."

"What?" asked Thyra, her regal appearance wilting by the second. Her golden crown began to melt, causing molten metal to cascade over her hair and jewels to clatter to the floor. "Impossible."

Zeva crossed her arms. Her bracers clanged together. "I felt it happen. Killer here showed mercy."

Thyra's gaze went distant. Her tri-colored eyes darted around like she was watching a movie.

Beside her, her sister Alethia grinned. "It's true."

Zeva grunted. "So much for him being some kind of killing machine. He couldn't even bring himself to squish a nasty little rodent no one would miss."

"He showed mercy," said Alethia, beaming.

"I don't get it," Zeva said. She studied him like he was some kind of science experiment gone wrong. "Why would you do that? Killing your curator was going to get you exactly what you wanted and yet you let her go. What the hell, man?"

Tristan realized that he was no longer bound by Thyra's will, trapped on his knees. He pushed to his feet, nearly dizzy with shock. "Jillian's hatred of me might have been misplaced, but I can't say that I would have done any differently than her if I'd been in her situation. I killed her husband."

"Not by choice," Alethia said. "Thyra forced your hand. *She* was the true killer."

Thyra waved her fingers as if the matter was insignificant. "Anyone who gets in the way of what I want deserves to die. Besides, all humans are merely toys for our amusement. And watching your curator torture you slowly for decades amused me greatly."

Zeva strode closer, her hammered silver eyes narrowing with curiosity. "I still don't get it. It's not like your curator was a child or some saint. She wasn't even kind. Why not end her life?"

How was he ever going to make a creature like Zeva understand? She was all about war, death and destruction. The concept of mercy was so far from her understanding, he might as well have been asking a fish to do calculus on the moon. "You wouldn't understand."

She put her face right up against his, her tone one of absolute demand. "Make me understand. It's the least you can do considering it was my clause that has freed you."

"Free? I'm still here, answering to your whims. How is that free?"

"I'll send you back to that blue marble in a minute—as soon as you tell me why you didn't kill the rodent."

He wasn't sure he believed her, or if this was some kind of a trick, but when it came to these women, it was always smartest to play nice. So he took a deep breath and tried to explain his actions. "If someone killed Bethany, I wouldn't care who issued the order. I would have hunted down the man who did the job and destroyed him. As much as I hate to admit it, Jillian and I are more alike than not."

"But she wanted you dead. It is your duty—your right— to destroy her. Why didn't you?"

"Because of Bethany."

Zeva frowned. "But she's…human. How does one miniscule girl change anything?"

"Because I love her. I knew that she would want me to show mercy, so I did."

The giant warrior snorted in derision. "Well, that's just stupid. I still don't get it."

"And you probably never will, sister," Alethia said.

Thyra jerked, shedding the remains of her withered velvet gown. "You're telling me that *Bethany* was the reason you're defying me?" She let out a scream of fury and burst into flames. "That bitch! I'll kill her!"

"No!" shouted Tristan, charging the woman who'd turned his life into a living hell. "I won't let you hurt her."

She whirled on him, teeth and fingernails growing to long points. "Try to stop me. I dare you. You're human again. Powerless. And my stonemen are already on their way to her."

Panic ripped at Tristan's calm, making clear thought nearly impossible. He might have spent centuries in battle, destroying whomever Thyra sent him to slay, but he'd only been a shell then, acting on pure compulsion.

He looked around, searching for some way to get back to Bethany and protect her. But there was not a single exit to be found. "Send me back. Please." He looked at both Alethia and Zeva, praying one of them would take pity on him.

"I would," said Alethia, "but I'd be sending you to your death. That I cannot do."

"I will," Zeva said. "For a price."

"No!" bellowed Thyra, the flames engulfing her body rising higher. "If you interfere, I'll make sure you suffer."

"Piss off," said Zeva, shoving her sister hard enough to send her careening through the billowing clouds that surrounded them.

She stared down at Tristan, her metal gauntlets creaking as she cracked her knuckles. "You want to save the damsel in distress?"

"I do."

"You can't do it like this—all fleshy and weak. Thyra's going to send as many stonemen as it takes to get the job done, now that you've pissed her off."

"Will you protect her?" asked Tristan, uncaring about how desperate he sounded.

"Depends."

"On?"

Zeva crossed her arms over her breast plate. "You're a decent enough warrior. You can join my army. I'll even let you be with the pretty human if you want, keeping her safe between battles."

"You want me to be your slave, don't you?"

She shrugged. "I prefer to think of you all as recruits, but whatever."

Alethia stepped forward. Her plain white T-shirt was singed from where Thyra's flames had licked the sleeve. "You can't do this, Tristan. You're a free man now. If you agree to this, your freedom is gone. You'll be back where you started."

"I can't let Bethany die," he said. "I love her. I'd give a thousand centuries of servitude if that's what it takes to keep her safe."

Alethia wrung her hands. "Think about what you're saying."

"I am. I'm not some wide-eyed child who has never been enslaved before. I know exactly what I'm doing." He pulled in a deep breath—the last free one he'd probably ever take. "I agree. So long as I'm able to protect Bethany, I'll serve you."

Zeva grinned, but it was all teeth and no humor.

Alethia hung her head and turned away to leave.

The floor beneath his feet shuddered. The sound of thunder filled the air, along with a deep, booming voice of authority. "*Girls!* What do you think you're doing?"

Alethia and Zeva looked at each other in horror. "Daddy?"

They started to scatter, but before they could, each girl was caged inside a cylinder of white, sparking strands of electricity. Tiny bolts of lightning popped and sizzled as it arced to the ground.

An instant later, a burly man in jeans and a plaid flannel shirt appeared. In front of him were all three caged sisters, lined up with their hands behinds their backs and their heads hung in shame.

The man paced in front of them. "Am I not indulgent with you? Did I not give you an entire world of playthings to entertain you?"

None of the women answered, and Tristan took that as his cue to keep his mouth shut, too.

"All you do is bicker and toss your toys around, breaking them. Well enough is enough."

Power cracked the air. Lightning streaked between cages, zapping each girl. They gasped in pain but didn't fight back.

Thyra's hair was in twin braids now, matching nicely with her fluffy dress and the pink teddy bear she was holding. "We're sorry, Daddy."

The man glowered and zapped the girls again. "I've heard that before. But once my back is turned, you'll be right back at it, sending your toys out to kill some innocent human. You know better than that, Thyra."

She twirled one braid and stuck out her bottom lip in a pout. "I promise I'll be good."

The man scowled. "Likely story. I'm sorry, Thyra, but you've pushed me too far. You're grounded."

"No!" she wailed, throwing herself to her knees. "Please, not that. I swear I'll make it right. I'll leave the bitc—beautiful lady alone and let Tristan go. He broke the contract fair and square."

"Do you think I'm a fool?"

"Of course not, Daddy. You're as wise as you are kind."

Behind her, Zeva poked an armored finger in her mouth and pretended to gag.

"And you," said their father, whirling around. "This poor man has spent centuries being Thyra's plaything. You don't even give him one day of freedom before demanding he serve you?"

"I'm sorry. I'll give him a whole week."

"You'll let him go free!" shouted their father. Each word was punctuated by a bolt of lightning.

"But—"

"No buts." He pointed a finger at Zeva. "You will let this man go and never bother him again." He turned his attention to Thyra. "And you will call off your toys and never again bother him or anyone he's ever known. Understood?"

Thyra pouted. "Yes, Daddy."

"And you," he said, pointing to Alethia, "I know what you're up to. Mark my words, it will end badly."

Alethia blinked in surprise. "I'm trying to be good, just like you said."

"And while I appreciate your efforts, your sisters won't. Watch your step. Don't anger them."

"Yes, sir."

"That's it?" Thyra demanded. "I get grounded and all Alethia gets is...*that*, whatever it was?"

Their father grew larger, looming over Thyra. The cage of electricity tightened around her. "Would you like me to take away *all* of your toys, *forever*?"

She was immediately cowed. "No, Daddy. I'm sorry."

"I should hope so. Now all of you, get out of my sight before I think up some new and interesting punishments for disturbing me."

The cages disappeared. All three sisters vanished, leaving only Tristan, and the little gray mouse that had once been Jillian.

The giant man looked at Tristan and sighed. "Daughters are difficult. You should try very hard to have only sons."

He wiggled a finger and the mouse morphed back into Jillian—a very naked and surprised Jillian.

A second later, Tristan was standing inside the burned-out shell of the house he had once thought of as home.

It took him a minute to realize that he was not held immobile atop his stone base. The base had vanished. He was no longer made of stone. He was flesh and blood.

He was *free*.

He looked around at the charred wooden building one more time before he walked away, knowing he'd never come back.

"Wait," said a voice from a long way off.

Tristan turned and saw Jillian standing there, wearing only a bath robe. Her gray hair was a wreck, and she was far too pale.

He stopped.

She tried to hurry over, but she was unsteady on her feet without benefit of her cane, and moved slowly across the uneven ground. He took pity on her and closed the distance, but stayed out of striking range. "What do you want? You're free of me now. You'll never have to see my face again."

"You could have killed me."

"Yes."

"I would have killed you had the tables been turned."

"I'm sure you would have."

"I spent the last three decades thinking I would be happier dead, so I could be with my husband. But I realize now that I'm not ready to go. I want to live. Thank you for showing me that."

He didn't know what to say other than, "You're welcome."

She looked around as if searching for words. Finally, she settled on, "I'm sorry, Tristan. For everything."

He was stunned silent by her apology. It took him a long minute to unglue his tongue from the roof of his mouth. "So am I."

And he was. He'd never meant to hurt her husband. Even as he'd tossed the man aside, knocking his head into the stone fireplace, he felt a deep, penetrating horror at his actions. He couldn't stop himself, but he'd always been sorry for what he'd been forced to do.

She held out her hand in an offering of peace.

Tristan took it.

A weight lifted from his shoulders, and a sense of peace settled into all the empty holes his regret and hatred had left behind.

He might never be whole again after what he'd been forced to do, but Jillian's forgiveness was a very good start.

CHAPTER 19

B ethany felt lost.

For a week she floundered, unable to function.

All the bluster of her attack on her brother had swept through her, leaving her feeling soft and empty, like a two-week old balloon. Not even her work seemed to drive away the grinding uneasiness that haunted her.

The assholes hadn't come by since the police had raided her house and carted one of them off to jail. She'd given the authorities every bit of information she had, cooperating fully. In return, she was free in her home, with uniformed officers driving by several times a day.

It wasn't a guarantee of safety, but it was the best she was going to get without a giant stone guardian camping out in her living room.

She missed Tristan—his constant vigilance, his endless patience, his excruciating care for her safety. But more than that, she missed the way he made her feel. She hadn't smiled since he'd left. Hadn't even felt like it.

How could a murderer make her feel like the safest woman on earth? Weren't her instincts better than that?

Apparently not, because while she knew he was dangerous, she never once thought he was evil or cruel.

Someone banged on her front door. She jumped, dropping the paintbrush she'd been holding.

"Who is it?" she called out as she pressed her hand over her skittering heart. She reached for a small chisel and gripped it in her fist.

"Dalton and Sue," said a deep voice.

Relief made her sag. No assholes yet.

Bethany really didn't want company, but they were paying customers—ones who'd paid her enough to make sure she'd eat for the next three months. The least she could do was open the door.

She pulled it open, standing in the way so they wouldn't think she was inviting them in. "What can I do for you?"

"Is Tristan here?" Sue asked.

"Why would he be here?"

The couple shared one of their secret looks that spoke volumes.

Sue's eyes were wide with hope. "We were hoping the news was true—that you might become his curator."

Bethany's voice went flat. "Sorry to disappoint, but that's not going to happen."

"Why not? Was the rumor wrong?"

"No, you heard right. I was offered a chance to become his curator, and I was even on board with the whole idea…right up to the point where I found out he was a cold-blooded killer with a heart of stone."

Dalton took Sue's hand in his. "I know it's hard to understand what it's like to have no will of your own, but it's not Tristan's fault. He was forced to kill."

"Not according to him."

"What do you mean?" he asked.

"He killed his own brother," Bethany explained. "I asked him and he said that no one made him do it. He did it of his own free will. And it wasn't in self-defense. It was premeditated."

"You're wrong."

"No, I'm not. He *admitted* it. If he can kill his own brother, he can kill anyone. I can't be around someone like that. I *won't*."

"Whoa," said Dalton. "Slow down there. You're going off half-cocked."

"You only say that because you're freakishly strong and have no fear of a man like Tristan. The rest of us aren't so lucky."

"You don't have all the facts," Sue said.

"Are you telling me he didn't kill his brother? That murder wasn't how he got turned into a statue to begin with?"

"No, he definitely killed his brother. But not until after the man killed his own newborn baby in a fit of rage, all because she'd been born a girl."

All the heat let out of Bethany's righteous fury. Her voice came out faint and weak. "What?"

"Yeah. Tristan's brother was a flat-out asshole—one who was winding up to beat the hell out of his wife—again—for daring to birth a girl. And all of this was within hours of her giving birth."

Bethany sank into the nearest chair as shock stole all her strength. "I don't understand."

"Clearly not," said Dalton, his anger coming through his tone.

"Are you sure?" she asked.

Sue nodded. "I checked the records and it was all there in black and white. Tristan may have killed a man, but he more than deserved to die."

"I still don't get it," Bethany said. "If Tristan did nothing wrong, then how did Thyra get her hands on him?"

Sue's mouth tightened in distaste. "Rather than thank Tristan for saving her life, his sister-in-law bargained with Thyra to enslave him. She was mad with grief over the loss of her child and husband—despite the piece of shit that he was—and offered herself and her lineage as curators in return for Thyra doing her worst to Tristan."

Bethany let it all sink in.

Tristan was a hero. He'd saved a woman's life and she'd damned him to an eternity of servitude to a crazy bitch.

And then he'd saved Bethany's life. Multiple times. And she couldn't even bother to step up and guard his stone form when he was helpless and unable to protect himself.

"How could I have done that to him?" she asked.

"What did you do?" asked Dalton.

"He wanted me to be his curator. All I had to do was convince one bitter old woman that she should let go of her anger. And I didn't even *try*. Not after I heard what he'd done—or what I *thought* I'd heard he'd done."

"Why didn't he tell you the whole story?" Sue asked.

"Thyra," guessed Dalton.

That deranged bitch had hidden the truth in order to get her way. She'd cut Tristan off, keeping him from speaking.

And Bethany had bought it.

"I have to see Thyra. I have to try again—beg her to let me try to convince Jillian to give me the job."

The two exchanged another one of those looks.

"We're not supposed to tell you this, but there is a way to see her," Dalton said.

Sue put her fingers in her ears and said, "I can't be a part of this conversation."

Bethany ignored her. "How?"

"Every curator has a ring, that when put into the base of the statue, will bring them right to the stoneman's owner."

"So, I just need to get the ring from Jillian and I'll be able to beam up to wherever Thyra is?"

He nodded. "But the sisters really don't like it when you use it, so be prepared for her to be pissed."

"Crazy *and* pissed," said Bethany with a sigh. "Good times."

CHAPTER 20

It took so long for Jillian Branch to answer Bethany's knock on the door that she was contemplating which window to break to get in.

The older woman was wearing a polyester pants suit in mint green, complete with stitched-in creases and a string of plastic pearls. As soon as she saw Bethany, worry lines creased her wrinkled brow. "I didn't expect to see you again."

"Ditto. I wouldn't be here at all, except, I was hoping you would do me a favor and let me borrow your curator ring for a few minutes."

"My ring? But that went away along with Tristan's stone base."

"Went away? Where?"

Her frown deepened. "I assumed he'd be with you. I got the feeling you two were...close."

"You're not his curator anymore?"

"No."

"Then who is?"

"You don't know, do you?"

"Know what?" Bethany asked.

"Tristan is free. His curse is broken."

"Free?" Until this moment, she hadn't realized just how worried about him she'd been. He was constantly in her thoughts as she replayed every second they shared, but the nagging worry in the back of her mind had stayed hidden. Likely as some kind of self-preservation instinct.

Worrying about a dangerous man she would never see again seemed like a futile waste of time.

Jillian beamed as she nodded. "Seems that one of the sisters wondered what mercy felt like, so she added an escape clause to Tristan's contract. If a deadly man like him could show mercy, she was sure she could figure out how it worked."

Bethany was still reeling too much from the news that he was free to digest any of that. Not that it mattered why he'd been cut loose.

"Mercy?"

Jillian took Bethany's hand and gave it a squeeze. "He could have killed me when Thyra turned me into a mouse." She shuddered at the memory. "I was out of my head with panic, struggling to think beyond anything but hiding. I ran for the only refuge I could find—Tristan's hand. All he had to do was squeeze and I'd be dead. He'd have been free to find a new curator."

"Clearly he didn't kill you."

"No. And that's when I saw the truth. I was punishing the knife when I should have been punishing the hand that wielded it."

"Thyra."

Jillian nodded. "He had no more control of his actions than I had control over her turning me into a mouse. We were all just her toys."

"So, if Tristan is free, then where is he?"

"I assumed he'd head straight for you. After all, it's not like he can make his way alone in this world. He has no car, no money. He can't even get a decent job without a social security card."

"How long ago did you last see him?"

"A few days ago. Maybe a week."

"We've got to find him," Bethany said.

"He can't have gone far unless he hitchhiked. He wouldn't let me give him money. All he'd take was a couple of sandwiches for the road."

The thought of him out there, alone and hungry in a world he couldn't possibly understand, made Bethany sick. "I don't even know where to look."

"A man like that can't be found, honey. Not if he doesn't want to. Go home. If he wants to find *you*, that's where he'll go."

"He's not going to want to find me. Not after the way I treated him."

"If he can forgive me for what I did to him for decades, whatever you did to him in a few days can't be all that hard to overlook."

Bethany wanted to believe her, but she knew the truth. She'd turned her back on Tristan when he needed her most. She'd done it in an effort to protect her heart, but that hardly excused her selfishness.

She hadn't wanted to love a murderer, and in the end, she hadn't. She'd loved a hero—one she was never going to see again.

Tristan found the man who'd been responsible for forcing Bethany to hide diamonds in the statues. Within minutes, he'd cornered him and killed him. It was a violent, messy encounter—over in seconds. But after watching the man for days and hearing of his plans to murder her for having his operation interrupted, there was no other option.

Some men needed killing, and it was the one thing at which Tristan truly excelled.

To be sure that no one took up where the dead criminal had left off, Tristan watched Bethany's house for two weeks, hiding in her elderly neighbor's tool shed.

There were no visitors, no signs of distress.

She was safe.

Why then, couldn't he move on? He'd earned his freedom, and after centuries of lonely solitude, he'd gathered up hundreds of ideas about what he'd do if he were ever free.

Now that he was, all he wanted to do was linger near the woman who consumed his every waking thought. And the sleeping ones as well.

He ached for her—the feel of her lips on his, the dulcet music of her voice in his ears, the gentle touch of her hands on his face. Having her close and being unable to be with her was the sweetest kind of torture.

Tristan had always believed that after everything that had happened to him—killing his brother, being cursed for eternity, having to obey the sick and insane commands of Thyra—his heart had turned as cold and hard as his stone prison. But it was hot now, beating fast every time he caught of glimpse of the woman who'd captured his hopes and dreams all in one beautiful package.

How could he move on when everything he wanted was right here?

He tried not to spy on her, being careful not to peer into her windows more often than necessary to ensure she was safe and happy. After all, she deserved her privacy, and he had no desire to make his heartache worse by longing for what he could never have.

Still, every once in a while, she'd stand at her kitchen window and peer out as if searching for something. Once, she stepped out onto her porch and stared at the spot where he'd stood in the rain, guarding her home while she slept.

There was pain in her eyes, and he knew it was his fault. He never should have involved her in Thyra's games.

A rustling drew his attention. He turned around, expecting to see a mouse scurrying through the tool shed, but instead, Alethia stood there in a fresh pair of jeans and pristine white T-shirt. Her plain features were softened with concern as she stared at him.

"What are you doing here?" he asked. "Haven't you women tortured me enough?"

"I'm not here to hurt you, Tristan. Truly."

"Then what do you want?"

"You to be happy."

He stood there, waiting for the rest of the joke.

Alethia sighed. "I'm not like my sisters. I'm…making amends."

"For what?"

"That's none of your concern. But Bethany is. She misses you."

His heart surged behind his ribs at the mention of her name. "You're wrong. All I brought her was pain."

"Go see her."

"And let her spit in my face? Or worse yet, scare her to death? I don't think so."

"Trust me."

He laughed, but he was out of practice, and it sounded more like a growl.

"Oh, for heaven's sake," she said. "You humans are so stubborn."

One second he was in the shed. The next he was at Bethany's front door. Before he had time to even figure out what had happened or how he got here, Alethia knocked.

Then she disappeared.

Tristan briefly thought about fleeing, but not only was it cowardly, he was concerned that it might worry Bethany to not know who had been at her door. She'd been dealing with a lot of bad men, and chances were she didn't know that he'd cut off the head of the snake.

Her door swung open and there she was, more beautiful than he'd remembered. Up close he could see the shimmer of her eyes and smell the sweet scent of her skin. He got lost for a minute while he soaked her in.

"Tristan," she said, and the sound of her voice swept over him like a warm ray of sun, so fresh and clean.

He closed his eyes and gripped the door frame to keep from swaying.

"What are you doing here?" she asked. There was no hatred in her tone, only surprise and curiosity.

"Alethia zapped me here. The sisters apparently haven't decided to leave me completely alone yet. I guess this is their idea of a joke."

Bethany's face fell as if he'd hurt her. "You didn't mean to come?"

Now that he'd insulted her, all he wanted to do was crawl under a rock. "I'm sorry to bother you." He glanced at the gray paste clinging to her fingers. "I can see you're busy."

"I'm not too busy for you, Tristan. I know you didn't mean to come by, but now that you're here, will you come in? I have something I want to tell you."

His gut clenched at the thought of what she was going to say. He'd upset her life, nearly gotten her killed, and involved her in the petty schemes of deranged sisters. The least she deserved was to have the chance to rail at him for what he'd done.

He nodded and stepped inside her cozy home. Instantly, he was bathed in light, and the intoxicating scent of the most alluring woman ever born.

"You look awful," she said. "Your clothes are hanging on you. When was the last time you ate?"

He'd scrounged up a jar of peanut butter and a loaf of bread, but it had been a long time since he'd had a real meal. "I'm fine," he lied. "Please, just say what you need to say so I can go."

"Oh." Her voice was faint. "Okay. I didn't realize you were in a hurry."

He had nowhere to go, but he wasn't about to tell her that. Better for her to think that he had forged the beginnings of some kind of life in his few weeks back among the human race. At least that way he didn't seem quite so pitiful.

She rubbed her hands on a towel covered in paint stains. "I guess I'll just get right to the point, then."

"That would be best." The more time he spent with her, the harder it was going to be for him to leave. Her warmth, kindness and artistic intellect were addictive. The more he had, the more he wanted.

She pulled in a deep breath that strained the front of her shirt, reminding him of just what sweet treasures lie beneath.

"I wanted you to know how sorry I am," she said. "I acted without having the whole story, leaving you behind to fend for yourself against those crazy bitches. I should have listened to my instincts about you and not what other people said. I should have stayed by your side and done whatever it took to become your curator. I'm so, so sorry that I abandoned you like that."

He was so stunned by her apology that he stood there, staring at her like a fool for far too long. "Abandoned me? Is that what you think happened?"

"It's what I know happened."

"No, Bethany. You're wrong. I was the one who got you involved in a bad situation when you were already up to your neck in bad situations of your own with those criminals. I'm a violent man. I know that my best skills can be measured in bloodshed."

"Those women were wrong. You're more than merely a killer. You're a protector. That's why you killed your brother. All the other people you killed while under Thyra's power are on her head, not yours. You had no choice."

"But I have killed of my own free will and would do so again if necessary." The image of the man he'd murdered a few days ago to protect Bethany was still fresh in his mind. "I feel no remorse for those deaths. No regret. And if given the chance to do it all again, under the same circumstances, I still would not let them live."

She nodded slowly. "There are people in this world that don't deserve to live. They prey on innocents, destroying lives and ruining families. It's good that there are protectors like you to stop them. Someone has to."

"I've done bad things."

She pressed her hand over his heart. "Maybe, but you're a good man—here, where it counts."

"The world needs more men like you." She stepped closer until her toes bumped his. "*My* world needs more men like you."

"How about just me?"

"Sounds perfect." She cupped his cheek with her slender fingers, smiled and went up on tiptoe to kiss him. "I love you, Tristan. The good, the bad…all of you. Will you stay?"

His whole world lit up, and if there was any stone left around his heart, it split and cracked away, leaving him feeling like the strongest man in the universe. For her he could do anything.

No matter what it took, he would spend the rest of his life proving that he was worthy of a sweet, beautiful, talented woman like her.

"There's nowhere else I'd rather be than at your side," he said.

Her smile turned sultry. "Good, because I've spent the past few days fantasizing about what I'd do with you if you ever came back. I've worked up quite a list."

He pulled her in tight and kissed her until both of them were breathless. "Whatever you want, Bethany. I'm all yours."

The End

THE
STONE MEN
SERIES

BOOK 1
> Rock Hard — Kathy Lyons
> Made Flesh — Anna Argent

BOOK 2
> Rock Candy — Kathy Lyons
> Heart of Stone — Anna Argent

Kathy Lyons

Kathy Lyons is the wild, adventurous half of USA TODAY bestselling author Jade Lee. A lover of all things fantastical, Kathy spent much of her childhood in Narnia, Middle Earth, Amber, and Earthsea, just to name a few. "There is nothing I adore more than to turn around on an ordinary day and experience something magical. It happens all the time in real life and in my books." Winner of several industry awards including the *Prism—Best of the Best, Romantic Times Reviewer's Choice*, and *Fresh Fiction's Steamiest Read*, Kathy has published over 50 romance novels and yet says she's just getting started. "It's the love story that gets me every time. There's magic powers and then there's the magic of love. The first is cool. The second is life."

Check out her latest news at www.KathyLyons.com, Facebook: JadeLeeBooks, Twitter: JadeLeeAuthor

Anna Argent

After spending years working in corporate America as an engineer, Anna traded it all in for a quiet life in the country. She lives with her husband on a small cattle ranch in the Ozark Mountains, penning stories filled with love, lust and a healthy dose of magic. She loves to hear from her readers at www.AnnaArgent.com.